Published by Piscataqua Press
An imprint of RiverRun Bookstore, Inc
142 Fleet St. | Portsmouth, NH | 03801

www.riverrunbookstore.com
www.piscataquapress.com

ISBN: 978-1-939739-67-4

Printed in the United States of America

https://www.facebook.com/D.H.Barnette

Loving Leda

Portsmouth Paranormal Romance #1

David H. Barnette

A Child's Birthday in Portsmouth

*What senses do we lack that we cannot see and
cannot hear another world all around us?*

- (Frank Herbert, *Dune*)

Portsmouth has always been a weird little town. Wherever you live,
you've probably heard the stories. When you ask the natives about those
stories, they pretend not to know what you mean. I'd learned not to ask.

My folks moved us away when I was in high school. I might never
have come back to Portsmouth if I hadn't gotten divorced and lost my
job all in the same year. The sour economy conspired against me.
Constant networking and a blizzard of résumés got me only a handful
of interviews. The interviews got me only *one* serious job offer. I wound
up in Portsmouth working for a start-up software company for a *lot* less
money than I'd been making in Washington. Thank God I didn't have
children to support, or an ex-wife who'd been awarded alimony. New
Hampshire was more expensive than I remembered. I could barely
support myself.

Not that I was complaining. Things were looking up. I was working

1

in my profession again. The company's stock was gaining steadily after a weak IPO. And it was nice to connect with family again, aunts, uncles, and several generations of cousins. I got invited to all the get-togethers and went to as many as I could.

So here I was at another birthday party. A Dora the Explorer birthday card and a modest check didn't exactly thrill the kid, but her parents appreciated my gesture. They'd welcomed me into their home and accepted me at face value. Who knows, maybe somebody would invite me to Thanksgiving dinner.

People look different when you've been gone twenty years. I was still putting names together with faces.

"Remind me, who's the older gentleman sitting in the corner?" I said.

"You mean Uncle Quincy?" my cousin Phyllis said. She was playing hostess; her daughter was this afternoon's birthday girl. Phyllis looked frazzled, and she had pink cake frosting in her frosted blonde hair. "You should go talk to him." Her tone implied *Good luck with that.*

"*Uncle Q,* of course," I said. "Thanks."

I worked my way through the crowd of adults and children, chatting and laughing with people as I went. I was either blessed or cursed with the gift of gab, depending on how you look at it. Eventually I got to the relatively quiet corner where Uncle Quincy sat with a copy of *Road & Track* on his lap. He was gazing in the general direction of the magazine, but it didn't seem to hold his interest. Occasionally he'd gaze out the window. The north side of Portsmouth didn't seem to interest him much, either. Quincy had the same thick, white hair he'd had twenty years ago, but the lines in his face were deeper. His eyes looked heavy, like he wasn't sleeping well. I can relate. He was the kind of gentleman who wears a suit to a little girl's birthday party. I have trouble relating to that.

"Quincy?" I said, holding out my hand for him to shake. He looked at my hand, sort of bemused, like he wasn't sure who I was or what it was, then remembered his manners and shook it. "I'm your grandnephew Jerry," I reminded him gently. "How are you, sir?"

"Jerry?" he said. "Oh, right..." He trailed off and looked out the window again. His expression was so vague and lost that I wondered if he'd started slipping into dementia. He turned back to me. "*How am I?* I'm not at all sure. I had the *damnedest* dream last night. You ever dream?"

"I must have dreams, but I don't remember them," I said.

"Hmm..." Quincy started to say. He was interrupted by a wild rout of hollering, cake-sticky children chasing balloons and each other around the living room. The little ranch house was heating up from all the people stuffed into it. Over the din of loud conversation, shouting and laughing, I heard him say, "Listen, I need some air. Care to join me?"

"Sure," I said.

We got our coats out of a pile in one of the bedrooms and told Phyllis we'd be back in a bit. She nodded distractedly and snapped at her husband to *take out the trash, for God's sake.* Quincy and I strolled up the street.

Normally I tend to chitchat about whatever comes to mind, but Uncle Q seemed so ... *bewildered* that I just walked along with him in silence. The quiet was a relief after Phyllis' noisy house. The sidewalk was covered in red, orange, yellow, and brown leaves, like you'd expect in New England in late October. It was the kind of day where we felt warm in the sun but cold when we entered the shade. A stream of cars passed us, heading for the joys of shopping at the malls.

It was good to be back ... *home.* Washington is awful in so many ways; it's best not to think about it if you have to live there. Portsmouth is beautiful and livable. There's an inevitability to the changing seasons here, and people cope gracefully with whatever weather comes. I remembered dreading the endless winters as a kid. Now I actually looked forward to the cold. Shoveling snow makes you stronger if it doesn't kill you, right?

After a few blocks, the sidewalk led past fields and woodland. A big sign said all the real estate was FOR SALE. I followed Quincy off the sidewalk into a field with rows of trees. He was wearing polished

3

wingtips, so I figured I didn't have to worry about mud ruining my new sneakers. Besides, it hadn't rained for weeks. The ground was dry.

He pointed at the lines of gnarled old trees. "This used to be somebody's apple orchard," he said. His voice was full of grief. "People used to *grow* things on this land and *eat* what they grew."

I nodded politely. I could think of nothing to say that matched his mood. The world changes. Portsmouth was no longer the city Quincy grew up in; the small family farms were gone. *How rich do you have to be before you're considered eccentric and not just nuts?* I wondered. I decided Q was eccentric.

We walked on through the field at his leisurely pace. If there was a path through the trees and thick grass, I couldn't see it, but he seemed to know where he was going. After a few minutes we came through a wall of pines to a small clearing. I saw no sign that anyone had been here recently, no flattened grass, no four-wheeler, dirt bike, or mountain bike tracks, no trash.

Quincy turned to me. "I dreamed about this place last night," he said. He pointed to the ground with the palm of his hand, a patting gesture. "Right *here*. Dreamed I was here in a *bed*, of all things. With a woman I used to love, of all people."

I just nodded and shook my head. "Dreams, huh?" I hoped I sounded sympathetic. Dreams have always seemed pretty random to me. I never worried about them, or thought they meant anything more than cerebral circuits powering up or down.

Preoccupied, Quincy moved slowly forward. He pushed the tall yellowed grass aside with one shoe before putting his foot down; then he did it again. He walked deliberately, like a heron stalking a frog. He didn't have to go far before he found something. Keeping his eyes on the ground, he beckoned me forward. Cautiously, I walked up next to him.

The grass in front of us was not crushed, but gently flattened, a square about seven feet on each side. It was hard to miss once I saw it. At the corners of the square, the dirt was compressed, four square indentations four inches deep and perhaps three inches square.

"Looks like the bed *was* right there after all," Quincy said. "Guess it wasn't a dream."

I had nothing to say to that, and he had nothing to add. In silence we headed back out of the little clearing the way we'd come. *Okay, so he's nuts*, I thought with an inner shrug. People get old and lose their marbles. Sad, but it happens.

As we entered the pine trees, I happened to look up at a patch of sky visible above the treetops. Instead of the cloud-streaked blue of an October afternoon, I what I saw was a rich dark purple predawn ... *firmament.*

The old word *empyrean* drifted into my thoughts. The thoughts themselves began to float like I'd been smoking marijuana. (I hadn't.) And were those stars or *planets* I saw high above us? They *swirled* in their courses. Was this what van Gogh saw and painted? Everywhere I looked was beautiful, and I could move my eyes only from beauty to beauty. My breath caught on its way into my chest: *Oh!*

Speechless for once, I put a shaky hand on Quincy's shoulder to slow him down. Glowering at this presumption, he turned. I pointed at the sky. Once he saw what I saw, he stopped scowling and his mouth opened. He looked down, took a deep breath, shook his head, and looked up again.

"It seems the dream still follows me," he said. He didn't sound a bit upset.

Quincy and I watched the incredible sky together as streaks of blue-green filled it up.

Out of that livid height flew something my eyes could make no sense of: hawk, owl, *lammergeier?* What kind of bird has a twenty-foot wingspan and the feathered markings of a human face?

Quincy grabbed my arm hard. It hurt. The old man was stronger than he looked. "This is very bad," he said. He meant the creature that was plummeting toward us. "We should run now. Whatever it says to you, for God's sake, *don't listen!*"

We ran. Quincy was breathing hard, but he kept moving ponderously along like a massive old steam-powered locomotive. I was breathing hard, too, shallow panic-breaths that didn't quite get me the oxygen I needed. You know those feet-stuck-in-mud nightmares? It felt like every weed and vine was trying to slow me down. My sneakers untied themselves, but I didn't dare take the time to tie them. I'm not sure I *remembered* how to tie them. I barely managed not to trip myself.

Above us a voice began ... *to speak.* That discourse became louder and clearer as the speaker flew lower. On and on it went in a high-pitched human-sounding male voice, rippling words, flowing sentences, entire coherent paragraphs. Whatever language the voice spoke plucked deliberately at my drifting thoughts as the grasses and vines clutched innocently at my feet. Slowed and hindered in mind and body, I fought the temptation to look up and engage the winged speaker in conversation. I was on the verge of understanding him. *Listening* seemed like the worst possible idea.

We got closer to the sidewalk. The voice from above grew fainter.

We stepped out of the field and looked up. The sky was pale New Hampshire blue, empty again; no one spoke from on high.

I bent over with my hands on my knees and fought for breath. Quincy did likewise. He brushed his tousled silver hair back into a semblance of order. He brushed burrs and leaves off his trousers. He shook his head in dismay at his badly-scuffed shoes. My hair was too short to get mussed, but I did pluck a few burrs off my socks. I retied my shoelaces. My hands shook. Neither of us had died during our ... escape. It struck me that we might have. Him because he was so old, me because I'd been scared to death.

Once we were breathing normally, we walked back toward Phyllis' house. I wanted to keep looking over my shoulder, but I didn't.

"I owe you an apology, Jerry," he said.

" *What?* Why?" I said.

"They knew me ... from before. Now that they've caught sight of you, they know *you,* too."

" *They?*" I may have sounded more skeptical than I meant to.

He stopped walking, so I stopped, too. Quincy looked me right in the eyes. His face was no-bullshit dead-serious. Old as he was, he looked stronger and more alive than me.

"Do you propose to *deny* what you just saw? What we *both* saw—and *heard*?" he said. I got the impression he expected me to say Yes and add to his lifetime collection of human disappointments.

"I saw *something*," I said. "I don't know *what* it was."

He looked at me closely for a while. I'd given him the right answer, or at least an honest one. "We have things to discuss, then. You should come to my house for supper," he said. "You know where I live?" I said I didn't, and he gave me directions. "I'll tell Pepsi you're coming. She'll be delighted—loves company, for some reason. Eight o'clock. Don't be late."

2

Uncle Quincy and Aunt Pepsi

Quincy stalked back into Phyllis' house, whispered into his wife's ear, interrupted her conversation without apology, helped her into her coat, and extracted her from the melee. Pepsi must have been used to unceremonious exits from family gatherings. She smiled happily, waggled her fingers at me from across the busy kitchen, and mouthed the words *See you tonight*. Then they were gone, driving off in a vintage black Mercedes sedan, all in about a minute.

Being who I am, it took me considerably longer to make the rounds, say my goodbyes, and thank my hostess. All the kids were now running around the back yard playing tag or something and screaming like kids do; they sounded like seagulls. (*Don't think about birds*, I told myself.) The adults had grouped up and were talking like grownups do: work, kids, politics, sports, gossip. Phyllis looked slightly less frazzled. At least she'd gotten the frosting out of her hair. She smiled at me over her coffee mug.

"You and Quincy seem to have hit it off," she said.

"I suppose we did," I said. I wasn't about to get into whatever the hell had just happened to me. "I'm invited to dinner at their house."

Phyllis' eyes got big. "*Really?* They never invite *anyone* over anymore. I was a little surprised when they showed up here today. Huh, now that I think about it, Uncle Q asked about you when I called to invite them. *Any*way. Quincy's ... a lonely man. Pepsi's his only company, but I think they live separate lives under one roof. One big *honkin'* roof. Have you seen their house?" I said I hadn't. "Well, you're in for a treat. Think *Architectural Digest* 1957."

I drove back to my little leased house on the south side of town, across the street from the South Cemetery. I was renting with an option to buy the place, once I managed to save up enough for a down payment. After being out of a job for months and then moving up here from D.C., I was still in a period of slow economic recovery. Me and the rest of the country. The ex had a better lawyer than I did. Despite having left me to, um, explore same-sex relationships, she'd still landed our house. After not getting screwed for months, I got screwed in divorce court, ha ha ha. I was too surprised to be bitter. Really, the whole situation was kind of funny, and I was relieved to be out of it. I hoped she was happier now than she'd been with me. I wasn't quite happy yet, but at least I wasn't *un*happy anymore.

These days I mailed monthly rent checks to a Boston law firm. Word around town was that the firm represented an organization Portsmouth folks just referred to as *the Friends*. They were *not* talking about the Religious Society of Friends, better known as the Quakers. Portsmouth natives didn't talk about who *the Friends* were friends *of.* That was simply *understood*—after all the troubles Portsmouth had been through.

I'd heard things. Everybody knew *something* had happened in Portsmouth. The truth was probably somewhere between the government's bland, plausible-sounding statements and the internet's lurid, implausible-sounding conspiracy theories. If I wanted to know more, I could ask, and the Friends would tell me. There were books I could have read, but why bother? The Friends even had a website; I avoided it. Honestly? I didn't really *want* to know. Whatever had happened in Portsmouth was old news and none of my business. I had a life to get on with.

So I quickly cleaned up the house. There wasn't much that needed doing. After the divorce, I'd quickly fallen back into my fussy bachelor housekeeping habits. Think Felix Unger from *The Odd Couple*. (I'd left my sneakers on a rack by the door.) I plopped down on the couch in front of the TV. There's nothing like channel surfing when you're trying not to think about something.

One channel was showing Alfred Hitchcock's *The Birds*; I surfed right past that. The universe seems to have a perverse sense of humor. I suppose seeing the Hawkmen in *Flash Gordon* would have been worse. (*Don't think about Hawkmen.*)

It being Saturday, I found a golf tournament to watch. Absolutely stupefying. I lay down on the couch, put up my feet, pulled a blanket over myself, and fell asleep to the hushed, reverent tones of the golf commentators. A world where a birdie was Christ's Second Coming. Perfect. (*Don't think about birdies.*)

A loud commercial for erectile dysfunction medication got me up in plenty of time to shower and get ready to go out. I shaved again and dressed carefully in a suit, tie, and dress shoes. If Quincy wore a suit to a child's birthday party, I figured I'd show up for dinner at his house in formal business attire. He'd have told me if it was a black tie event, wouldn't he?

Quincy's directions were excellent. I followed them until I saw an open black iron gate in a low stone wall. I turned my little car off the shore road into his driveway just before the appointed hour. When I caught sight of the house at the end of the drive, its facade lit up by spotlights hidden in sculpted hedges, I stopped the car and gaped.

"Holy shit," I said to the empty car, "that's not a house, it's a *mansion.*" The car didn't argue with me. Word in the family was that after buying IBM stock since the 1950s, Quincy had also started buying Apple and Microsoft stock in the 1980s and had never budged off this simple strategy. He was living off the fruits of his investments, God bless America. Three stories, weathered gray stone and red brick, slate roof, green shutters. Detached stone garage with chauffeur apartment over. And what must have been a gardener's cottage, also stone, with attached glass greenhouse. You get the idea.

I drove slowly up the crushed stone driveway. Someone had recently raked it. Painstakingly. By hand. I could see the rake marks. I parked near the front door, locked my little Honda (big city habits die hard), and rang the bell.

Aunt Pepsi answered the door. "Jerry!" she said as she hugged me. "So good to see you, dear." Neither her education (Radcliffe) nor her travels with Quincy (the contemporary Grand Tour) had altered a syllable of her pristine New Hampshire accent. She still pronounced "dear" as DEE-yah. Her real name was Penelope, a name that has come back into fashion in recent years, but nobody ever called her by anything but her childhood nickname. I suppose that's a custom of the wealthy. Pepsi *came from money*, as they say around here, married Quincy when he was poor, and managed to stay married to him after he got rich. The years had taken their toll on Pepsi, but she wore them as gracefully as anyone can. She dressed well (black with pearls) and rocked her short rich-lady haircut, if you know what I mean. A chic Washington woman of her generation would have *had some work done* by now. Pepsi seemed to have skipped the cosmetic surgery.

She still looked stylish and elegant. It seemed to me that the world of rich white people was once a better place, and that Pepsi was an envoy from that place. All five feet of her. I hugged her back gently. "It's good to see you, too, Pepsi," I said. I really meant it. I'm not much of a Family Values guy, but without kin what's the point, you know?

Quincy strode into the foyer, shook my hand, and pulled me into the house. Pepsi shut the door and shooed us both into the dining room.

Q nodded at my suit approvingly. "You clean up pretty good, kid."

"When in Rome..." I said.

"A gentleman fits in wherever he goes," said Quincy.

"Psh," Pepsi said to me, "as if *he* was a gentleman before *I* got my hands on him."

Quincy surprised me by leaning over, throwing his arm around his wife, and kissing the top of her head with real feeling. "These have been good years," he said. "I'm fortunate to have spent them with you."

Pepsi seemed flustered by this display of affection. "*Now* he tells me," she said. Embarrassed, she gave him a quick hug back.

I didn't know what to say, so I stood there smiling vaguely and feeling awkward. The gift of gab doesn't guarantee a talent for actual connection with other human beings. Also, the conversation seemed to have developed a worrisome *undercurrent*, and we hadn't even had dinner yet.

Speaking of worrisome, the entrée was tuna wiggle, Pepsi's specialty. It seemed their cook/housekeeper had the weekend off. Whatever I'd been expecting of dinner at my rich relatives' house, it was not a bygone generation's bygone comfort food. It wasn't horrible, but how good could anything be that involved canned peas and canned tuna? I'm no food snob, so I said Thank You Very Much and cleaned my plate. I politely declined a second helping. I'm no martyr, either. You ask: What kind of wine goes with tuna wiggle? Pepsi served a nice New York State Chardonnay, chilled in a silver wine bucket full of ice. The wine helped, but only a little. I followed the example of my host and hostess and nursed one glass throughout dinner. I've never been much of a drinker.

After dinner, Pepsi emphatically declined my offer of help with the dishes. Quincy led me to the library and slid the dark oak pocket doors closed behind us. I looked around for a bust of Pallas like in Poe's "The Raven," but didn't see one. (*Don't think about ravens.*)

The house, I'd learned during dinner, had been lovingly restored a few years ago. I'm sure it cost a bundle, but Pepsi was of a generation and a class that thought it vulgar to discuss money with guests, even relatives. The library hadn't needed much work, except for what looked like new forest green curtains (thick as comforters). The thick old-school wood-slat Venetian blinds might have had new cords. I noticed because Quincy closed the blinds in all four of the library's high windows. Lest we be observed?

He turned on some lights and waved me to an old soft-leather chair, the twin of his, next to the cold fireplace.

"No fire in the hearth in this house anymore," he said. "Probably a metaphor."

The house felt warm enough to me. We were both wearing suits and ties, after all.

I tried to match his tone. "Well, nothing's coming down the chimney tonight, right?"

Quincy looked startled. "Jesus, I *hope* not," he said, staring at me as if I knew something he didn't.

It was about time to get to the point, I thought. "Uncle Q, I really appreciate being invited to your home. After our little walk this afternoon, I have to ask, are you in any danger? Am I?"

Q looked away from me and into the empty fireplace, thinking about how to answer.

"Physically, probably not—or not yet," he finally said. "Spiritually? Very possibly."

I couldn't think of a single polite thing to say, so I kept quiet. Strategic deference to my elders was something I'd learned from all the well-bred Southern boys I went to college with.

Quincy looked up at me. "You think I'm evading your question," Quincy said.

"I don't know much about the things of the spirit," I said in what I hoped was a neutral tone. *Don't give a shit about that nonsense*, is what I meant.

Quincy waved his hand; he knew what I meant. "These things are hard to talk about. People resort to poetry or painting or song and dance when plain words fail them. I'm not a religious man, either, in any sense of the word." He looked at me like he was studying me. "But after what we saw today, is it so hard to believe that there might be another world?"

"I *still* don't know what happened out in that field," I said. "I can't make any sense of what I saw. And I'm afraid to think about what I heard."

Quincy nodded encouragingly. He wanted me to talk this out.

"By *another world*, are you talking about Heaven and Hell?" I said.

"*No!*" With one big hand he made a sweeping horizontal gesture to cut off that line of inquiry altogether. "Look, I've always just called it *the Other World.* It was there long before Christianity. The Other World was there before Judaism. *It's always been there.* It's a dangerous place, sure. It's dangerous to go anywhere you don't know the laws and the customs. But don't you *want* to know? Why *else* do we live but to learn things?"

"I guess I've never thought about it," I said. *I never wanted to think about it,* is what that usually means. It's certainly what *I* meant.

Uncle Q observed me for a long, uncomfortable interval, assessing me. For an odd moment, I saw myself as he saw me: average height, thin build, thinning sandy hair cut short, hazel eyes, unlined face, no distinguishing tattoos, scars or other physical characteristics. In a word, *unprepossessing.* In the heat of the moment, women have called me *weaselly* if they were angry with me or *foxy* if they were happy with me. Finally Quincy shook his head, "You're a nice enough fella, Jerry, but you're *untested,* still a boy. You're how old now, forty?"

I could feel my face heat up. "Thirty-five," I said. "*Sir,*" I added.

"Military service?"

I shook my head No.

"Married?"

"Divorced," I said. Quincy grunted. He didn't say *Quitter,* but disapproval was all over his face. I didn't much like what he was saying, but he wasn't wrong about me. Except for the one ill-fated marriage, I'd spent my life avoiding danger, commitments, and entangling alliances. Avoidance was part of my survival instinct.

Quincy, by contrast, served as a young infantry lieutenant in the Korean War. Typical of his generation, he never talked about what he'd seen, done, and suffered. All the family knew is that he'd come back covered with medals and so badly wounded it took him a year to recover. If anybody ever recovers from that kind of thing. So I was inclined to give him a break; he deserved some respect from his younger relatives.

He continued watching me. Finally he smiled and said, "Well, you may have escaped the fire thus far in your life, but your manners are impeccable and your impulse control is first-rate. At your age, if one of my elders had talked to me like I just talked to you, I'd have told him to fuck off."

I laughed, couldn't help it. He laughed along with me, then turned serious again.

"Here's what I learned in the Army," he said. "Everybody dies eventually. *Everybody.* The thing is to make your time count. Cowards, villains, and idiots will send you in harm's way, but only if you let them use you. There's no virtue in being cannon fodder. The best you can do in this life do is look out for your friends and family."

"And yourself?"

"Nothing wrong with that," Quincy said. "No particular virtue in it, either." He held up a hand to indicate the house we were sitting in. "The things I learned from my ... *dealings* with the Other World have made me rich..." He trailed off, staring into some inner distance.

"But...?" I prompted.

"Well, look at me," he said. "I'm eighty-four years old, strong as a horse, live in a stately home overlooking the Atlantic. But none of that will last—*I* won't last—forever. Houses can be restored, but not people. I'm starting to think that during my travels in the Other World I may have incurred a *debt,* or that I may have broken some *law.* A law of which I was ignorant, but still."

The conversation was starting to scare the hell out of me. The tuna wiggle I'd eaten threatened to make a curtain call. "Where's Aunt Pepsi in all of this?" I said, breathing deeply and swallowing hard.

Q glared at me. "She's *nowhere* in all of this," he said. "I've kept Pepsi out of it. I expect you to do likewise. This discussion is just between you and me."

"That's fine," I said, "but what if something happens to you?"

"Then you still say *nothing*," Quincy said. "Is that so hard to understand?" He paused for a long moment. "They have seen *you*, but I don't want them to see Pepsi. And they won't—if you keep your own counsel."

"Who are they?" I said. "If you know, I mean."

"I don't know exactly, but I can guess," he said. "We visit them in their world—briefly, at first, for all the reasons people travel anywhere on Earth. Then they mask themselves in our desires and memories and begin to visit us in our world. They visit us first in our dreams. And finally, their physical world begins to manifest in ours."

"And that's what happened—what we both saw—in that field?"

Quincy nodded sadly. "I dreamed of my lost love—everybody has one—dreamed we lay abed together in that field. I tried to embrace her, but she turned away before I could see her face. Above us the dawn sky filled up with more stars than I'd ever seen before. Out of that sky flew something like an owl with a dog in its beak. It ... *greeted* me. I woke up in horror with my heart racing. Some of that was just dream-nonsense, of course. But then, today I saw marks that might have been from where that bed sat in that field."

"I don't know what I saw," I said.

"We see the Other World and those who live there, not as *they* are, but as *we* are," said Quincy.

"Why did you tell me not to listen to that ... *bird*, or whatever I thought I saw flying down at us?" I said.

"Well, it was calling us, wasn't it? Didn't you feel yourself being *summoned?*"

"What right does something from *your* dream have to summon *me*?" I was angry again. Anger feels manlier than fear.

Q looked sad. "It's never about *rights* in the Other World, only *power.*"

Power to do what? I wondered. I didn't ask. Maybe I should have.

Confusion Worse Confounded

Wandering between two worlds, one dead
The other powerless to be born,
With nowhere yet to rest my head
Like these, on earth I wait forlorn.

- (Matthew Arnold, "Stanzas from the Grande Chartreuse")

Quincy and I talked on into the night, but I don't think we got anywhere. He was either evading my simple questions or wasn't sure how to answer them. Did he not *know* what had happened to him? But why would he withhold information from me?

In the middle of this unsatisfactory conversation, Pepsi knocked quietly, stuck her head into the library, said good night to me, and told Q not to stay up too late. I thanked her for dinner. Pepsi smiled, waggled her fingers, ducked back out, and slid the door shut again.

Around midnight, seeing that Quincy had told me everything he knew or everything he was willing to tell me, I told him I had to get going. He walked me out to my car.

Above us the sky was clear. It was the ordinary sky of Earth, as far as I could tell, full of the same old blurry stars. I saw the navigation lights of an international flight heading north up the East Coast before flying out over the Atlantic to Europe. I wondered if any passengers were looking down to see the light illuminating the house and spilling out of Quincy's open front door.

I finally asked the question I'd driven down here to ask. "What the hell do I do now, Quincy?"

Q observed me closely. "What you do depends on what you *want*, kiddo," he said.

I wasn't about to get into that with him. I said Thanks and Goodnight, shook his hand, and drove back down the drive.

I resisted a sudden urge to stomp on the gas, spin my front wheels, and mess up his driveway. As he'd correctly observed, my impulse control was first-rate. Uncle Q was a bridge. I wasn't going to burn him just because I was frustrated.

I slept late Sunday morning, had a light breakfast, and went for a long walk. I quit running a couple of years ago when my knees began to hurt all the time. I can take a hint. Once I started walking instead, my knees felt fine. After the walk, I did some gentle yoga and some tai chi. I don't know if these things do any actual good, but they make me feel better.

Sunday afternoon, showered and feeling virtuous, I drove in to the office to solve some minor software problems customers had complained about. Amazing what you can get done in a quiet building without interruptions from phones and colleagues. It also doesn't hurt to send your boss an email status report outside normal working hours. Had the approach of middle age made me cynical and manipulative, or was I born that way?

Sunday night I had a date. Well, okay, it was a tentative agreement to meet a lady for an early beer at a bar downtown. Maybe after the drink we'd decide to go out for pizza, who knew? But it was more like a date than anything I'd done since the divorce. I wasn't nursing a broken heart, exactly, but I had a renewed distrust of human connection. Better to have loved and lost, I suppose. Anyway, rather than going home, I hung around the office laying out my work for the coming week until it was time to drive into Portsmouth.

I shut off the lights, locked the door, and walked around to the employee parking area in the back. Our building was one of many that had been built near the airport formerly known as Pease Air Force Base. In 1991 the Air Force had returned most of the land to civilian control, and—except for a small Air National Guard contingent—flown away to bases elsewhere in the country. The airport was a lot quieter than the airbase had been. My boss would rather have rented office space downtown, but you can do software development anywhere, and rents were cheaper here.

If I was thinking about anything as I walked, it was whether Leda, the lady I was meeting, was my type. I wasn't sure I *had* a type, exactly. It was more like: was I attracted to the woman in question and was she attracted to me? I guessed we'd find out.

The paved parking area was surrounded by bushes, a barrier between our building and an identical white office building next door. The bushes grew thickly. Many were still green in October, and the evergreens planted among them would stay green all winter.

I was surprised to see a tall naked woman standing in the bushes maybe thirty feet from my car, holding the branches apart with spread arms. She watched me intently without shame and without fear.

I felt an echo of what I'd felt in the field with Quincy when I saw that impossible sky above us. A brightly-lit dread filled up the center of my body from groin to throat. I was seeing something that couldn't be there. The woman stood in the middle of the flames of my burning yellow dread (my *holy* dread?) and claimed it for her own. We were two, yet somehow we were one.

She was here, it seemed, to claim *me*. It was clear in the way things in dreams are clear that she wanted me to enter the Other World with her. Clear from the way she looked at me with something that transcended desire. *Is this what a theophany is like?* I wondered. The sky behind the woman was not of Earth; I'd seen it before.

My feelings were clear as pond ice, but my thoughts grew muzzy. Once again it was like being drunk or stoned. What I remembered and held on to were Quincy's words: *they mask themselves in our desires.* I stood still on the asphalt.

"Who *are* you?" I asked the impossible woman. How sturdy her arms and legs! How magnificent her breasts! Her bare sex, I saw, was swollen and wet with her desire. For *me?* Why? She was like something out of the ancient world. "*What* are you?"

The woman made a gesture with her left hand that communicated exactly: *Come with me and find out!* I saw her arm move, but the bushes in which she appeared moved not at all, as if her mere presence held them apart like a strong wind.

"Not tonight," I managed to say. "I've got a date."

Somehow I managed to get myself into the Honda. It started with one turn of the key. Thanks, new battery. As I drove past the woman and out to the street, I saw her expression change from Archaic smile to unutterable sadness, still shining with the light from what Quincy had called the Other World.

Even before I was gone from the parking lot, she was gone from where she'd been standing. The streetlights came on in the autumn dusk. I suppose I should have gone back to see what traces she'd left behind, but I didn't dare.

Bad news if I'd only imagined her. Worse news if she'd actually been there.

4

Hitting the Escape Key

I drove a mile or so to one of the malls and parked under one of the lights in the very center of a big parking lot mostly empty of cars. I sat in my car shaking and breathing hard like I had hypothermia, trying to get myself under control. Half of my panic was fear, but the other half was painful raw desire. It took a long time to calm down. I played that scene with the naked woman (she sure *looked* like a woman) over and over in my head, but got no closer to understanding it. To grasp what had happened, I'd have to have followed her into the Other World.

As I was shaking my head to dismiss that idea, my phone buzzed with an incoming text message. It was Leda asking where I was. Instead of texting back, I called her. That's a possible guy-girl protocol breach, but I was having a hard time coping tonight.

She picked the call right up. "Jerry? Weren't we meeting for drinks tonight? You're not blowing me off, are you?" She sounded more resigned than upset. I guessed she'd been blown off before.

"Look," I said, "I'm kind of freaking out here. Something very weird just happened. I'm not sure a bar is a good idea."

She didn't miss a beat. "You still feel like pizza?" I said I did. "How about if I pick one up and meet you somewhere?"

"Forgive me," I said, "but ... my place or yours?"

"Yours," she said. "You sound pretty shaky. I don't think I'm in any danger." I could hear the smile in her voice. It made me feel better.

23

"I promise to be a perfect gentleman," I said. "I'll even pay for the pizza."

"Yeah, right," she said. "Like I haven't seen *that* porno more than once."

We laughed. I gave her my address, said goodbye, and drove home.

Forty minutes after I got there, Leda showed up in her little Chevy. I walked out the kitchen door to meet her in my driveway. She got out of her car and without preamble, simply hugged me. That was a pleasant surprise. Women are actually kind of awesome, I remembered.

I held my door open for her and carried the big pizza box in behind her. I set it on the table, figuring we'd just grab slices out of the box, but no, Leda would have none of that. She got me to break out dishes, napkins, silverware, and beer glasses. Bachelor Boy Scout that I am, I had a couple of cold six-packs in the refrigerator.

By unspoken agreement we sat on opposite sides of the little retro Formica kitchen table, just enjoying pepperoni and mushroom pizza and talking of this and that. It was nice to share a meal with someone again, a meal that wasn't a working lunch or dinner with a client.

Leda and I had worked together briefly before she left the company for a better administrative job with a firm downtown. She knew I was divorced; I knew she was between relationships. I thought she was cute, but I never date colleagues. When we'd talked at work, I got the feeling that she might not find me totally repulsive. I waited exactly two days after Leda left before calling to suggest we meet for drinks. "Glad you called," she said. "Thought *I* was going to have to call *you.*" She never dated colleagues, either, smart lady.

She told me all about her new job, her bosses and her coworkers. I told her what had happened at the company in her absence, how Bob, my boss, had apparently hired Leda's replacement for breasts, not brains.

Leda laughed. "Yeah, Bob kept looking for my boobs, but he never found them."

"I don't think there's any polite response a gentleman can make to *that,*" I said.

She laughed, I smiled. It struck me how *comfortable* it felt to be sitting here with her. Maybe it was a delayed reaction to yesterday in the field with the scary flying creature in the air and tonight in the parking lot with the scary naked woman in the bushes. I felt very much at home with Leda, as if I'd always known her. Being who I am, I tried to chide myself for this sentimentality, but my heart wasn't in it tonight.

Once we'd finished eating, I made two aluminum foil packs of the leftover pizza, one for each of us, and put them in the refrigerator. Which reminded me. "What do I owe you?"

"Don't be silly," she said. I know enough about women to know she didn't mean that. Whatever she was making in her new job, it was a lot less than I was being paid. Professional and clerical salaries around New Hampshire are fucking ridiculous. And by that I mean *low.*

"Nah, you did me a huge favor," I said. "I'd feel better if I paid tonight. You can pay next time, okay?" I handed her enough money to cover any conceivable pizza, but not so much she'd think I was being creepy. One learns these nuances in the dating wars. But "next time"? What was I thinking?

"Well ... *okay,*" she said and took the money, as if reluctantly. I got the sense I'd done the right thing and passed an unspoken test. Women are actually kind of a pain in the ass, I remembered.

Leda watched as I rinsed off the dishes and stuck them in the dishwasher. We took our beers into the living room. She looked at the couch and did an exaggerated double take.

"Whoa! Wouldn't have thought you were the floral print type, Jerry," she teased. "Interesting choice for a straight guy."

I laughed. "Very funny," I said. "No, I rented the house furnished. That hideous couch came with it. I generally just ignore it and it doesn't bother me."

She looked around the living room and poked her head into the little hallway. Uninvited, she took a quick tour of my bedroom, the bathroom, and the guestroom. She saw what I'd seen when I rented the place: some woman had decorated the house according to her very particular, very girly taste. I wasn't sure how much latitude my lease gave me to change things. Beyond keeping things clean and orderly, my surroundings didn't matter to me, and I'd been pretty busy since I moved in. Leda nodded her head to herself as if she'd confirmed something, either about me or about the previous owner. Or was she checking out my housekeeping, for God's sake? Women are actually awfully nosy, I remembered.

But we weren't here to talk about cleaning tips or the color scheme, were we? Again by unspoken agreement we sat down on opposite sides of the flowery couch. Now it was me she was watching closely. I watched her closely, too. She was nice to look at, almost as tall as me, shining dark hair, blue eyes, hourglass figure stuffed into jeans, a loose green sweater over what she'd implied were original equipment human breasts.

"So what happened today?" she said. She sounded curious, not skeptical or judgmental.

"It wasn't just today," I said. "Something bizarre happened yesterday, too." For some reason (family loyalty?), I decided just to tell my part of the story and to leave Uncle Quincy out of it. I gave Leda an abbreviated version of what I'd seen in the field on the north side of town—and what had chased me back to the safety of the sidewalk.

"Wait," she said, "before that happened, you were at *a little girl's birthday party?* That is *so sweet.*" She wasn't teasing, not at all. I started to worry about Leda just a little. It would not be unheard of for an almost-thirty-something never-married woman to have biological clock issues coloring her view of the world—and of me. If so, uh-oh.

"My folks moved us away from Portsmouth years ago," I said. "They died when I was in college, first my mother, then my father." Leda said the things you say to acknowledge someone's old loss. I continued, "After college, I had a series of jobs around Washington, clawing my way to the middle. After I moved back here, I wanted to get to know the family again. Whenever somebody invites me, I *go.* Birthday parties, barbecues, holidays, the whole nine."

Leda nodded. That made sense to her.

"So anyway..." I went on to tell her in more detail what had happened to me—outside the office building where she used to work, for God's sake. In Portsmouth, New Hampshire. On a Sunday.

As I told the story, she watched me as if she was thinking about how to help. It was a relief to talk to someone. I told her almost everything I'd seen, heard (or not heard), and felt.

I held my hands out, palms up. "You think I'm crazy? I don't *feel* crazy, just confused."

"You sound pretty sane to me," she said. "You weren't drinking either time?" I said I wasn't. "No pot?" I shook my head No. "Prescription drugs?"

"The universe has given me bad luck with women, but excellent health," I said. "It's rare that I have to take anything more than aspirin."

Leda nodded. "You've probably already thought of this," she said, "but would it make sense to go see a doctor?"

I liked the way she said it. She was smart enough about male psychology to know we resist being *told* what to do. "You know, I never thought of that," I said, "a loose wire in the brain or something?"

"I can recommend a good GP," she said. "If you don't already have a doctor, I mean."

"I don't, so that would be very kind of you," I said. She dug around in her purse, found the doctor's business card, and handed it to me. Women's purses are like magicians' hats.

"Seems like the least I can do in return for you buying the pizza and beer," she said.

We smiled at each other for quite a long time. It felt good—awkward, but good. *What is happening here?* I wondered. Were we about to meet in the middle of the cabbage rose couch and kiss chastely like frightened teenagers? Repair to my lonely bedroom for some lusty adult activities?

Leda broke the stalemate first by looking away from me, looking into her half-full beer glass, looking at the floor, and finally looking around the room before looking back at me again.

"I haven't been entirely honest with you," she said.

"Whoever *is* entirely honest?" I said. I wasn't being cynical. I hadn't told her *my* whole story, either. Honesty doesn't have much to do with the human condition as I understand it.

"Oh, I know people who never lie," she said. "*Never.*" Then in an apparent change of direction, "Do you know whose house this is?"

I told her the name of the Massachusetts law firm I paid rent to.

Leda shook her head No, that had not been what she meant. "I guess I should have asked if you knew whose house this *used to be.* I wasn't sure myself till I looked around a bit and finally put two and two together."

I tried to make a joke of it. "Am I gonna want to know this?"

She wasn't willing to joke or change the subject. "You told me what happened to you. I don't understand it, either. If I had to guess, I don't think my doctor will find anything wrong with you. But I *do* think you're in some kind of danger." She moved down to my end of the couch next to me and put her hand on my thigh, not a sexual maneuver, just a reassuring gesture, one human being to another. "Jerry, I know people who can help and advise you—I'm ... a *Friend* of those people."

I'm not totally obtuse. "Oh, so one of *those people* used to own this house?" Leda nodded. "And you belong to the, um, *organization* that manages their, um, worldly affairs, their estates or whatever?"

"Yup." She moved back to her own end of the couch. I could still feel the warm spot on my thigh where her hand had been.

I shook my head in sheer frustration. "Dammit," I said, "instead of telling me that, I'd almost rather you'd asked if I've *accepted Jesus as my personal savior.*" The opening gambit of many a pious husband-hunting Southern gal. And an ironclad guarantee I'd never call her for a second date.

Leda tilted her head, pouted her lips, and batted her crossed eyes at me: a world-class duckface. "Well? *Have* you?"

I told her what I'd told Quincy. "I'm not very religious, I'm afraid. I don't know much about the things of the spirit." Both those things were facts.

"Who is and who does?" she said. "Not me, that's for sure." She sounded a little sad; I wondered why.

"But you *know people*," I said. I hope I didn't sound nasty, but fear makes me edgy.

"I do," she agreed calmly. "I know people who know things I'm afraid even to think about. I can arrange an introduction. Interested?"

I didn't answer right away because I was locked in indecision. Leda knew not to press me. Her expression was somewhere between concern and disappointment. I'd been disappointing women my whole life; I'd never liked doing that, but I'd gotten used to it.

Part of the problem was that this situation looked to be lousy with danger, commitments, and entangling alliances, all the things that would mess up my new start in life.

Another part of the problem was that I couldn't tell where my best interests lay. Quincy wisely pointed out that whatever I chose to do would depend on what I wanted. Beyond making enough money to live decently, I didn't *know* what the hell I wanted. I'd started to like Leda and wanted to get to know her better, but...

The last part of the problem was that I didn't know where my duty to my family lay. What obligation did I have to Quincy? How could I ask Leda for help without betraying what Uncle Q had told me in confidence? Without kin, a man doesn't amount to much. Without loyalty to family, a relationship with them is impossible.

And with that thought, I began to wonder about Quincy. A man who'd gone to the Other World and acquired power, at least the power to make himself rich in this world. A man who'd done that, traveled back and forth between worlds and supposedly kept it secret even from his own wife since the 1950s, it seemed to me, was unlikely to have involved his nephew in that secret entirely by accident. What obligation did Quincy feel to *me?*

I might treat my elders with respect, but I'd always tried to be nobody's fool. Good luck with that in twenty-first century America. And good luck with that in any marriage, by the way.

Not wanting to be rude to Leda, I finally said, "I'm at least a little interested, but I'm also scared shitless, pardon the vulgarity." I smiled at her. "I really appreciate your coming over and bringing pizza to comfort me, but what you're telling me scares me almost as much as ... whatever it was that happened to me."

Leda grinned at me. "Yeah, the Friends get a lot of that," she said. "We *choose* to be friends with ... people who often scare us. And we're all scared of something, aren't we?"

5

Dire Straits Sings "Skateaway"

Between two worlds life hovers like a star,
'Twixt night and morn, upon the horizon's verge.

- (Lord Byron, *Don Juan*)

I walked Leda out to her car. We hugged in the driveway with what felt like real affection. She kissed me on the cheek. What did *that* mean? Had I just been friend-zoned? Was she offended that I hadn't invited her to spend the night? Did I care?

"What happens now?" She was observing me in the yellow glow of the light next to the kitchen door, a wounded soldier in the dating wars conducting reconnaissance on a wounded enemy.

"I want to see you again," I said. It felt good to tell the truth.

"*Good*," she said. She was smiling at me. "When? And who calls who first?"

"Tuesday," I said with pretend seriousness. "Either of us can call or text first, no harm no foul. But no phone stalking and no crazy behavior."

"Agreed," she said, matching my silly poker face. She started to open her car door, then turned back to me. "Is there some reason you didn't attempt to, um, *seduce* me tonight?"

"I like you," I said. "I didn't want to mess things up between us when you came over here under a white flag of truce and bearing pizza."

Her face softened. "I like you, too," she said. Pause. "Would you for God's sake give me a real kiss, please?"

I held her tightly and kissed her. She held me and kissed me back. It was wonderful. Neither of us wanted to let go first.

"Huh, you *do* like me," she said. "I wasn't sure. Don't believe I've ever met a gentleman of the old school before."

"And you like *me*," I said. "This mutual liking business is kind of a new experience for me. I want to take things slow—before I take you into the bedroom for the final disappointment."

Leda looked me up and down. "Patient, kind, *and* modest," she said. "This is going to be epic."

"You forgot 'handsome'," I said. "God, you pretty girls are *so* self-centered."

She inhaled sharply. " *'Pretty',* is it? You better stop flattering me, or I'll drag you into the bedroom right now and disappoint you all night long."

That night I dropped off to sleep as soon as my head touched the pillow. Alone. No dreams came, thank God.

As it happened, both Leda and I got busy at work and didn't get together again until Friday night. Remember the forty-hour workweek? Yeah, me neither.

We went to a movie, a stupid romantic comedy. We enjoyed sitting in the dark making fun of it. Then we strolled around downtown in our winter coats, hats, and gloves. The weather had turned cold early, dropped below freezing, and stayed there day after day. Farewell, fashion; hello, layers.

Portsmouth is a pretty town, especially now that it's been lovingly restored to its colonial prewar glory. Most of us simply pretended the city had always been this way, that no wars had ever happened here. Is that the Piscataqua River flowing past us, or is it *denial?* Har har har.

Leda, of course, would know all the details of what had happened here. Learning the city's true history had to be part of membership in the Friends. Leda knew my true history, too, at least its recent episodes. But I couldn't make myself talk about the incomprehensible danger I faced. Denying the threat's existence had built a wall between us.

The next move was mine. I was afraid to make it. She knew people. I was afraid to meet them. And so far, the Other World had not intruded again into mine, so I delayed and delayed deciding what to do. Leda gave me time and space to figure things out. I appreciated that, because I was really stuck.

If there's any advantage to *not* sleeping with a woman you're attracted to, it's that you don't have to have The Talk with her. You know the one. *We really have to talk,* she says. *Oh, shit,* you say. *That Talk: Where Do We Go from Here?*

We talked about everything else, though. Personal histories (the PG-rated versions). Education. Books (mostly her), movies and television (mostly me), and music (considerable overlap). Likes and dislikes. Somewhere during our extended conversations, we became, not lovers yet, but *friends.* It wasn't at all like being sidelined in the friend zone. It was more like we had things to *say* to each other and things to *learn* from each other. We actually *talked* on the phone, rather than texting inanities. I liked hearing her voice, and I think she liked hearing mine.

She wouldn't wait forever for me on the other side of the wall I'd built, not if I knew anything about women. But while she waited, we went on walks around Portsmouth (still below freezing), saw the latest movies (still not so hot). She took me on a tour of the public library. I appreciated the thought; I even got a library card just so she'd smile at me. I recognize how pathetic that sounds. She showed me where I might find the books about the people she was Friends with, should I wish to learn more, hint hint. *Maybe later for that,* I thought.

There was certainly a sexual subtext to our relationship, but sex wasn't the whole point of it. Leda and I discovered we agreed about most things, disagreed about a few things, respected each other's opinions—and always enjoyed spending time together.

I was surprised how disappointed I felt when she called to break our afternoon date. We'd planned to go ice skating on a frozen pond down by the beach.

"Hey, if you have to work, you have to work," I told her. "That's the world we live in. No hard feelings here."

"*You're* still going, right?" she said. "You really should go. You've got the afternoon off, and the skating won't be any good after it snows."

"I think I will," I said. "I haven't skated for years. This way you won't have to watch me stumble around and fall down while I break in my new skates and get used to the ice again."

"Ha!" she said. "You've never seen *me* skate."

"Listen," I said, "could I interest you in spaghetti and salad at my house tonight?" I'd never cooked for her before.

"Sounds great," she said. "I'll bring some wine." I could hear that she was smiling.

I thought we might have to change our Facebook status to "It's Complicated."

The pond was a wide body of (I hoped) shallow water, three or four acres surrounded by cattails. All the kids were in school and nobody was skating on it this afternoon, but there were skate tracks all over the ice. The ice itself looked smooth and thick, even near the shore. I stepped off the bank onto the ice, first one boot, then two. I bounced gently up and down. No noise, no movement, no bubbles: safe to skate on.

Still, the pond looked ominous under the November overcast. The day was really cold and mostly windless. My breath swirled around my face.

Right, nothing for it but to do it, I thought. I sat on the bank and laced up skates for the first time in over twenty years. The leather was stiff and uncooperative in the cold, but I managed to get the laces tied securely before my hands went numb and useless. I put my gloves back on, left my shoes where they were, and cautiously stood up.

I don't think of myself as athletic, but my coordination is pretty good. It didn't take long before I got the hang of skating again, forward and backward. I was very proud of myself. It didn't take long before I got overconfident. I went sliding across the middle of the pond on my ass, coated with shaved ice. I didn't hurt myself, and falling down like a little kid made me laugh. My laugh echoed into the distance, into silence. I was *very* glad the fates had brought me back to New Hampshire.

I got up (*that* was harder than I remembered) and began skating at a deliberate pace around the outside of the pond. I'd also forgotten how good it felt to glide. The easy rhythmic effort of my arm and leg muscles kept me warm, moving on the knives on the bottom of my shoes, knives that glided on a thin layer of meltwater beneath the blades.

It was cold magic. Cold sun shone briefly through a rift in the clouds. The hiss of my skates. The smell of the saltmarsh, still unfrozen. A breeze off the Atlantic carrying the scent of ocean. I moved, I flew, with breath coming in cold and going out warm, smooth and easy. In the distance, red-tailed hawks wheeled high above a tall, old pine tree. The tree grew in the center of an island in the middle of an adjoining marsh on the far side of the pond. One hawk cried to another, a call with no words; I'd never heard the sound in real life. I was amusing myself estimating the number of movies where I might have heard a hawk's cry (not to mention *The Simpsons*) until...

The sky on the north side of the pond *opened up*. The sun of the Other World shone into this one, onto me. I felt its desert warmth.

Beneath me, thick ice groaned as that other sun heated the near side of the pond. I heard the sound but didn't know what it meant.

The sun of the Other World illuminated a mighty city, a city-state as it seemed to me, but modern, with tower roofs of metal and tall glass windows. Above the towers, flags flew. My vision worked in that world like a telescope. The more I looked at anything in that splendid city, the more of it I saw. That beautiful city spoke strongly to something in me, as strongly as if it had been built for me alone.

The flags held the image of the winged creature who had flown down at Quincy and me in the field. It seemed the city was the creature's, that the creature had much to tell me. That if I would only consent to enter the city of the creature, it would teach me everything there was to learn about the Other World.

Atop the battlements of the creature's city, I saw the goddess who had appeared to me in the parking lot behind my office. When she saw me, even at that great distance, her gaze locked with mine. Smiling her Archaic smile, she dropped her robe and stood naked. She offered her splendid, vibrant, naked self to me, it seemed, if I would only consent to enter the Other World and parley with her and with the winged god of her city.

This time I was more tempted than fearful. All I had to do was skate *that way* and the Other World would gather me in. Transcendent knowledge and transcendent bliss would be mine. Eternally? That was less certain. *What you do depends on what you want,* Quincy told me. What did I want?

Being who I am, I was far surer of what I *didn't* want. I didn't want to be someone's fool. Not the flying creature's and not the glowing goddess'.

Not *Quincy's* fool, either. What I really wanted right in this moment when I was caught between two worlds was the truth from Uncle Q. This Other World offer was too good to be true.

"Thanks, but no thanks, my lady," I said to the woman I saw with such paradoxical clarity on the gleaming battlements at that infinite remove from me.

It seemed she yearned toward me, extending both arms in my direction: *Fear not, my love will make you strong.*

As I shook my head, thinking *Sorry, no,* the eternal warmth of that strange world faded and was gone. I found myself back in cloudy ten-degree New Hampshire November.

I also found myself still standing atop the ice, but with my skates covered by meltwater. The whole slab of ice on my side of the pond had broken away from the rest, and it was tilting me into the cattails, sliding me into the water.

Winter misfortune only becomes an adventure if you survive it. I discovered how hard it is to skate uphill with your feet under water. If I fell this time, I wouldn't be laughing at myself. It's all fun and games till you find yourself on the underside of the ice. The slab made alarming cracking noises three feet beneath me.

I got mad. "*Really?*" I yelled at the denizens of the now-invisible Other World. "*That's* the deal here? If I don't do things your way, you fucking *drown* me?"

Nobody answered. All that happened was that I made few yards' progress toward my car, maybe a hundred yards away. My feet were now so cold from the ice water that they hurt. As long as you feel pain, you're still not dead. That's good, right?

I slipped and fell to my hands and knees in ice water. Swell, wet feet, and now wet jeans. I didn't feel like laughing. The additional discomfort only made me angrier and more determined. I got back up again. Step by arduous, slippery step, my car got closer and closer.

I made it off the tilted slab of ice, back onto the part of the pond that was still frozen hard and flat. *Finally.* With a feeling of enormous relief, I skated the last fifty yards back to the bank. I was *very* cold by the time I got to land. My vision was blurry. I might have been weeping in relief.

The rest of my skating survival story was mostly low comedy. I had to sit in the car, shivering, running the engine and blasting the heat until my red, chapped hands got warm enough to undo the frozen skate laces. Then the icy laces didn't want to come untied. I finally started laughing at myself again. I suppose I could have called 911, but what would I say? "Come help me untie my skates"? I'd almost rather die.

By the time I got my skates and wet socks off (blessed relief!), put dry boots on my burning red feet, and drove away alive and uninjured, I knew what I wanted.

And He Can Cook, Too

There's a love, I want to say, that's new,
Fresh forever, surging through each minute

- (Robert G. Tucker, "Imagine Beast-Wings")

I had a pot of water on the stove and was washing salad fixings when I heard Leda drive up. She let herself in the unlocked kitchen door, put her purse and a bottle of Chianti on the kitchen table, hung her coat over a kitchen chair, and immediately stepped in to hug and kiss me. I was smiling as I kissed her. Halfway into this very pleasant ritual of greeting, she stepped back and looked at me.

"What?" she said. "Did something else happen to you?"

Her instincts were excellent. "Something did happen," I said. "Those people you're friends with? I want to talk to them."

And with that, I took down the wall I'd built between us. She knew it, too.

"I think we've postponed *the ultimate disappointment* long enough," she said. "Dinner can wait." She took my hand and led me into my own bedroom.

I guess we'd come together at the end of long dry spells, but we still moved slowly to, um, slake our thirst. She turned on the bedside lamp. I took that as a good sign; she wanted to see me as much as I wanted to see her. So beautiful. So beautiful.

There was a lot of smiling and touching. There was even some laughing, the happy kind, not the nervous kind. I found I was having trouble keeping enough air in my lungs. I wasn't running away from anything this time, though.

"Look," I said hoarsely, "I really hope this goes well. I love you." I was not entirely surprised to hear myself say the words.

Tears came to her eyes, but she was still smiling. "I loved you first," she said.

"Nuh-uh," I said.

At an early stage of the proceedings, we had a brief, honest exchange of sexual health data (good *and* good) and birth control planning (IUD *and* condom, at least for tonight). This sort of thing is much easier when you don't have an extensive history of random drugged and drunken sex. I'm sorry if that sounds judgmental, but welcome to the twenty-first century, everybody.

Normally, becoming intimate with someone new is an exciting but awkward voyage of discovery. Usually the first trip to the bedroom is an early part of getting to know the other person as a person. But Leda and I had spent so much time together and gotten to know each other so well that we were able to concentrate on pleasing each other—and on being pleased. The old-school courtship we'd fallen into has much to recommend it.

You like that? Very much. *Do you like that?* Oh, yes. *Would you mind doing that a bit longer?* I'd love to. *Please don't stop.* Not till you beg me.

When you like someone and come to love them for who they are, sex is more like play. But even when it's playful, it's still lovemaking. It's making love. Together, Leda and I were making something new in the world. I'm not talking about conceiving a child, we'd decide about that together in the future. I'm talking about *creating* something with our own bodies and minds.

But all that mystical stuff aside, there are things a man can do to synchronize his sexual rhythm with a woman's. If you're an ordinary man like me, it might take some extra effort to learn how to please a woman. Let me just say that it's worth the effort.

I wouldn't claim to know about all women, but Leda seemed more willing to *be* pleased than anyone else I'd ever slept with. Not that there had been all that many. She was wise and aware enough to see how much it pleased me to please her. There was probably a song about that, but damned if I could remember it.

When she looked at me, she saw someone who was happy at her happiness, someone who saw her, unique in all her human beauty, shining as no Other World goddess could. When I looked at her, I saw someone who was glad to gladden me, happy to give me what I wanted, herself, to give herself to me completely, knowing that I treasured the gift.

A long time afterward, we lay side by side, naked and happy, breathing deeply, one hand on each other's hips. She turned her head to look at me.

"I've never been disappointed *that* many times in one night," she said. "I'm still shaking from that last string of disappointments." She wasn't kidding. Her thighs and abdomen rippled gently a few times as she relaxed. Women are awesome.

I turned to smile at her. "I may have just had the single biggest disappointment of my life," I said.

"Unless I'm flattering myself," she said, "you had a couple of minor disappointments earlier in the evening, too."

"*That* has never happened to me before," I said.

"Should I sing 'Like a Virgin'?"

"I beg you not to," I said.

We showered quickly. I gave her a pair of my pajamas to put on (she looked cute) and put some on myself (I looked clothed). I boiled the water, threw in the spaghetti, heated up some jar sauce, put out the salads while the garlic bread baked in the oven.

While we ate, I told her about my Other Worldly skating adventure.

She was suitably horrified. After dinner, she made a phone call; I agreed to meet one of her friends on Saturday.

She stayed over that night. Before leaving for work in the morning, we both changed our Facebook status to "In a Relationship." Funny how serious that felt.

If life were like the musical theater, I would have burst into song. Nothing by Madonna, though.

7

A Friend of the Friends

Saturday afternoon, Leda and I found ourselves in a remodeled 1950s bungalow on Portsmouth's west side, sitting at her friends' dining room table. Our host and hostess, a white-haired retired couple, made us feel right at home. They served us strong tea and hot, crispy oatmeal raisin cookies. The other guest was Peter Brown, a wiry mixed-race gentleman with more white than black in his hair. He wore the black suit and Roman collar of a priest. I don't know why that surprised me so much. Maybe I felt underdressed. Leda and had I planned to go skating, so we were in jeans and sweaters.

We didn't talk about fashion. We talked of this and that, the economy and unemployment, the stock market, the weather, the American healthcare debacle, the local elections, and what mischief the 424 state legislators in Concord might be getting up to. Nobody ventured any strong opinions about any of these topics, although it was easy to guess they might have some.

"Well, hey," said our host, getting to his feet, "nice meeting you, Jerry. Always a treat to see *you* again, Leda. I'm informed we have some shopping to do. We should be back by full dark—I hate driving after sundown. Stay as long as you like. I'll set the door so it locks behind you."

"Are you sure you don't want to stay the night, Peter? We'd love to have you." said our cheerful hostess. He smiled and said No thanks. "Bye, then!" she said. And out the door they went, entrusting their immaculate home to us. New Englanders are full of surprises.

Peter smiled at Leda and me. His smile was melancholy. "I'm sorry I *can't* stay here tonight," he said. "I love Portsmouth. This may be the last time I ever see it."

"You're not *ill*, I hope?" I said.

He laughed. "No, no, not at all. It's just time for me to go home. You know how it is with us, right?"

I indicated Leda with a nod of my head. "I'm sure the lady would be willing to tell me—if I were willing to listen."

Brown looked at the two of us closely. He grinned as if whatever he saw pleased him greatly. "How wonderful," he said. "You two are *spoken for!*" I thought he might clap his little hands together in glee, but no.

His words made me oddly uncomfortable. I reached over and took Leda's hand. "I don't exactly know what you mean by *spoken for*," I said, "but I love her." It seemed rude to talk about a lady like she wasn't sitting right there, so I looked her in the eye and said, "I love you." Like I was further explaining something she hadn't already heard or hadn't understood the first time I said it.

The lady gave me a look that made it clear that, despite the presence of a clergyman, I'd given her cause to consider jumping my bones right here and now. Women can be unpredictable.

Brown laughed *for* us in sheer joy. I'd never heard anything like that, the deep amusement that springs from wisdom. "Ah," he said, "just *look* at the two of you with your whole lives ahead of you. I've been a single fella far too long. When I go home, I think there's a lady who might have a thing or two to say to me. We'll see what happens."

"May I ask where *'home'* is?" I said. Having heard the stories, I thought I knew what he'd say.

"My own true home is the next world over from Earth," he said.

"But you knew I'd say that, didn't you?"

"Thought you might," I said. "Wouldn't be surprised if you asked us to come along."

Leda gave me a look I couldn't interpret. Frightened? Hopeful? Had I said something offensive? "Peter's invited me to visit his world with him more than once," she said. "I've always been too afraid."

I caught her eye. "I wouldn't go without you," I said. "Hell, it scares me even to talk about this." I held her hand tightly.

She squeezed my hand in sympathy. We wouldn't be traveling anywhere today, except maybe back to bed. There, she may have felt she could protect me from anything that frightened us.

Peter nodded again, sadly. "I see how it is with you both," he said. "It's a pickle. I can't stay here much longer, and you can't go with me. Well, okay, let's do what we can today. Leda said something's scared you badly—and more than once?"

I outlined my three Other World *visitations*, if that's the right word. This time I told the whole story of how *Quincy* got me into this by leading me into that field on the north side of town. Leda was hurt that I hadn't told her everything, but Peter reassured her.

"I'm sure Jerry's circumspection was only possibly-misguided family loyalty and nothing more," he said. "What's your uncle's game, I wonder? Assuming he has one, I mean."

I shook my head. "Quincy said the Other World was about *power.* I don't exactly know what he meant, except that he said his trips over there have made him rich."

"Knowledge is power," Peter said. "First law of real magic."

"I thought that was just a cliché," I said, "the kind used by jerks who withhold essential information from the people they work with." There's one in every company. I'd even had bosses like that.

"There's magic and then there's magic," said Peter. He spoke simple words in a language I'd never heard before. Although I didn't speak a word of that language, I understood instantly that he was saying *Knowledge is power.* The afternoon sun had been fading from the quiet dining room; the words hung in the air and *lit it up.* A language that could do that even briefly was wonderful, powerful—and scary.

I saw his point. "I guess there's knowledge and then there's knowledge," I said.

"Smart fella," Peter said to Leda. He meant me. "If I were you, Jerome," he said, "I'd find out what your uncle is *doing* with all this power he gets from his dealings with the Old Gods."

Why hadn't I thought of that? I didn't even know what Q was doing with all his *money.* "Good idea," I said, "but *'Old Gods'?*"

Peter waved his hand. "A term of convenience, nothing more. Before there *were* any human beings, other kinds of creatures walked upon the Earth, or flew above it, or burrowed under it. The arrival of humankind changed things in some fundamental way so that those older creatures went ... *elsewhere.* There are myths, folktales, and even scriptures about those who exiled themselves. Even today, powerful non-human beings sometimes manifest themselves to people in this world. Perhaps those beings hope to return. I'd say they were *beyond* good and evil if the Old Gods didn't have such bad effects on those who seek them out."

"Why would they be bad for us?" I said. Beyond loyalty to family (assuming they remain loyal to you), I thought of life as a war where you take any advantage you can get.

"Do you know my story, Jerome?" I said that I didn't. I suspected Peter's story might have been in those books I had yet to read, the ones Leda had urged me to borrow from the library. "Well, long story short, I was a priest of the Church before I found my true home in the next world over. My teachers in both worlds taught the same lesson: that a man has to avoid the evil and choose the good. Free will, you see—that's what it's *for,* to make that choice."

"What happens to the man who refuses to choose?" I said. I hate forced choices; what's free about that?

"If you don't choose the good, what's left?" he said. "There's nothing there for you. Nothing good, anyway. How'd you feel when you saw that bird-thing flying at you?"

"Scared." I didn't mind admitting it.

"How'd you feel when you saw the beautiful lady shining in the shrubbery behind your office?"

"Like I'd knocked back a shot of rye whiskey and it was making me dizzy and sick."

"How'd you feel about the ... shining city on the hill?"

"Like maybe it would be interesting to go there, never a dull moment, but that it was a bad place to go." He was really backing me into a corner here.

"How'd you feel when Miss Leda here came to your house the day you almost froze and drowned in shallow water?"

I looked Leda full in the face. "Like I was home," I said. "Like I'd made the right choice." She smiled at me. I didn't care that Peter Brown had read my mind. I'd done nothing to be ashamed of.

Peter sat back in his chair and pointed one index finger at my heart. "Nothing I've learned in either world tells me anything but that we were *created* to choose the good. And the good is very good indeed. You have no idea. Well, *I* had no idea, put it that way. I've seen real evil at work right here on Earth and stood against it. Because I *chose* the good, chose to oppose the Fallen and all who serve them. As I am now, I suspect most Old Gods can't even *see* me, the way they can see Quincy. The way I suspect they now can see *you.*"

"I'm confused," I said. "I thought you said I'd made the right choice."

"You did," he said. "Human love's a very good thing. But it's not the *best* thing. It confers no protection. When we love, we give hostages to fortune." He sounded sad.

The old couple kept their house too warm, but I felt chilled. "Sorry to be dense," I said, "but I'm still not following you."

"I'm sorry to be so blunt," he said, "but if you and Leda want to be safe from those beings your uncle has got you mixed up with, you'll have to come to *my* world. And sooner rather than later."

"What happens if I—if we—stay here?" I said.

"I don't see into the future, my brother," Peter said, not unkindly. "Only the greatest of us ever glimpse what might be. If you stay here, you'll have to take your chances, like everyone who lives in Portsmouth always has. The walls between the worlds are *thinner* here, you know."

He looked from Leda to me and back again. He must have seen that we weren't leaving Earth any time soon. If ever.

Peter Brown's smile was a benediction. He waved goodbye and simply faded out of that Portsmouth dining room like the Cheshire Cat.

8

501(C)(4)

Leda and I let ourselves out of her friends' house, making sure the door lock engaged behind us. I drove us away in silence. We were both shivering, imagine that, and it took the heater a few miles to warm up the car. The weather had stayed very cold, but no snow had yet fallen. It wasn't even Thanksgiving yet. Welcome to New Hampshire.

"That was a hell of a thing," I said.

"I knew they *could* do that," she said, "but I've never seen anyone actually *do* it."

"Kind of makes me think the man was telling the truth," I said.

She swiveled toward me as best she could, given that she was securely belted into a bucket seat. "He wouldn't lie," she said firmly. "*They don't.*" It was important to her that I understand how seriously she took the commitment she'd made—and how much she respected those she'd committed herself to. I took *Leda* seriously; that'd have to be enough for now.

On the other hand: disappearing priests. "Maybe that's why people call them *elves*," I said, "even though they're just human beings who know things the rest of us are afraid to learn."

She smiled at me. "You're smarter than you look."

"Good thing," I said.

Down by the beach we skated on the pond where the Other World had mugged me. The pond had completely refrozen solid, level ice from top to bottom and side to side. Leda fell down more than I did, and once we fell down together, laughing like loons. There were other people out skating, kids and two small teams of adults playing hockey. Everyone was having fun and nobody bothered anybody.

No gods and goddesses arrived to spoil our fun. I could still see the hawks' nest in the top of the tall pine tree on the islet back in the marsh, but I saw neither hawk.

After skating till the daylight was gone, we drove back to the house Leda rented along with two housemates, Beth (tall, blonde, and thin) and Janjan (short, red-haired, and chubby). I hadn't done much more than say Hi to the housemates in passing. It seemed silly for us to spend the night in Leda's one room when I had a whole house. Tonight Beth and Janjan were making a big pot of stew for the four of us. Leda and I stopped off to pick up jugs of red and white wine and some warm loaves of crusty bakery bread, our contribution to the feast.

I'm a little slow on the uptake sometimes, so it wasn't until we were all sitting at the battered old kitchen table drinking wine that tonight's *agenda* dawned on me. I was to be subjected to thoroughgoing female scrutiny, a classic game of Analyze the Dude's Intentions. Having been off the market for five years, I had forgotten that these days a young lady's friends act *in loco parentis* to protect her from cads, bounders, mashers, slackers, drunks, druggies, users, pervs, violent offenders, and still-married men. In fairness to Leda's housemates, our courtship *had* suddenly accelerated from zero to warp speed. Being who she was, Leda would not have told her friends about my, um, metaphysical difficulties. So all they had to go on was my demeanor and testimony before the court of female opinion.

We talked about work (everyone was happy to be employed, unhappy to be underpaid). We laughed about hapless coworkers, (everyone had at least one). We talked about our Thanksgiving plans. Beth and Janjan were going down to Beth's parents in Providence; Leda was torn between flying home to her mother's house in Chicago and staying with me. In the event of Leda's absence, I was considering frozen lasagna and TV football, unless one family member or another invited me to dinner.

And inevitably, we talked about (dunnn dunnn *dunnn*) relationships. I said that I was recently divorced, without getting into details. Leda patted my thigh in that comforting way she had; she meant a lot more by it now than the first time she put that move on me. Beth said she was dating a charming guy with no ambition and no prospects who played a lot of video games. She didn't see much of a future for them. Janjan had just unloaded a guy who drank too much too often and who was selfish in bed. She was contemplating changing teams and sleeping exclusively with women, or so she said half-jokingly under the influence of two glasses of rough red wine.

Janjan then turned to me. "So, Jerry, our little Leda says you're ... a *gifted* lover?"

How is a gentleman to answer such a question? Surprised, I turned to Leda with two fully-raised eyebrows. "You said *that?*"

Leda *blushed.* I'd never seen that before, and it made me smile. She glared at Janjan. "Jeez, all I *said* was that I was *happy!*" she said. "Miss Thang here drew her own conclusions."

I decided to answer Janjan more or less directly. "Believe me, I'm nothing special," I said. "My ex-wife left me for one or more other women. After I got over feeling sorry for myself, I *learned* from the experience. Thanks, internet!" The nugget of truth in my little joke defused the tension, and we all laughed. I reached out, gently brushed Leda's hair aside, and cupped the side of her face in my palm. She closed her eyes and rested her face against my hand like a happy cat: *more, please.* My heart leaped up. Among other things. "There *is* something special between Leda and me," I said to Janjan. "It's *liking* each other— a lot. That's the secret ingredient." I was honestly surprised it had taken me so many years to discover such an obvious thing.

Janjan looked at Beth. Beth looked at Janjan. Leda opened her eyes, looked at me, sat up straight and looked at Beth and Janjan. "*See?*" she said.

I guess they saw. They made that *Awww...* sound women use to show how adorable they think something is. Or to pretend that's what they think. Women can be kind of awful.

Leda said she'd never seen *me* blush before, either.

The stew involved chicken and vegetables and noodles and spices. It was so good that I went back for seconds. The cooks beamed with pride. In the middle of the second bowl, my phone buzzed. In my profession, that's never a good thing on a Saturday night, so I excused myself, got up from the table and walked into the living room (dark and cold compared to the kitchen) to take the call. As I answered, I saw that the screen of my phone said *Restricted Number.* Probably not Bob calling me with a work emergency, then.

It was Quincy. *How'd he get this number?* I wondered. *I didn't give it to him.*

"Jerry?" he said, "Quincy here. I apologize for interrupting your Saturday, but I have been derelict in my avuncular duties. I quite forgot that Pepsi asked me to invite you to Thanksgiving dinner—that is unless you already have plans?"

"That's very thoughtful of you, sir," I said. "I'm honored that you remembered me." I can sling the bullshit with the best bullshitters who ever bullshat their way through the American South.

Leda stuck her face into the living room and mouthed *Everything okay?*

I nodded Yes and mouthed *Quincy!* This time *her* eyebrows went all the way up. "Uncle Quincy," I said into the phone, "would it be an imposition if my, um, *fiancée* were to come to dinner with me?"

"What? Not at all, no imposition whatever! Pepsi and I will be delighted to meet the young lady. Drinks are at noon, dinner's at one."

He paused. "Oh, and lest I forget my other reason for calling you, would you be able to drop by my office when you leave work on Monday? I have a business matter to discuss with you."

That was a surprise. I didn't know that Quincy had an office or that he was anything but a retired investor. "I'd be happy to meet with you, sir. Where and how late?"

Quincy said he'd be in the office till seven on Monday and gave me the office address and the phone number. We said our goodbyes and hung up.

By this time Leda was standing in her living room watching me. She reached over and turned on a floor lamp next to a battered old armchair. I still couldn't quite read her expression.

Then she smiled. "It looks like I'll be celebrating Thanksgiving with you and your crazy-rich relatives," she said. "But *'fiancée'*? Did you just propose to me ... *by proxy*?"

I'm no fool. I walked over and took her in my arms. "Quincy and Pepsi are the definition of *old-school*," I said. "They would not understand why a mere *girlfriend* would be spending a major holiday away from her own family of origin."

"You really want me to be there, don't you?"

Smart girl. "Something's up with Quincy. I figure you can help me figure it out. Unless you'd rather go see your mom in Chicago."

She made a face. "My brother and I always fight. Nobody'll miss me if I stay here and help you play *Ghostbusters*. Or is it *Scooby-Doo*?"

I laughed. "It's definitely *Happy Thanksgiving, Scooby-Doo!*" I said. In hindsight, *Thanksgiving Terrors* would have been more accurate, but I had somehow missed that episode.

Leda put her arms around my waist. "So we're *not* getting married? A gal needs to know these things. What with the trousseau and the wedding-industrial complex and so forth."

"I think we ought to get married eventually," I said. "That's what people who love each other do, right? But I'd like us to live together first, maybe wait a year to set the date. You know, see if we can stand each other?"

"Oh. My. *God.*" she said. "You're not kidding, are you? Did you just ask me to move in with you?"

"Only if you want to," I said, "and only when you're ready."

She kissed me long and hard and with great attention to detail. It went on quite a while. Beth and Janjan finally spoke up from the kitchen.

"Are you two having some sort of *sexual intercourse* in *my* living room?" Janjan asked plaintively.

"If so, can we come watch?" said Beth.

"Hell with that," said Janjan. "Can we come *help*?"

"Is a foursome the same as changing teams?" Beth asked Janjan. They argued about that, finally concluding that it might be, but not necessarily, because it depended on who did what and to whom. Thanks again, internet.

"Is it okay if I tell them?" Leda whispered in my ear.

"Sure," I whispered back.

"You guys?" Leda said, "Jerry just asked me to move in with him."

Then there was a lot of girl shrieking as we walked back in to the kitchen arm in arm. The fuss was pretty embarrassing, but I guess my embarrassment was self-inflicted.

Ever the good employee, I got to the office at seven o'clock Monday morning, planning to get all the paper ducks in a row before my younger colleagues started straggling in, dazed and confused. Without documentation, the boss doesn't know what you've accomplished and the clients don't know what they're paying for.

I was surprised to see Bob, better known as Mister Nine on the Dot, waiting for me near the door from the hallway we shared with two other small businesses. He looked tired. *Haggard* would be a better word, although he was freshly shaved, besuited, necktied, and smelled of cologne. His thick black hair looked clean, but it was sticking up all over the place, like he'd dressed and driven here right out of the shower.

"C'mon in the office," he said and led the way. As the company owner and the boss, he had the only office with a door. The rest of us worked in low-wall cubicles with modular furniture and used a conference room for meetings and client work sessions. Sometimes we worked from home, but that's hard to do regularly in a small company.

Bob held his office door open for me, gestured me to one of the two chairs in front of his compact desk, and shut the door behind us. As directed, I sat in one of the chairs. Instead of sitting in the comfortable Aeron chair behind his desk, he sat in the guest chair facing mine. I had a sudden attack of the Mondays. This did not look good at all; I'd been through this ceremony before.

"Oh, crap, Bob," I said, "are you *firing* me?"

He shook his head sadly. "We've been *acquired*, Jerry," he said. "If anything, I'll be firing *me*."

So many questions. I looked them all at him. "'Scuse me?" I said.

"Ever see *The Godfather*? They made me *an offer I couldn't refuse.*"

He looked so distraught that I felt worse for him than I felt for myself. I'd always landed on my feet, hadn't I? "Who are *they*, Bob?" I said. I said it gently, though. I'd come to like the guy.

He pulled himself together and sat up straight in the cheap-ass guest chair. The secret to open-door management is not letting your visitors get comfortable. "*They*," he said with just a trace of bitterness, "are a 501(c)(4) organization whose name I am at present contractually unable to divulge to you. *They* offered me far, far, *far* more for this company than it's worth. Probably more than it'll be worth in ten years—I don't think there's room in the market for us to get much bigger than we are right now. I've been in negotiations with *them* all weekend, hammering out the details. Once our part-time strip-mall lawyer got a load of *their* lawyer—excuse me, their *lawyers*, their white-shoe Washington *legal team*—and read their offer, he told me it was a once-in-a-lifetime deal and that I'd have to be a fucking idiot to turn it down."

Bob paused, obviously exhausted. He clasped his hands together and studied his shoes (both shiny, both tied). He looked up at me. "I have a wife who loves me, two little kids and a huge mortgage to support," he said. He didn't mention the new admin with the astonishing chestal area, so I figured either he wasn't sleeping with her or she didn't matter to him. "As it stands right now, *I* can retire in June, pay off the mortgage and send both kids to medical school. And you've still got *your* job, right? So where's the problem?"

I didn't know where the problem was, exactly. If there was a problem between Bob and his conscience, that wasn't for me to tell him. "What happens now?" I said.

He smiled. "Right to the point. Good man," he said. "On a personal note, I've never regretted hiring you, Jerry, not for a second. Your technical work is as good as anything the new graduates do for me. You work your ass off, don't think I haven't noticed. More importantly, you can *talk* to people without pissing them off! Do you have any idea how rare that is in this business? Anyway..."

He went on to explain that our operations would continue unchanged until the phase-in of the transition team from our mysterious (to me) new parent organization. The transition was scheduled to start in January. By June, Bob's little company would become part of a greater whole. *It doth not yet appear what we shall be,* I thought.

Meantime, we'd continue working our existing projects and servicing current clients. Any prospective new business not sent our way by our new masters would have to be approved by those masters before we took it on. Bob asked me not to say anything to the customers just yet; he'd take care of that personally this week.

Oh, and: in the coming weeks, everyone in the office would be asked to sign employment contracts committing us to stay with the company at least a year after the transition. After signing, we'd all get significant salary bumps. Happy New Year. I'd be able to exercise my option to buy the house I was leasing.

Being who I am, I was suspicious. It all sounded too good to be true. Only one shoe had dropped.

"Any problem if I tell my girlfriend about this, Bob?" I said. He really didn't need to know I was dating Leda.

He grinned. "Tell her whatever you like, dude," he said. "You don't really *know* anything yet, do you? I suspect your new contract will have some kind of nondisclosure agreement, though."

"Hell, Bob, it can't be any worse than the non-compete clause *you* made me sign."

"We're in a highly competitive business," he said. "I tried so hard not to hire anybody who'd steal the company out from under me." He slumped and looked at his shoes again. "And now I've sold it out from under myself."

9

The Business of America

I made coffee and got to work as though nothing unusual had happened. In between doing the tasks that just couldn't wait, I couldn't help speculating about the future. Bob briefed everyone individually as they came in. Nobody laughed, nobody cried. Everybody was as puzzled as I was. It was all *vewwy mystewious*, as Elmer Fudd would say.

After talking to all of us, Bob went home for the day. He was dead tired and suffering mixed emotions from selling the business. He'd spent the last ten years of his life launching the company and then successfully taking it public. What would he do now?

Which reminded me: he hadn't cautioned me about insider trading. I was a key employee, if anybody was. Could I sell the stock Bob had given me in lieu of bonuses? And if I could sell it, *should* I? The stock market had been going great all year, but pessimists talked about another bubble about to break. Really, speculating in stocks is just gambling unless you buy into an index fund and let your money go with the market flow for the long term. Maybe even then. The ex had gotten our house, but I'd fought off her raid on my 401(k) retirement account, which was doing great at the moment. Thanks, index fund.

Everybody in the office talked things out, as best we could in the absence of any solid information about how the change would affect us.

As the oldest employee, the young'uns looked to me for advice.

"I've been through this kind of thing before," I said. "I'll keep working like it's business as usual. I'm also going to update my résumé, just in case."

"On the other hand: *raises in January!*" said Mike, our new-grad network engineer. "We should close the office at noon and all go out to lunch!"

A chorus of *woo-hoos*: everyone but me agreed with Mike. Our productivity declined sharply after that. It's hard to get anything done Thanksgiving week, anyway. In the end, I went out to lunch with the kids. Thank God for voicemail and email.

Since it was Thanksgiving week everywhere in corporate America and in government, I was able to get out of the office by four o'clock, imagine that. I called Quincy's office number. A lady with a husky voice answered. She told me my uncle was available and that I was expected.

I drove south on U.S. Route 1, which runs along the East Coast from Fort Kent, Maine to Key West, Florida. *The road*, as J.R.R. Tolkien sang, *goes ever on and on*. Most of Route 1 is commercial real estate, which in practice means one business after another, ice cream, restaurant, furniture, electronics, landscaping, motel, office building, grocery store—you get the idea.

Quincy's office was in an unpretentious four-story building that looked like 1990s vintage, not that I'm any kind of expert. In front of the building was one of those annoying signs that identified the building's tenants in fancy gold script that's too small to read as you drive by. (I *do not* need glasses.) As instructed, I drove around back and found myself in a large parking lot.

I parked. As I was hustling through the cold toward the building, I noticed two of those wide-angle fisheye security cameras above the double entry doors. The damn things are everywhere. I pulled on one of the doors and found it locked. The other door was locked, too. A metallic voice spoke from a speaker hidden in the base of one camera: "Mr. August?"

"Um, yes?" I said hopefully. *August* is my surname, after all, but it's also my uncle's last name, hence my hesitation. There are a lot of Augusts around the New Hampshire seacoast, most of them not related to me in any way.

"You're expected, sir. I'll buzz you right in."

I heard a muted buzz and the door unlocked. I pulled it open and stepped into the warm lobby. It's good to be expected.

Not far inside the lobby was a security desk. Two uniformed guards stood behind it. The desk looked more like a contemporary version of an Art Deco bank teller's cage, glass (bulletproof?) and steel.

One of the guards, a gentle-spoken guy in late middle age with a white buzz cut, politely beckoned me forward, saying, "May I see some ID, sir?" in tones that suggested he knew it was an imposition. I showed him my New Hampshire driver's license. "Thanks so much, Mr. August," said the guard. "Sorry about all the formality, but it's a tough old world these days, isn't it?"

I agreed that it was. I noticed that the other security guard, a younger man whose dark blue uniform was packed with muscle, had come partway out from behind the security desk to witness the ritual showing of the driver's license. I couldn't see the man's hands and therefore assumed he was holding a weapon, or for all I knew, a brace of flintlock pirate pistols. I nodded at him, but he didn't nod back. All business, this guy.

Smiling, the older guard directed me to the elevator. Stone-faced, the younger guard watched to be sure I actually got into the elevator. If Bob hadn't already given me a case of the Mondays, these guys definitely would have.

The lady with the husky voice met me at the elevator with what I'm sure she thought was a smile. It wasn't anything like a smile, and she didn't trouble to introduce herself. By this time, all my inner alarm bells were clanging noisily. It didn't help when I saw the holster at the waist of the lady's short jacket as she let me into Quincy's office. The pistol might have been a compact Smith & Wesson LadySmith or something similar. The lady looked like she knew a lot more about firearms than I did and could easily have handled a heavy Colt Python. How big an office gun do you really need, though?

What the hell have I wandered into? I wondered. I hoped Quincy would tell me.

Q's office was big with a substantial oak desk and four high-end satellite chairs in front of it. In the far corner sat a full-sized conference table surrounded by padded conference chairs. *This is where all the magic happens*, I thought, remembering *MTV Cribs*. Despite the good furniture and the thick beige carpet, the office was fairly spartan by the wretched-excess standards of corporate America. Oh, the things an IT guy sees, from vast marble desktops and shining display cases full of looted Egyptian *ushabti* to badly-executed life-size oil paintings of naked trophy wives. I wish I was kidding.

From behind his gleaming, immaculate desk Quincy waved me to one of the side chairs while he finished up a phone call. My armed escort did a crisp about-face, went out the door, and shut it behind her. I sat and continued my inspection of the office. The walls were bare dark wood, I noticed. No ridiculous motivational posters. No art, good or bad. No I-Love-Me wall with awards and pictures of the modest occupant in the company of the famous and the powerful. No family pictures, either on the wall or on Quincy's desk. Had he just moved in? My nose picked up no new-furniture or new-carpet smell.

Quincy said a polite goodbye to whoever was on the phone and hung up. He gave me a big smile. "Jerry!" he said. "Thanks so much for stopping in." He was a hard guy to read, but I thought he sounded sincere.

"I had no idea you were ... in business still, Uncle Q" I said. *In business ever*, is what I meant.

"If it's all right with you, I'll get right to my *plans* for this business, so we can both go home to our suppers."

"Of course," I said. Why else had I driven down here?

"Am I correct that your employer told you today about a

forthcoming change in his company's ownership?"

"That's correct, sir."

"Did he inform you who had acquired the company?"

"He did not."

Quincy sat forward a bit in his cushy executive desk chair and put his forearms on the desk. "I'm happy to hear that you work for someone who honors a contract. I asked for his discretion because I wanted to tell you this personally. The August Association, *my* organization, is the purchaser."

Sometimes you don't know how to feel about the things that happen to you. I fell back on the cynical assumptions that serve me in place of wisdom: there are no coincidences in business; if it sounds too good to be true, it's not; and *cui bono* or Who benefits here? Everybody wants something. What did Quincy want?

"May I ask *why*, Uncle Quincy?"

Quincy sat back in his chair. "My technology people advise me that we *need* your company's unique expertise so the Association can continue to grow and prosper. The fact that you dominate your niche of the market is just icing on the cake."

"I'm surprised to hear that a nonprofit like yours needs anything but networking, hardware maintenance, and basic web services," I said.

Quincy gave me a look of distaste that said I'd just stepped over an invisible line. Or possibly tracked dog shit onto his immaculate carpet. "Yes, well," he said, "before we get too far into *specifics*, I suppose we should call in the lawyers." He picked up his desk phone and hit three buttons. "Oliver," he said into the phone, "if you would, please?"

A youngish blond man in an expensive suit entered the office without knocking. He held a thick spiral-bound document in his left hand. Quincy didn't bother to introduce us, the exquisite rudeness of the very rich and very powerful. The lawyer looked a question at Quincy. Quincy nodded his approval: *You may speak, minion.*

"Mr. August," the lawyer said to me in the peevish tones of a man who has always gotten his own way and expects to continue getting his own way for all eternity, "this is a *draft* of your prospective employment contract. This document cannot leave our offices."

"Understood," I said as I took the contract from his hand. I skimmed through it and saw that it had twenty-five sections, if I still remembered my Roman numerals. Each section had at least five pages, some had more. Holy crap.

"If you wish," Oliver said, "I can brief you on the main points now...?" I didn't respond to that. "Alternatively, or in addition, I can give you an opportunity to review the document in detail...?" I didn't respond to that, either. My silence seemed to upset him. Good. "I should also disclose that I am employed as part of the legal team who serve as counsel to, and therefore represent the interests of, the August Association. This contract appears to me to be very much in *your* interest, but that, of course, is not for me to decide."

I'm smart enough to know when I'm outgunned. I knew all the words in the document I'd skimmed, but not what they'd commit me to. "I'd like to have a lawyer look at this before I consider signing it," I said.

"Should you choose to retain counsel," said the lawyer, "you may call Mr. August's secretary to arrange an appointment for you and your attorney to review the contract."

I handed him back the contract. "Good idea," I said. "As you say, it's a draft. Once I understand the provisions, I'll be in a better position to negotiate with you."

"We'd like to have signed employment contracts from you and your colleagues by the tenth of December," said the lawyer. "Besides an immediate raise, you may have noted that the contract provides for an additional bonus for signing by the deadline."

Sometimes the carrot *is* the stick. "I'll let my colleagues decide for themselves what's in their interest," I said. "I can probably give you my decision before the end of the year, depending on how the negotiations go."

Oliver didn't like that. He was hoping he could get my signature on the contract tonight in exchange for the bonus—and for the enormous favor he would do me by explaining what was in it. Quincy was smiling. He liked my style. "Thank you, Oliver," he said to the lawyer.

"Good night, sir," Oliver said. He might have closed the door a little harder than necessary. Not quite a full flounce, but as much of a display of temper as he thought he could get away with.

Quincy shook his head. "Another K Street prima donna," he said. "The Ivies just keep pumping them out. Oliver was overheard complaining about his accommodations ... at the *Hilton*, if you can believe it. Well, it seems we've done as much business as we can do tonight, Jerry. You and your intended are still planning to come for Thanksgiving dinner?"

"Wouldn't miss it, sir." I paused. "I probably should have asked your lawyer," I said, "but I was wondering if I should do anything with the shares of company stock I own."

Quincy grinned at me. I imagine that grin was the last thing a fair number of North Korean and Chinese soldiers had seen on Earth. "You can do whatever you like with your stock," he said. "I suggest you hang onto it, though. The Association's going to be doing a stock repurchase next year. We're taking the company private again. You'll make out handsomely on the deal, kiddo." He paused. "Between you and me, now, if we can reach agreement on your employment contract, you'll end up managing the operation for me after Bob transitions out. You'll be our Information Technology Managing Director—with a salary to match that impressive title."

I had not seen the offer coming. Nor had I gleaned it from my quick scan of the densely-worded contract.

"I appreciate your confidence, Uncle Q," I said, not knowing what else to say.

10

A Disquieting Telephone Call

When I moved back to Portsmouth, I left most of my friends behind in Washington. Not that I'd ever had many close friends. Human connections don't just happen, and except for Leda, I hadn't taken the time to make new friends in New Hampshire. But these days it's easy enough to stay in touch with people you care about. Thanks, Facebook and smartphones.

Leda was working late again, poor girl, so I came home to my empty house and immediately got on the phone to my friend Max. *Miracle Max* we called him, not because he looked anything like the wizard in *The Princess Bride*, but because he had apparently-magical sources of information. He'd parlayed his talent for research into a very lucrative position with some beltway bandit corporation in Suitland, Maryland. Government contracts, the intelligence-industrial complex. Max's line of work was all very hush-hush—until a certain contractor employee ran off with a suitcase full of scandalous U.S. secrets and started leaking them to the press.

I used the house's landline. Very old-school, I know, but I get weary of cell phone echoes, fragments of sentences, and dropped calls. Max picked up his private line right away, probably saw my name on his caller ID box.

"J-man!" he said. "How's my favorite Catholic Jew?"

"Miracle Max!" I said. "How's my favorite Jewish atheist?"

"Ah, who *is* a Jew?" he said. "It's a race! *No, it's a religion!* Wait, you're *both* right!"

It was our running joke. Neither of us cared much about either race or religion. We spent some time catching up. He was still single and dating up a storm, but he was delighted for me that I'd found somebody special. I promised to invite him to the wedding, if and when. Like the song says, it's good to have friends.

"Hey, listen," I finally said, "I need some information, and I figured if anybody could help me, it'd be you..." I sketched out what had happened, how Bob had sold his company to my Uncle Quincy and his August Association; how Quincy had offered me a job that sounded too good to be true. "Problem is, if I can't find anything much about the August Association on the internet, how do I know who I'm saying Yes or No to?"

Max went quiet for a long moment. I heard the sound of laptop keys in the background.

"It's a 501(c)(4) lobbying organization, right?" I agreed that was true. "You know what *dark money* is?"

"They don't have to disclose their donors?"

"You got it," he said. "Politics is all about dark money these days. Supreme Court, *Citizens United,* blah blah blah. The question is, my friend, what's your uncle *buying* with all that dark money?" More sounds of laptop keys. I heard a sharp intake of breath on the other end of the phone.

"Max? You okay?"

A pause, then slowly. "Yeah. Yeah, *I'm* okay, J-man. *You're* not, though."

"*Bascuse* me?"

"Jerry, if it was me in your shoes? I'd take my girl, change my name, and move far far away from Portsmouth, New Hampshire."

I smiled to myself. There's a lot of imaginary drama which only exists inside the Capital Beltway and has no effect on anyone in the rest of the country. "Might you be exaggerating just a tad?" I said.

"I wish," he said.

11

We Gather Together

Thanksgiving morning, I drove through cold, sunny, quiet streets to pick Leda up at her house. By ten o'clock I was all exercised, showered, shaved, and dressed carefully in a charcoal gray business suit, a blue button-down Oxford cloth shirt with a red tie. Formal but not stuffy. The suit was somewhere between a baggy grandpa suit and one of those weird tight-pants-tight-jacket deals that, mark my words, will be out of style in a year. I might be wrong; I was wrong about designer beard stubble, which is still with us. But *you can't go far wrong with the traditional look*, my father used to tell me.

Beth and Janjan were already on the highway to Providence, so Leda and I had her house to ourselves. I was glad I showed up early. I found her staring into the closet, obviously in the throes of a crisis of confidence. I tried to tell her how delightful she looked standing there in her underwear, but she would hear none of it. The prospect of meeting my rich uncle and aunt had temporarily shaken her composure. She wasn't crying yet, but a full meltdown was imminent.

"For God's sake, Jerry," she said, "I *cannot* decide what to wear. Help me out, I'm *panicking* here!"

I kind of saw her point. She had plenty of work clothes and a supply of club or party clothes, but all the non-work things I saw would show a fair bit of her flawless skin. I embraced her from behind, rocked her gently from side to side, and kissed her ear. She relaxed against me just a little. "You'll do great, sweetness. Do you have something conservative, something you might wear to a funeral?" She said she did. "Minimal cleavage, not too much leg showing?"

"Cleavage? *Me?* Who do you think you're talking to?" A dickweed ex-boyfriend had actually tried to talk her into breast implants; I was glad she'd dumped him and kept what Nature gave her. Leda pointed to a black dress. "I'd wear *that* one, but it seems weird to wear black on a holiday. Also, that dress makes me feel *dowdy* for some reason, dunno why I bought it." She shook her head, mystified by her own shopping decision.

"Would a scarf or jewelry help?" I said. "Possibly both?" I have observed that women resist having their fashion choices *dictated* by straight men, although we are free to offer suggestions.

"You're a genius!" she said.

She turned around and kissed me. I kissed her back like the gentleman I aspire to be.

She quickly located exactly the right accessories. Boots wouldn't do on this occasion, it seemed, so she had to decide on shoes with heels, using the Goldilocks method: *these* were too high, *those* were too low, but how about this pair? Now that I looked closely, almost *all* of them looked like porn star shoes to me. When the hell did *that* happen to women's footwear? *O tempora! O mores!*

"Think *funeral*, sweetie," I said. "Quincy and Pepsi are about as old-school as you can get and still be on the topside of the grass."

"Kitten heels it is, then," she said with a sigh of resignation. I wondered, *What in the world are kitten heels?* But I nodded supportively as she grabbed a pair of shoes whose low heels looked nothing like kittens to me. She finished getting dressed, put her shoes on, and held out her hands, "Ta-da!"

"You look stunning," I said. I meant it, too. She *glowed.* The dress suggested her curves without flaunting them. Very pretty *and* very ladylike.

She hugged me. "You'd say that if I were naked," she said.

"I certainly would," I said. "By the way, does this suit make my penis look small?" With her confidence restored, it was safe to tease her again.

She put her hand on me below the belt and squeezed gently. Then she knelt and kissed the front of my trousers with real affection, greeting an old friend.

She stood back up and kissed me on the lips again. "It ain't how it *looks*, my dear, it's how it *feels*," she said.

It certainly felt good to me; I was glad if felt good to her, too. I was happy that we suited each other right down to the ground, front to back, top to bottom, and side to side. So to speak.

Crisis averted, we drove south to Quincy and Pepsi's. I'd told Leda all about my meetings, Bob in the morning and then Quincy in the afternoon. Leda knew even less about mergers, acquisitions, and finance than I did. Neither of us knew what to make of all the secrecy surrounding this deal.

I didn't tell her anything about the rather scary conversation with Max. I thought perhaps liberal politics had finally overwhelmed his normal good judgment. Was my uncle *really* the head of a thuggish criminal conspiracy to undermine American democracy, destroy the healthcare system, cut the socioeconomic safety net, bust all the remaining unions, pillage the middle class, transfer all the wealth to the very rich, and wreck the country's infrastructure—all while ballooning the national debt? Max's claims seemed, well, *hyperbolic.*

Being who I am, I couldn't just leave the smaller mysteries alone, though. "A couple of things keep nagging at me," I said. "How did Quincy get my cell phone number?"

"Maybe *Bob* gave it to him?"

I laughed at myself. "Occam's razor! That *is* the simplest explanation, isn't it?" She agreed it was. "There's just something about this whole situation that doesn't smell right, though. Why does my uncle need an armed personal assistant? Why does the August Association need armed security in its lobby?"

"Knowing you, you've done your homework on this."

"Yeah. I couldn't find much on the association in the public domain, though. Google told me very little that was helpful. The association's own website says they're 'a civic and educational corporation'. The website claims to be 'under construction', and doesn't say much else, besides listing a single phone number that probably goes to their switchboard." I could understand why Quincy might not want the public to know how committed his organization was to fighting tax and healthcare reform—and how much money he was pouring into the fight. I was sure Max had gotten his facts right. When Max said *billions of dollars*, he *meant* billions.

"Why would a tax-exempt organization in a downmarket Route 1 office building need armed guards?" Leda said. "Who are their enemies?"

"Hell," I said, "I don't even know who their *friends* are yet." *Dark money*, I thought. Max was right about that part; it was in the tax law.

"This is *New Hampshire*, for God's sake, not Chicago," she said.

"Maybe it bothers Quincy that people can carry weapons openly in New Hampshire without a license. So he needs some actual good guys with guns to protect him from all the potential bad guys with guns." I was just baiting her with National Rifle Association propaganda. Gun control was one of the things Leda and I had fun disagreeing about.

"Don't start with me," she said. She was smiling, though.

"I was strongly tempted to start with you back at your house," I said. "It's not often a gentleman gets kissed on the zipper."

"I'll, um, *make it up to you* later," she said with a stagy leer. "Know what I mean? Nudge nudge, wink wink, say no more."

In answer, I reached over and put my hand on her thigh. So hot.

"Dude," she said, "I'm *begging* you not to make me wet right here in the car."

Reluctantly, I put my hand back on the steering wheel. "*That* really doesn't take much, does it?" I said. It was a kind of miracle, it seemed to me, the way men and women could touch the depths of each other. Figuratively and sometimes literally.

"It's *you*," she said with sudden feeling. "Nobody else. Ever. Don't make me talk about this right now." She pretended to fan her flushed face with one hand, the way girls do.

"Should I sing 'Like a Virgin'?" I said.

She smiled back at me, grateful for the change of topic. "Maybe later."

"We have so much to be thankful for," I said. A joke that also happened to be true.

We pulled into my aunt and uncle's crushed-stone driveway. Leda caught sight of their house for the first time. "Hooley *CRAY-up!*" she said through her nose. It was the first trace of Chicago accent I'd ever heard from her; I found it charming. Having lived in different parts of the country, neither of us had much regional accent left. I suppose we could have worked in television, misreading the news.

"Yeah, it really is a mansion," I said. "Pepsi's old money. Quincy's old and *has* money. But somehow those two crazy kids from opposite sides of the tracks have made it work."

Pepsi and Quincy met us at the door and ushered us into the grand foyer. Quincy's assistant, the husky-voiced lady, nodded at me and took our coats. She was either pretending not to know me or felt it wasn't the place of staff to speak to guests in her employer's home in her employer's presence. It was all very *Gosford Park*, if there's an American equivalent. She didn't seem to be armed today, so that was something.

I made the introductions. *Manners maketh man*, my father often reminded me.

"*Leda?*" said Pepsi. "What a lovely name! People don't appreciate the Greek and Latin classics anymore, do they?" Pepsi gave Quincy a look, just a flash of expression not meant for me, and one I couldn't interpret. Quincy smiled back at her blandly. Whatever the message was, he'd received it.

"Why, thank you!" Leda said. Pepsi was quite a charmer. "It's an old family name. And my father taught English literature at the University of Chicago. He loved mythology, Mrs. August."

"Oh, piffle," said Pepsi. "'Mrs. August' was *Quincy's mother*, may she rest in peace. *My* name is Penelope, but everybody calls me Pepsi. I hope you will, too."

"Especially since it seems you're going to be part of the family, Leda," Quincy said, ever the paterfamilias.

By this time we'd allowed our host and hostess to herd us into the living room. It was nearly as big as a hotel lobby. I was gratified to see that we wouldn't have to walk more than a quarter mile of hardwood desert and cross too many dry lakes of oriental rugs before we reached the polished antique sideboard, the oasis where the drinks were.

"When *is* the wedding, dear?" Pepsi asked Leda.

Discreetly panicked, Leda looked to me for guidance: *Help me, Obi-Wan Kenobi; you're my only hope!* I *had* gotten her into this, after all.

"We haven't set the date yet, Aunt Pepsi," I said. "Once we do, I promise you'll be among the first to know."

"Tsk," said Pepsi, "you young people today are *shockingly* informal." She managed to sound thrilled with our scapegrace, devil-may-care, caution-to-the-winds lifestyle, and even secretly approving of it. "But what a *lovely* dress, dear," she said to Leda.

The conversation ebbed and flowed. Pepsi, Leda, and I drank white wine. Quincy seemed irked that I'd violated his generation's man code by not joining him in a Thanksgiving drink of whiskey.

"Good stuff," he said. "Single-malt. Sure you won't join me?"

Under the circumstances, this was the last place I'd drink anything stronger than wine. "Sorry, Uncle Q," I said, "have to keep my wits about me. You know how the police are."

He nodded, angrily it seemed to me. "Damned *nanny state*," he said.

Here come those undercurrents again, I thought. I wondered if my uncle would confirm Miracle Max's theory that the August Association wanted private enterprise to replace all public police and fire departments. Not that Quincy would ever talk business in front of the ladies.

Just after one o'clock, the four of us sat down together at one end of the huge dining room table. Plenty of elbow room. Quincy and Pepsi's table could have accommodated all the adults from the party at Phyllis' house. Maybe my uncle really hated having a house full of guests and my aunt indulged him in that splendid isolation.

The cook, a lean fortyish woman, and her assistant, a gaunt young man, began bringing in platters of turkey and side dishes. They both wore black pants and white shirts, like caterers.

"Would *you* like to say grace, Jerry?" Pepsi said. I'd forgotten what a mischief-maker she was.

I wouldn't like that at all, I thought, but it seemed churlish to say so. Instead, I held up my hands in the classic Catholic *Orans* posture. Quincy and Peps bowed their heads. Leda gave me a surprised look and then bowed her head also. It took a couple of seconds for the words to come back to me.

"*Barukh atah Adonai Eloheinu Melekh ha'olam, she'hakol nih'ye bidvaro*," I said, then translated: "Blessed are You, O Lord, our God, King of the universe, through Whose word everything comes into being." Just to nail it down for the Christian side of the house, I threw in a bit of Dickens: "God bless us, every one. Amen!"

Everyone looked up at me in polite confusion. With our servers' assistance, we began putting food on our plates.

"Mom was Jewish and Dad was Catholic," I told Leda. Quincy and Pepsi already knew, of course. "None of us went to services, but they still taught me how to say the Jewish and Catholic blessings before meals. We used to alternate." Leda smiled at me; she thought Judaism and Catholicism were as funny as I did. She may have wondered why I hadn't mentioned it before. I'd probably hear about that later. The lady had issues with the withholding of information. I was not looking forward to telling her about Max.

"*Hebrew*, was it?" said Quincy. I said it was. "First time *that* language was ever spoken in this house." He might have thought he was merely employing the famous New England style of dry understatement, but his undertone gave him away. I'd been listening to that kind of crap all my life, safe in the disguise of my unprepossessing goyish looks. That I was a Jew only in the narrow, technical sense of the word mattered not at all to the bigots and nutjobs who freely voiced their hatred, believing they were safe among their own kind.

Respect for one's elders doesn't imply taking any shit. "Jerome, the *Catholic* saint for whom my father named me," I said, "taught that the *Hebrew* was the inspired text of the Old Testament." Sometimes nothing says *Go fuck yourself* like a dry statement of facts.

"That was a *lovely* prayer," Pepsi said, before this minor social awkwardness could escalate. She gave Quincy another significant glance that said *Stop being yourself in front of the guests.* "*Thank* you, Jerry! Doesn't this turkey look *tender?*"

Dinner went on and on. I ate less than I wanted to, strategically saving room for pie. Pepsi learned all about Leda's childhood in Chicago (happy!) and the Clayton family's nominal religion (Episcopalian: classy!). Pepsi told stories about growing up in New Hampshire, as it used to be, when men in suits and straw boater hats and women in long dresses took electric streetcars to the beach. Quincy told stories about the grand old men, mountebanks, and crooks of New Hampshire politics. In deference to my host, I refrained from the obvious Old Man of the Mountebanks joke.

While the servers cleared away the food and the dishes, Pepsi took Leda off on a tour of the house. Quincy led me back to the library.

"Don't mean to spoil the holiday with business," he said, "but have you given thought to that little matter we discussed?"

"I have, sir," I said. "My attorney's office will call your office on Monday for an appointment."

"Good, good!" he said. He seemed to think no rational person could resist his munificence. That was very close to being true. "I may have pointed out that what a man decides to *do* in life depends upon what he *wants.*"

"Are we talking about the Other World, Uncle Q?"

Quincy looked over at the open library doors to see if the ladies had returned from their expedition. They had not. I hoped they'd taken a topographical map, a compass, and a cellphone, or we might never hear from them again. Seeing that we were still alone, he said in a low voice, "Have you gone ... *exploring* over there?"

Quincy seemed just a little too eager. There was something voyeuristic about his question. I decided to err on the side of discretion. "No, but I *have* had a couple of *very* odd experiences."

"Mm," said Quincy, encouragingly, hoping I'd say more.

I can do New England style understatement when the situation calls for it. "What I saw, or *thought* I saw, didn't seem to have much to do with the world we live in."

Quincy leaned forward expectantly and gestured with an open hand. *"Numinous,"* he said. *"Wholly other."*

I nodded agreement, hoping he'd say more, but he didn't. Quincy watched me as if he was still trying to decide about me, or about something. "Well," he finally said, "you'll make up your own mind in your own time, I suppose."

"Power," I said. I can do oblique and elliptical all day long, even on a full stomach.

"Power," he agreed, as if I'd asked a question or made a statement. "Once you decide you want it, you meet its conditions."

"Hmm," I said, as if I understood what he meant.

The conversation went on awhile in awkward fits and starts. He *wanted* something from me and knew he wasn't going to get it, not today.

Before we were quite reduced to grunting and hooting at each other each other like the pre-human hominids in *2001: A Space Odyssey*, Pepsi and Leda returned. We went back to the dining room for pie and coffee.

"Well, *that* wasn't too stressful or anything," Leda said as we drove out of the Augusts' driveway and onto the winding shore road. She meant the exact opposite of what she said; the lady had a black belt in sarcasm.

"Now that you've met my aunt and uncle," I said, "what do you think?"

She didn't hesitate. "Something's *wrong* there, but I can't put my finger on it. Like you said, they're very charming, very old-school formal, but I didn't feel *safe* in their house."

"Undercurrents?"

"Exactly," she said. "There's something going on, but I don't know what it is."

"What makes you say that?"

She gave me a sharp look and saw I wasn't mocking her. "The same way I know Peter Brown and our other *friends* are in the right. On the right side of things, I mean."

I had to agree. "Yeah, Peter's a good man. I felt *safe* sitting there with him, you know? I felt sad when he ... had to leave. And not just because I hoped he could help us."

She nodded, glad to see our instincts were in agreement. "You *do* know. I *knew* you would."

"Okay, you're not gonna like this next part..." I said. I went on to tell her Max's possibly-paranoid theory about what Quincy and the August Association were up to.

Leda started out glaring at me for having left her out of the loop, but as she heard me out, her face filled up with sympathy.

"I didn't want to freak you out before we had dinner with Quincy and Pepsi," I said. "Wanted to give you a chance to make up your own mind. My own recent experience has kind of *colored* my perceptions of my aunt and uncle."

"This isn't just political," she said.

"Not if the Other World is involved." I told Leda about my cryptic conversation with Quincy. "He used the words *numinous* and *wholly other* to describe the place," I said. "I always worry when people start up with the spiritual stuff and leave their reason behind."

"What are you going to *do*?" she said. "Knowing what you know, you can't just go to work for your uncle like a good little nephew."

"This really isn't much of a problem," I said. "Quincy keeps telling me that what I want should govern what I do, like that was some big mystery. What he doesn't know is that I've already found what I want: *you*. Besides you, what else do I need—besides a way to make an honest living, I mean?"

Traffic was light on the shore road, but I still had most of my attention on driving. When I looked to my right, I was surprised to see Leda looking straight ahead through the windshield and crying quietly.

"Sweetie, *what?*" I said. "What's wrong?"

She dug some tissues out of her purse, wiped her eyes, and blew her nose. She turned to me. "You make me so *happy*!" she wailed. She started crying again.

"You certainly *sound* happy," I said. "And I've never seen you *look* happier."

Leda started laughing at herself through her tears, and I laughed along with her.

"If you're happy and you know it, clap your hands!" she said.

I got laughing so hard I couldn't see straight. I pulled the car into a turnout next to the ocean to catch my breath.

"Listen," I said when I could speak, "how about a short walk on that nice, smooth paved walkway?" I felt overfull; typical Thanksgiving. I probably should have skipped the pie, but I figured saying grace in Hebrew was provocation enough for any guest in my uncle's house.

"A *short* walk sounds great," she said. "Fair warning, I'm good for no more than a half mile in these shoes. Kiss me before we get out of the car, okay?"

"Happy to oblige, ma'am."

12

A Confluence as of Mighty Rivers

Arm in arm and hip to hip, we strolled along a tarred sidewalk that bordered the landward side of Odiorne Point State Park. Over a hundred lightly-wooded acres included hiking trails, a breakwater, and even a beach. During World War II, the government had built low man-made hills to conceal the massive concrete bunkers and the big guns that were part of Portsmouth Harbor's defenses. In recent years, I gathered that a criminal conspiracy, ostensibly and illegally acting on the federal government's behalf, had commandeered the park from the state of New Hampshire. The conspirators had greatly expanded the underground facilities and then had systematically violated the civil rights of thousands of people. I also gathered that Leda's friends, Peter Brown among them, had done their best to right the many wrongs committed at Odiorne Point.

Those must have been bad times, indeed, but you'd never learn anything about the Second Portsmouth War from listening to the residents. Many of the conspirators who'd worked to overthrow the U.S. Government had been tried for treason, imprisoned, and forgotten. (We heard about the treason trials, even in Washington. Then we, too, managed to forget them.)

These days all the underground installations, new and old, were safely sealed up. The razor-wire fences were gone, and the park had reverted to the state once again. Our tax dollars at work, doing the right thing for once after underwriting so many wrongs. Those who pay attention to such things would tell you that the convicted traitors had been quietly released from prison one by one; most had left the country, their crimes strangely forgotten. It was a part of our history nobody wanted to remember.

But really, are people wrong to focus on the present and the future? That's what Leda and I talked about as we walked. How glad we were to be together. The things we'd do next year and thereafter. When I'd introduce her to the rest of my family. When we'd fly out to Chicago to meet her mother and her brother.

The past is whatever it was, and there's no changing it now, I've always thought. You can't live there. Although I know people—people of my own generation, not all of them even Jewish—who can never seem to escape the shadow of the *Shoah*; it follows and haunts them. Those people believe that certain events change the world forever in some fundamental way. I've never understood what any of that old news has to do with the day-to-day business of living an ordinary life.

The lady on my arm begged to differ. She felt it was her mission to educate me about Portsmouth's recent past.

"Your house?" Leda said. "The woman who owned it—before she traveled where Peter Brown went—was the *political officer* in charge of Odiorne Point back when the New World Order ran it as a prison camp."

I *really* didn't want to know any more about that, but when you love somebody, you have to hear them out. "Doesn't it scare the hell out of you even talking about this stuff?" I said. "When Peter told us that *the walls between the worlds are thinner here*, I about jumped out of my skin."

She looked at me and saw I was sincere, or at least as sincere as I ever am. She grinned. "I have to respect a guy who admits when he's afraid. Do you know how rare that is?"

"How would I know that? Look, in my experience, it's possible to *avoid* most of the things that scare me. I'm saving my courage, if I have any, for the scary stuff I can't escape. So far, so good."

"That comes *so close* to making sense," she said. "Riddle me this, then. What made you tell me you loved me before we'd even slept together?"

I didn't have a good answer for that. "Riddle me this, then," I said, "I'm nothing special, just an ordinary guy with a working brain. What made *you* love *me?*"

Leda raised one eyebrow. She was *very* cute. "Fishing for compliments, are we?"

"Nope. Stay with me here." I stopped in the walkway, held her at arm's length, and looked straight at her. "Ordinary life is full of mysteries. Why *do* people love each other? What good is someone who can't find the courage to own up to loving you? It takes guts just to get through the day."

She nodded. "Point taken. And to answer your question, I love you because you're fucking awesome."

"No, *you* are," I said.

"I think we can agree to agree on both those things."

"Would it be all right if I kissed you in token of that agreement?"

"I think you should," she said.

After one of those smiling, cold-nose kisses, we walked on a hundred yards further holding gloved hands against the freezing day. At least there was no wind. We said Happy Thanksgiving to other walkers we met, two other couples, a young woman pushing a kid in a stroller, four older people, and a string of inline skaters. They all smiled and greeted us.

As we turned around to head back to the car, I heard a dull thump and felt an impact through the ground under my feet. A gust of impossibly hot wind struck my face.

I had the odd thought that we'd walked into a construction accident in which a poorly-framed wall had fallen over, just missing us.

What had fallen was one of the thin walls between the worlds, between cold, overcast New Hampshire and the hot desert sun of the

Other World. I heard the sound of rivers that met each other and the roaring violence in which they rushed to the sea, and the sea to them.

Again I had that odd, stoned sense of slowed thoughts drifting past and away from me. Where were they going? Where *was* I? I felt the presence of other people surrounding me, but could see no one. Even my vision had slowed; it focused itself upon random dust motes blown into the air by the sudden wind.

Slowly I turned in Leda's direction to ask if she saw and heard what I was seeing and hearing. Although I couldn't see her, I still felt her hand gripping mine as tightly as I held hers. "Do you...?" I started to say.

Leda's hand pulled, or *was wrenched,* sharply out of my grasp. (Did I hear her involuntary "*Ah*" or only imagine it?) The pain brought me back closer to my ordinary self. My eyes filled up with a sudden light so bright I thought I would never see again. My ears filled up with a roaring sound like wind, yet not.

Blinded, mourning the loss of my eyesight, fearing the loss of my love, I waved my hands through the dazzle in front of me—or was it actually inside my head?

I yelled, "Leda! Where are you?" She didn't answer. No one answered. I hardly heard my own voice.

The heat went away as suddenly as it had arrived. The roaring in my ears faded and disappeared. The cold returned. My hands found, not Leda, but only piled stones on the border of the park, a dry-stone pillar, as tall as I was. I felt the rough rock edges.

My vision returned bit by bit. I was alone. More accurately, I saw that I was now alone on Earth.

This was on me. After I refused their summons three times, the denizens of the Other World had taken Leda instead.

Having heard the uproar, one old couple now returned to my side. They tried to ask me questions, but I could make no sense of their words. They tried to reassure me, but I was beyond comfort.

☙ 13 ☙

A Refusal to Cooperate with the Umvestigation

From the fugue state engendered by the Other World, I went quickly into shock. The everyday world narrowed around me. I sat in cold, dry grass and leaned up against the dry-stone pillar. I'd escaped the fire for thirty-five years, as Quincy put it. Now the fire had sought me out. Why was I so cold, then?

Somebody with their wits about them called police and paramedics. A police car was first to arrive on the scene.

"My girlfriend," I told the cop as he helped me to my feet. I felt bad that he had to work on Thanksgiving. He was so young, and his hat was slightly too big for him. "We were walking. She just *disappeared.*"

"A bunch of ... people *took* her," said one of the old guys. He was stamping his feet and banging his mittened hands together against the cold.

"*Who* took her, sir?" said the cop.

"Well, I didn't exactly see *who,*" the old guy admitted, "but there was a whole *bunch* of 'em swarming around the girl."

"Then all of them were *gone,*" said an older woman I assumed was the guy's wife. "I couldn't see where they went."

The cop nodded. He looked skeptical. I didn't blame him. A truck with two paramedics showed up. The cop led me over to it so the EMTs could check me out.

As my wits began returning, I decided not to say much more than I'd already said. A man would have to be ten kinds of stupid to learn nothing from watching every movie Alfred Hitchcock ever made, not to mention *The Fugitive*. I felt bad now, but I'd feel worse if I talked myself into jail or into the state mental hospital. I thought I knew what had happened. If I was right, the police couldn't help me with this. Even if they believed me.

And lo and behold, the young cop got on the radio and on the phone. To share his Thanksgiving misery far and wide? Nah, he was just doing his duty as he saw it. Before long, more police cars and a crime scene van showed up.

It turned into a circus. Crime scene tape was strung. Witness statements were taken from everyone incautious enough to have stuck around. The putative victim was identified from her New Hampshire driver's license, retrieved from her purse under the passenger seat of my car by a begloved evidence recovery technician. Everyone looked gratified by this significant result. Could the young lady's recovery be far behind? Two satellite news vans full of TV people showed up to gawk at the scene and broadcast video of the melee from outside the police perimeter. Coordinated searches of the state park and its surroundings were organized. Statements to the media were promised.

Although I'd stopped shivering and my vital signs had returned almost to normal, the police directed the EMTs to take me to the hospital—with a police escort, of course. Cops impounded my car. Off the convoy went to the hospital. I was pushed into the emergency room in a wheelchair. After consultation, the wheelchair was pushed into an examination room whose door was locked behind me. I got out of the wheelchair of my own accord and sat in a more comfortable chair. A harried fiftyish physician's assistant showed up to check my pulse and blood pressure, ask a few questions, and tell me what I already knew, that I was basically okay and that I'd feel even better after a night's sleep—whatever had happened.

"You may occasionally feel weird for a couple of days," the PA said.

"That's perfectly normal." Being human, he couldn't help being curious. "What *did* happen to you, anyway?"

"I was walking with my girlfriend down in Rye," I said. My eyes filled up with tears. Jesus, how I missed Leda. My heart hurt. "Something happened, I don't know what, and she was just *gone.*"

"Jeez, I'm sorry, dude," said the PA, shaking his head sadly. "What a world, huh?"

I guess emergency room staff see more than their fair share of suffering. No escaping the fire for them.

"Let's go over it again," said the detective. The cops had driven me from the hospital to the police station. A perpetually-annoyed middle-aged man wearing hunter's camouflage was taking my statement. Supposedly.

What he was actually doing was interviewing the only suspect. I'd told him everything I'd seen, heard, and smelled when Leda was ripped away from me down at Odiorne Point. Actually I'd told him all of that twice. I'd said nothing about what I knew or what I suspected; how foolish would that be? And since the police can lie to a citizen but a citizen cannot lie to the police, I was not about to let this guy put words in my mouth and trip me up.

Especially not in front of the fish-eye camera up in the corner of the interview room.

"Get your deer yet this year?" I said, hoping to build a little rapport with the detective.

Some people *have* no good side for you to get on. "*No,*" he said, "and you're not helping me get back to camp. Now how do we get the *truth* about what happened to Leda? An *innocent* man would be willing to take a polygraph..." Hint, hint.

Hearing her name coming out of his mouth pissed me off. Enough is enough. I stood up. "Am I free to go?" I said.

He growled at me. "Siddown, I'm not through talking to you!" Ooh, scary.

I remained standing. "I'm through talking to *you*," I said. "Since you're not charging me, I'm leaving. And how about giving me back my fucking car?"

The fish-eye digital video camera was probably all that kept him from punching me; I saw him consider the idea and reject it. Seeing that he couldn't bluff me, and seeing that he had nothing on me, because there was nothing to have, he let me go. He grudgingly ordered a subordinate to return my car keys. If he couldn't arrest me, at least he could get back to the woods before the end of deer season.

I was unlocking my car when a classic Mercedes Benz pulled into the space next to mine in the police station parking lot. Quincy's husky-voiced, short-haired assistant hopped out of the driver's side and opened the rear passenger door for my uncle. As lost and lonely as I felt, it was good to see a familiar face.

"Jerry, are you all right?" Quincy said. "I came right over as soon as I heard."

How had he heard? I wondered. "I'm okay, Uncle Q," I said, "just a little shaken up. It didn't help that the police started in on me like they think *I* kidnapped Leda. Ridiculous."

"Well, I suppose they're just trying to eliminate every possibility," he said. "But what *did* happen to the poor girl?"

He watched me closely as I gave him the short version of what had happened: the bright light, the loud sound, Leda's hand yanked out of mine. I said nothing of the Other World, not that I knew anything for certain. If I read his expression and body language correctly, Quincy approved of my reticence in front a member of his staff.

To my surprise, Quincy's assistant spoke up. "Sounds like flashbang grenades," she told him.

Quincy nodded at her to acknowledge the possibility. "Myra has a distinguished military background," he said to me. *Who names a kid Myra?* I thought. "She knows whereof she speaks. But why in the world would anyone want to kidnap your fiancée?"

Something about that question didn't sit well with me. The

undercurrents again.

"I can't imagine," I said. "I'm not rich. Neither is she. Neither is her family."

"If I may, sir," Myra said to Quincy, "the young lady's kidnapping may be aimed at *you.*"

"We should not discount that possibility," he said. "We'll have to await further developments, see if we receive a ransom call, and so forth. But what'll you do now, Jerry?"

"I'm not sure, Uncle Q. The police don't seem to have any idea what happened. Nobody mentioned anything like a stun grenade to me."

"I know it's bad form to bring up business during a *family* crisis like this," Quincy said, "but the Association has certain investigative *resources* that would be at your disposal if you were to, er, accept the new role you and I discussed. Resources that might succeed in locating Leda if the authorities were to fail."

The undercurrents had reached the surface. Was my uncle trying to bribe me? Yes. Yes, he was.

"That's very generous of you, sir. I'll certainly keep that in mind this week. You'll have my decision, as we discussed."

"Good, good," said Quincy. "Remember what you *want,* Jerry. Keep *that* in the forefront of your mind and you'll know what to *do.*"

I know a thinly-veiled threat when I hear one. "Sound advice, sir," I said. My friends, finding me unreadable, all stopped playing poker with me years ago. One more reason I don't gamble.

Quincy (kindly?) invited me to stay at his house—just to be on the safe side, as he put it. I declined politely, and we said our goodbyes. Myra drove Quincy off. I drove home.

The *Mysterious Thanksgiving Kidnapping at Odiorne Point State Park* made the evening TV news. Leda's driver's license picture filled the screen; it sort of looked like her. The idiot newscaster read: "At this hour, Ms. Clooton is still massing. Police continue to interview witlesses and are perusing all leads. An unnamed souse close to the investiture reparts that Ms. Carlton's fiancé has refused to cooperate with the umvestigation. If you have any wanformation, please call…"

Refused to cooperate, huh? The *unnamed source* was that fucking detective. Unable to solve the mystery of Leda's disappearance, he was covering his ass with the news media. I hoped he got a big buck in his sights and missed the shot. Or better yet, that he came down with buck fever and failed to *take* the shot—so all his buddies would make fun of him forever.

14

New Friends

In times of trouble, some people fret, stew, and obsess. I take action so I don't have to feel painful feelings and think troublous thoughts. The next day, Friday, I called the old couple at whose dining room table Leda and I had met and talked with Peter Brown.

The husband answered, and I said who I was. There was a pause, the sound of a hand being held over the mouthpiece of the phone, and a muffled exchange of talk.

He came back on the line. "How can we help you, Jerry?" he said. His tone was pretty frosty. Nobody does frosty like New Hampshiremen. I guess he'd heard about Leda's disappearance. Given who his friends were, he may have known where she *hadn't* gone. Maybe he blamed *me* for not letting Peter Brown take her to a place of safety.

Hell, I blamed myself. I got choked up for a couple of seconds, couldn't speak. Oh, poor *me*, right? *Leda!* I thought and pulled myself together.

"Leda was kidnapped, sir," I said. "The police have no idea who, why, or how. I don't really know where else to turn. I thought maybe you folks could point me in the right direction?" Hint, hint.

A moment of silence. "Timing's terrible," he said, talking to himself as much as to me. "We're ... traveling, leaving tomorrow, got a million things to do. Still, Leda obviously thought a lot of you, 'scuse me, *thinks* a lot of you. Tell you what, come over tomorrow after supper, around seven. You can see us off, and we'll see if we can think of something that might help you."

"I appreciate it, sir."

"Look, Jerry," he said, "This is gonna sound unkind, but I don't have time to screw around and worry about hurt feelings here. Leda said you were scared of learning more about the Friends—and about the people we're friends *with?*"

"That's true," I said. It killed me to admit my cowardice to a stranger.

"You know where to go and what to read to learn more, right?"

"I guess the library has all the books?"

"'Course they do," he said. "Or you can buy the books online like the kids do these days. Leda said you've been away from Portsmouth for twenty years? A lot happened here during those years. *A lot.* I don't have time to spoon-feed you the history. Go do your fucking *homework*, son." *Click.*

"I'll see you Saturday," I said into the now-dead phone.

Today being the day after Thanksgiving, the library was closed, so I found the books online, downloaded them to my laptop and began skimming rapidly through them. I don't read much for pleasure, but this was a survival situation. The books had information I needed. I dived in like I was researching a software problem somebody might have solved before.

I stopped to make coffee when my eyes got weary. (*Don't think about drinking coffee with Leda.*) I went back to the books. I started to understand all the things the citizens of Portsmouth—except the Friends—never talked about:

Three Portsmouth Wars in which people died and the city was more or less flattened.

Who'd started those wars and who'd won them.

Who the good guys were. How bad the bad guys were.

How high, deep, and wide into government the bad had spread.

How long ago that started.

How the bad guys deceived one of the Old Gods into working for them.

What happened when the good guys recruited the Old God.

What (supposedly) happens after death—to ordinary men, anyway.

The nature of power and magic, and how those imponderables relate to body, mind, and spirit.

And (as the late-night TV ads would have it) much much more! Other worlds! Invisible Mountains!

Enough, already. I was getting tired and sulky. Not for nothing had I spent years ignoring all the history I'd just spent hours learning. I'd put a wall around myself; reaching out to Leda had breached it. *Okay, okay,* I finally thought, pushing away from the laptop. *If even half of this is even half-true, then Peter Brown was right. I have to pick a side.*

Once you know the truth, or even begin to suspect it, you have to act. You have to do what you can to help. That's what the Friends did. *The Friends* was just local shorthand for a worldwide organization, one Leda was part of. When the people of Earth spoke about those who had saved them, they called those people *elves*, an old word from folklore; they called their support network on Earth the *Elf Friends*. *Terms of convenience*, to use Peter Brown's phrase, like *the next world over*, as the elves called the place they lived. Whatever sort of human being the elves were, you could learn everything about them simply by entering their world and becoming one of them. They invited everyone to share everything they knew. *Everyone* on all of what the elves call the *human worlds*.

That was when I lost it. Dammit, I missed Leda so much. I was so frightened of what I'd have to do to get her back. Being who I am, I knew I'd trade my life for hers, if it came to that. I wept for Leda, who I loved. How lost and confused she must be in a world that made no sense to her senses. And I wept for myself, walking blindly into a future unlike anything I'd ever imagined and unlike any past I knew. Except maybe for that part of history I thought had nothing to do with me.

Yea, though I walk through the valley of the shadow of the *Shoah*...

⚒ 1 5 ⚒

Cold Water

*The thief cometh not, but for to steal, and to kill, and
to destroy: I am come that they might have life, and
that they might have it more abundantly.*

- (John's Gospel)

My cellphone showed 6:59 when I rang the doorbell of the West side
bungalow. I stood in the cold under the front porch light. The inside
curtain over one of the glass sidelights twitched aside. I pretended not
to notice as somebody checked me out. The curtain snapped back over
the glass. Weird. This was Portsmouth, not 1940 German-occupied
France.

Instead of inviting me in, my host and hostess, wearing bulky winter
coats, joined me out on the porch. They both hugged me. Actually, they
hugged each other and I just happened to be in the middle. That was a
surprise. Had my reputation had been rehabilitated after we spoke on
Friday?

"*Jesus*, it's cold," he said.

"Go get the *car*, then, she said. I have observed that husbands and wives often speak to each other like their mates are charmingly wayward.

She sounded nervous or excited—or both.

He walked slowly over to the detached garage, bent over very slowly, and painfully lifted the door. He turned sideways, lowered himself gently into the seat, pulled his legs in, started the car, and backed it out.

"Would you...?" she said, indicating the garage with one gloved hand.

"Sure," I said. I went over and closed the door.

"Thank you," she said quietly. "His hip just kills him in cold weather. Not that he'd ever say anything, but I can tell. He never lets anybody *open* the damn door for him, though. Won't *let* me buy him a garage door opener."

The lady got into the front passenger seat next to her husband and buckled her seat belt. The gentleman powered his window down.

"Hop in the back seat," he said. "I'll drive and we'll talk."

"Okay?" I said. I did as he asked, though. It's not like they were going to kidnap me.

"Here's the deal," he said as he backed the Cadillac out of his driveway. "After you see us off, just drive the Caddy back here, park it in the garage, lock the garage door, let yourself into the house, hang the keys on the hook in the entryway, set the lock, and let yourself out. If you don't mind, I mean."

"I can do all that," I said, relieved I wasn't going to have to call a cab or walk back to retrieve my own car. Portsmouth also has public transportation, but I'd never broken the code.

I figured we'd be driving to the Boston shuttle bus, or further west to the Manchester airport. But no, he headed downtown.

"Are you taking the bus to Portland?" I said. "Or is it the train?"

"Not exactly, dear," she said. "We're going to meet someone. Being picked up, you might say."

"You asked us for help, Jerry," he said. "We passed your request to our friends. We're meeting someone tonight who can help you find Leda."

"If anyone can help, it's *Them*," she said. She reached over and patted her husband's cheek. He smiled at her and put his attention back on the road.

Seeing this quiet display of husband-and-wife affection just about killed me. *Don't think about Leda*, I thought for the thousandth time. I hated the idea of crying in front of people I'd just met, even friendly people.

I'd thought he was driving downtown. Instead he turned the big car south at the cemetery.

"There's the house I'm renting," I said as we passed it.

"Yup," he said. "You know whose house it used to be, right?"

"I do *now*," I said. "I've done all the required reading for this course, sir."

He laughed. "Good for you, kid. The More You Know."

"Donita Danton," she said in a tone of wonder. "*Lady Donita*, the New People call her."

"Don't see many New People around Portsmouth anymore," he said.

"I'm not surprised," I said. What did surprise me was that people had actually moved to Earth *from another world*; I thought it best not to mention my surprise. Portsmouth residents just pretended the New People who'd moved to Earth *from Agharti*, for God's sake, were ordinary immigrants who'd come here from elsewhere on Earth. Abroad, possibly.

"Guess they moved inland," he said. "I would have, too, after what happened."

"American citizens are free to move wherever they want," she reminded him.

What they left unsaid was that the New People community had been built on the lower slopes of the Invisible Mountain. When the Mountain subsided, their settlement sank with it, or who knows, simply got buried.

So many things that were common knowledge among Elf Friends were never discussed in Portsmouth's polite society. *Never*. As if the ordinary world around us would vanish without that denial. I refused to deny my own experience. First Peter Brown left Portsmouth for the next world over, disappearing in front of Leda and me. Then Leda was abducted into the Other World, disappearing in front of me before we'd even started our life together. I was done with denial; it couldn't pull Leda out of thin air.

Before long we were on the coast road. He parked the Caddy in a turnout on the north side of the Odiorne Point State Park. Uh-oh.

"We'll hike in from here," he said.

We all got out of the car. He locked it with a beep and handed me the keys. The still air around us felt even colder to me, but that might just have been fear. I pulled a knit hat out of my coat pocket and put it on before my ears turned brittle and broke off. Winters were considerably less brutal in D.C., I now remembered.

He took his wife's hand and led the way into the park, keeping us on the path with a narrow-beam penlight. The path took us through a stand of trees beside a little tidal creek. When we came back out of the trees, the half-moon shed enough light on the path that we could see to walk. A hundred yards along, we walked off the path onto tide-smoothed rocks that clacked and crunched underfoot as we approached a short stretch of soft, wet sand. We crossed the sand and clambered up onto the land side of a long breakwater that stretched out into Little Harbor where it meets the Piscataqua River and the Atlantic Ocean.

The breakwater was built of giant rocks piled up on the harbor bottom until they reached ten feet above the high tide line. The old couple helped each other walk carefully along the top, avoiding the narrow clefts in the flat surface.

I walked close behind them, carefully watching them for slips and trips, and watching where I put my own feet. *What are we doing here?* I thought. I was pretty sure I knew.

"You're going to the next world over, aren't you?" I said quietly, knowing how far sound carries over water.

"Yup," he said, matching my tone. "Once you know what the choices are, it's either stay here and die or go there and … be transformed."

"Thought we should go before we got too banged-up to walk or lost our marbles," she said. I heard the smile in her voice. The lady had all her marbles; they both did. But *"walk"*?

We got to the end of the breakwater. Did I mention how cold it was? A little wind blew in from the east and made us feel even colder. *Now what?* I wondered.

We didn't have to wait long. He pointed out to sea. At first all I could see was a line of moonlight on the quiet surface of the water. I heard little wavelets washing against the massive stones we stood on.

A distant sphere of light appeared in the darkness. It moved toward us at a rapid walking pace. Inside the globe of light I saw a human figure, a black-clad woman, walking atop the water.

She saw us, smiled and waved. The old Elf Friends waved back. I waved, too. Always the gentleman, I scrambled down the side of the breakwater to meet her. She took my hand and stepped off the water and onto the stone, not that she needed any help. She wore loose black trousers, a black turtleneck, a black sweater, and boots. She had dark eyes and dark hair. The light that surrounded her showed me she was beautiful. *Leda!* I thought. Of course, she wasn't Leda.

"Jerome August," she said, giving me a big smile. "Well met, brother. Peter Brown told me all about you. Once I've taken our brother and sister safely home, may I visit you at your house?"

"I'd be honored, ma'am," I said.

"Jerry," said the lady from the stone above us, "allow me to introduce Aimee Amory, our escort."

"Pleased to meet you, Ms. Amory," I said. I knew her story, too.

"How about if I call you Jerry and you call me Aimee?" she said. I said that made sense to me. *As much sense as anything's made lately,* I thought.

Aimee and I helped the old couple climb down the breakwater.

"You can leave your coats with Jerry," said Aimee. "You won't need them where we're going."

The husband and wife did as the shining woman suggested. She held their hands and whispered words in that mysterious language Peter Brown had used, words I couldn't catch. Words that lit up the night around us. The light around her expanded around the old couple, and she led them out onto the surface of the water.

They all stood there. None of them sank into the water. I saw it, but I couldn't quite believe it. They moved gently up and down as the waves moved under them, like boats would do.

I climbed back to the top of the breakwater, holding the coats like the hired help at Quincy's house. I watched the three of them *walk* out onto the Atlantic. They walked a moonlit path toward a land mass I'd never seen before, an island that loomed up from the ocean bottom at the mouth of the harbor. An island mountain that *simply couldn't be there.*

But there it was, the top of the World Mountain, better known as the Invisible Mountain to those of us who lack the vision or the grace to see it. With their elf guide holding their gnarled old hands, the Elf Friends walked out of Portsmouth on top of the waves.

I stood there watching in disbelief until I saw the three faraway figures walk onto the Mountain's lower slopes. There, unless all the books were lying, they entered the borderlands of the next world over.

The light vanished. The Mountain, if that's what I'd seen, became Invisible again. No one now moved upon the face of the waters.

16

Housecleaning

My eyes had gotten used to the dark; it was easy to see the path. I got back to the Cadillac without difficulty. Luck was with me. No police showed up to investigate why I, of all people, happened to be present at the scene of yet another mysterious disappearance, of all things.

I aimed the big car toward Portsmouth. I didn't stop shaking until I crossed the city line. Cranking the heat on high didn't seem to help. I wasn't shaking entirely from the cold. I noticed my eyes were wet. I blinked the tears away.

Luck stayed with me back at the Elf Friends' house. I locked their car in the garage, hung up their coats and keys in the house, locked the door behind me, and drove home in my own car. I hoped their neighbors were used to guests coming and going and would ignore one more. *The Lives of Others* never got much traction in Portsmouth; most people mind their own business.

At home, I sprawled on the hideous cabbage rose couch in front of the TV, trying to distract myself until my visitor arrived. Whatever programs were on, I couldn't focus on any of them. My head was full. I couldn't deny what I'd read and learned and heard. I'd met someone who shouldn't exist and seen her do something that shouldn't be possible. It now seemed beside the point that she was also supposed to have done other things I couldn't believe in worlds other than Earth.

Grief and stress make you tired. My eyelids might have briefly closed a time or two, then closed for a longer time as I slid into uneasy sleep.

A faint noise and a feeling of disturbed air woke me up. The young woman I'd met on the breakwater simply *appeared* in the middle of my living room.

I was about to speak when she locked eyes with me and held a finger over her lips: s*hush*. As I sat on the couch and continued to ignore the TV, Aimee Amory searched my house for listening devices. She uncabled my router, cutting my internet access. She *sniffed* my laptop. She climbed the narrow stairway to the attic bedroom I used for storage. She went down to the cramped little basement. She made the universal "telephone" gesture with her thumb and little finger. I handed her my cellphone, which she also sniffed. She powered it off and handed it back to me.

She'd saved my landline phone for last, and that's where the bug was, behind a couple of screws inside the base of the phone. It didn't look like much when she found it, just a black plastic rectangle. I would have figured it was just part of the phone; I'm not much of a hardware guy, no pun intended. She held the device up to me with two raised eyebrows: *See?* I nodded to indicate that I saw.

She held up one finger: *Be right back.* She disappeared again.

I couldn't imagine I'd ever get used to that.

But she was as good as her word, reappearing twenty seconds later on the exact spot she'd left.

"Whew," she said. "I'm glad that's over."

"Well," I said, "do I need to know what you did with it? Not that I'm thrilled to learn my phone was bugged."

Aimee grinned. "I threw it in that tidal inlet at the bottom of the cemetery across the street."

"Thanks," I said. "Would you like something to drink? I have wine, beer, coffee, and tea."

"I'd like tea," she said, "but can I have a hug first?"

I stood up and hugged her. She hugged me back with easy strength, like she had a powerlifter's muscles shaping her compact body. She was perhaps an inch shorter than Leda. Like Peter Brown, Aimee appeared to be of mixed race, perhaps partly Asian. Peter's skin had been paler, though, while Aimee's was a darker gold.

I stood back and looked at her. I didn't mean to stare rudely, but there was something very *attractive* about her and she had a pleasant spicy scent I couldn't identify. The perfume of her own world?

Beautiful as she was, she wasn't Leda.

Smiling, Aimee looked back at me. "I see how it is with you," she said. "Your Leda is lucky to have found someone like you. You're as spoken for as my husband Daniel and I."

I knew their story. Now. How she had saved Daniel Ryun's life until he could become an elf. How together they had saved Portsmouth and the East Coast of North America from disaster. Supposedly.

"I guess I *am* spoken for," I said. "Can you help me find her?"

"Let's have tea," Aimee said. "We'll talk."

17

Tea for Two (No Tap Dancing)

I made us mugs of bitter green tea. We sat at my kitchen table and drank it. A white-faced electric wall clock buzzed faintly as its second hand circled the dial. *Time's a-wastin',* I thought. But it wasn't my move, was it? I didn't know what action to take *instead* of wastin' time; that's why I'd asked for help. Aimee seemed content to sit there holding the warm mug in two hands, savoring the smell of tea in hot water, and looking around the kitchen. Finally she broke the silence.

"Donita Danton, the woman who once owned this house, helped save my life," Aimee said without preamble. "Before she came to the next world over, she was working for those who hate mankind."

I knew that story, too. "If my horrible living room sofa is any evidence, it's clear she was a monster."

Aimee laughed. She had perfect teeth. I guess all the elves did. It was probably worth traveling to the next world over just for their dental plan. "My *point,*" said Aimee, "is that when she encountered summary evil face to face, she chose the good instead. Most people do."

I shook my head. "Sorry, I don't get it," I said.

"The choice between unhappiness and happiness is easy for most of us," Aimee said. "It's simple self-interest, once we see that's what the choice *is.* The Old Gods, though, seem to be a different story."

"Peter Brown said they were *bad* for us in some way."

She nodded. "There's a kernel of truth in all those myths and folktales. People who traffic with the Old Gods always seem to fare badly. *Always.*" She reached over and put one hand on my forearm. "I'm not sure yet how to help you, Jerry. If you come to my world with me, *you'll* be safe from the Old Gods. But if those gods and their servants can't find *you*, how can you find Leda?"

I found her touch reassuring. "My uncle thinks his dealings with what he calls the Other World are all about *power*," I said. "As if power's morally neutral, like electricity."

Aimee grimaced as if she found the thought painful. "I was taught that power *corrupts*," she said. "Nothing in my life has convinced me that power *over others* remains morally neutral."

To show that I knew her unhappy history, I patted her arm. "I'm sorry for your trouble, Aimee," I said.

"Huh," she said with a smile, "that's what Daniel always said. Back when we only spoke English together, I mean."

"I think I'd like Daniel," I said. "If—I mean *when*—we get Leda back, maybe the four of us could double-date?"

She laughed. "*Double-date?* Dude, you are *so* old-school!"

I pretended to have hurt feelings. "Fine, we'll all *hang out*, then, as you *kids* say. First, though, can you teach me how to deal with power without letting it corrupt me?"

Aimee sat up straight and smiled at me. "Peter Brown *said* you were a smart fella."

18

"Pain is Weakness Leaving the Body" and Other Popular Misconceptions

I didn't have to go back to the office till Monday. Aimee and I had the rest of Saturday night and all of Sunday to work together. I was young and strong and highly motivated to learn what she had to teach me. Well, that's what I thought.

Thirty minutes in, I felt old, weak, dim, and *resentful* of all the knowledge she was forcing on me. I followed her direction grudgingly, thinking *Well, this is stupid.* It took an enormous initial effort to learn the basics of something that seemed completely irrelevant to finding Leda.

Those we miscall elves see things differently from the way the rest of us perceive the world and ourselves. Boy, is that an understatement.

My father had been an Army Ranger who fought in Vietnam. The sadness of all he had done and learned there was always with him. He told me I'd have a happier life if I avoided military service. He taught me to think things through for myself. When I was a boy, Dad taught me the bleak basics of self-defense: walk or run away unless trapped; break away if you can; injure, maim, and kill if you must. *Once you see there's no other way, you have to choose to kill the enemy*, he said. *Making that choice is the hard part; the rest is just technique.*

I'd only had one fight in high school. A huge, aggressive, ahem, "student-athlete" took an irrational dislike to me. He said I had no right to keep breathing his air. He swung, missed, and tried to grapple with me, looking to get me on the ground and pound me unconscious. I got inside his guard and punched him in the side of the neck. The fight ended with him lying on the floor and fighting to breathe. I got suspended for a week, either for defending myself or for risking damage to the star, I was never sure. That he had a hundred pounds on me and would have put me in the hospital was deemed irrelevant. He survived. Word got around that wiry little Jerry was nobody to fuck with. I discovered that I would have killed the bully without hesitation if I'd had to. Sometimes you have to *insist* on your right to live. I was fine with that.

Aimee had quite different ideas about conflict, though, and about the human bodies through which conflict is expressed and resolved. I told her about what I'd done with what my father had taught me. She said, "Your father was right that fighting is all about intention or mind-set. But you can't kill everybody you go up against, can you?" I admitted that was true. "Let me show you something..." she said. She proceeded to demonstrate how the human energy system, let's call it, could be used to deflect attention from yourself, to deflect an attack away from you, to discourage people from attacking you, and if all else fails, to destroy their ability to attack, as my father had taught me.

She went on to show me how all that worked. From inside myself I watched how all the inner lights lit up like a Christmas tree, or if you prefer, a menorah. So therefore if one pushed *here*, then *there* on the energy supporting someone's body, *this* would happen...

...and she caught me before I fell, lowering my helpless body to the floor. I started laughing as she helped me up. Once I finally saw how simple her teaching was, at least in theory, I started feeling young and strong and highly motivated again.

Learning the complicated part would have taken years and required studying magic that can be expressed only through the language of the next world over. I just wanted to learn enough to help me get Leda back—without giving up my life on Earth.

"Why is Quincy so intent on getting you to explore the Other World?" Aimee said.

"I'm not exactly sure," I said. "And I think my refusal probably got Leda kidnapped."

"Something about power, maybe?" she said. "Peter Brown asked what your uncle was doing with his power. What have you learned?"

I told her everything Miracle Max had found out about the August Association. I also told her what Max suspected, hoping to make her laugh. She didn't laugh. In fact, she looked worried. Uh-oh.

I told her all about the apparently-generous offer Quincy had made to bring me into his organization. "Do you think he's trying to buy me?"

"Sounds like it," she said.

"Damn, I was hoping you'd talk me out of thinking that," I said. But I'd known.

"Are you seeing that maybe the Old Gods *have* been bad for your uncle?" she said.

"Bad for this country, too, it looks like. Pardon my liberal politics."

She didn't try to talk me out of that, either. "It'd be nice to know your uncle's intentions," she said.

"I'll know more this week. How can I contact you?"

"If you're willing, I'll meet with you every night," she said. "Besides the pleasure I get from escorting our friends home across the water, I came back to Portsmouth for *you.*"

"I'm, like, a *job assignment?*" I wasn't sure I liked that idea.

She shook her head No—emphatically. "It's something I feel *called* to do."

Aimee spoke sincerely, so I didn't make a joke. For once. If I asked her where *the call* came from, she'd probably tell me something I wasn't ready to hear.

"When you talked to your friend Max, what phone did you use?" Aimee said.

"Oh, crap," I said, "I used the house phone. The one you took the bug out of. The phone was here when I moved in; I just got the phone company to give me the number. Should I be worried? Should he?"

"Maybe you should call and tell him why you think he should be on his guard." She paused a moment, thinking. "I'm no electronics expert. All I know about that black device I threw into the water is that someone with bad intentions stuck it in your phone. For all I know, the New World Order planted it back when this was Donita Danton's house."

I smiled. "Yeah, the National Security Administration is already sweeping up all the internet and telecommunications traffic in the country. Anybody with enough influence could probably just sit in Utah or Maryland and listen to my phone calls. My secret has always been to have no secrets."

"He's ... the Most Uninteresting Man in the World," Aimee said. "*Stay boring, my friends.*"

I laughed. She was a good teacher.

"The more I think about it, the more it looks like I'll have to go to the Other World to get Leda out of it. Wish I could take you with me," I told Aimee.

"I can do better than that," Aimee said. "How about taking me *and* Daniel with you?"

I will admit goggling at her. "I must have misunderstood what you and Peter Brown said about the Old Gods. I thought they couldn't even *see* you guys—or that you were like oil and water and didn't mix." I meant the elves.

She shook her head. "I don't think we can travel with you in the body. What we can do, if you're willing, is share thoughts with you mind-to-mind."

That sounded awful. *My mind,* I thought, *is often a cramped and dirty place, quite unworthy of such distinguished guests as Aimee and Daniel Ryun.* But what I said was, "Um..."

Aimee looked at me in her direct, disarming way. "I read many of your thoughts now as we work together, my brother. There's nothing in your heart or mind that makes you unworthy of my company."

Again, although I'd read about mind-to-mind communication, it was quite another thing to have Aimee demonstrate that she'd been reading my thoughts.

She watched me closely. "I can see that you're unhappy with the idea," she said. "I don't blame you. How about this, though? I think if Daniel and I work together with you, we may be able to get a line on Leda. Where she is. *How* she is."

"Why didn't you say so?" I said. "Let's do it."

19

Messages

Late Sunday night—actually early Monday morning—we decided I'd had enough. Aimee bid me goodnight and just ... *left*. Poof, gone.

I needed sleep, but I felt too wired. I turned my cellphone back on. My voicemail contained four messages each from Beth and Janjan, bottom line: *call us as soon as you get this*. There was another voicemail from a blocked number, bottom line: twenty seconds of silence with the sound of a TV in the background. I thought I knew who that was.

Before facing up to my responsibilities to Leda's housemates, I plugged the internet cable back into the router. Most of my email was work-related and could wait for the workday, but one message was from a mail website I didn't recognize with a random string of characters in the "subject" line. When I opened it, all it said was:

> *Interesting visitors today. Had to invoke Godwin's*
> *Law of Nazi Analogies. Watch yourself, son.* ^_^

The silent voicemail and the anonymous email with the smiley face were both from Max, covering his tracks to show me he was serious. The Nazi reference told me his visitors were federal agents. Bottom line: *we're being watched.* Thanks to Aimee, I knew Max wasn't just being paranoid.

I didn't bother to answer Max's email; I'd talk to him later.

Right now it was time to call Beth and Janjan. I used the house phone. Because why not? I had a landline, but the girls' house had inexpensive voice-over-internet, not terribly secure.

Janjan picked up after two rings. "Jerry?" she said. Poor kid sounded sleepy.

"Yeah," I said. "Guess you heard about Leda?"

"Just a minute," Janjan said. I heard her yell to Beth to pick up the other handset.

Great, they were going to double-team me. And not in a good way.

Beth picked up. "Jerry? What *happened?*"

I told them the little I knew. I told them what I'd seen and heard.

"The police were here *waiting for us* when we got back from Providence," Beth said.

"They were asking about *you,*" Janjan said. "I told them you'd never hurt Leda."

"'Cause you *love* her," Beth said. She wasn't teasing.

"I do," I said. "I love her."

Beth and Janjan began to cry in each other's ears and in mine. That went on for quite a while.

"That's what we told Leda's mom when *she* called," Janjan said. "The police called her in Chicago to see if the kidnappers had made ransom demands. What the hell, Jerry? Mrs. Clayton doesn't have any money."

"Nobody's contacted me about ransom, either," I said. That wasn't quite true, but close enough.

The conversation went around and around a couple of times before we agreed to call each other if we heard anything, as soon as we heard it.

I found it oddly restful talking to two people who also loved Leda, who understood how much I cared about her, how much I missed her, and how much I wanted her back. I undressed, set my alarm, fell into bed, and went immediately to sleep.

A Dream of My Lost Love

I don't usually remember my dreams, but this one hit me hard. Perhaps because Aimee's teaching had sensitized me to inner currents I'd never noticed before. Or perhaps simply because I was so tired and sad and frightened for Leda.

Had Quincy's words been prophetic? With the perfect recall of my undistracted sleeping mind I heard him say again:

> *I dreamed of my lost love—everyone has one— dreamed we lay abed together in that field. I tried to embrace her, but she turned away before I could see her face.*

And then:

There was a naked woman beside me in my own bed in my own bedroom. The mattress sank a bit under her body. Her back was to me. I heard her breathing quietly in her sleep. Leda?

Leda's disappearance was just a dream, I thought. In the way of wish-fulfilling dreams, that thought made perfect sense. Why *couldn't* I have whatever I wanted? Didn't Quincy say *What a man decides to do in life depends upon what he wants?* To get that power, all I had to do is meet the *conditions* of power.

All I had to do was keep my eyes closed, reach out, and touch her.

And she would *be* Leda.

But there was some *wrongness* there. An undeniable feeling of something badly amiss ruined my sleep, like stomach cramps or nausea in the middle of the night will do.

My eyes began to open.

I saw the outline of someone next to me.

Whatever I was dreaming, whoever I'd dreamed up, I wanted to *see* her. I opened my eyes all the way.

I felt the other side of the bed rise. I saw no one.

It was just me in the bed.

What would have happened if I'd kept my eyes closed and reached out for ... whoever it was that had been lying next to me?

I smelled a faint trace of something like musk or hot sand, but the scent quickly faded.

I felt empty. Leda, my own true love, was still lost.

21

Legal Counsel

I left work early on Monday. Well, early for me. With one thing and another, I had trouble concentrating on the tasks at hand. Bob didn't seem to care about project status updates. He was having trouble focusing, too. He still hadn't gotten around to telling customers about our regime change. He just nodded when I said goodnight.

I met with Steve in his office in a stately nineteenth-century Portsmouth home that had been remodeled into business suites. We'd gone to grade school together in our long-ago childhood, which is why I picked his name out of the yellow pages. That, and the fact that his prematurely white-streaked beard in the photo ad looked very lawyerly. He showed me to a comfortable client chair and sat with a clean yellow legal pad on the desk front of him. Judging by the new stone sections of foundation, the building had suffered damage and required repairs because of the geologic upheavals attendant upon the Portsmouth Wars. I didn't expect Steve to discuss that, and he did not disappoint.

"Nice office," I said looking around. "Beautiful building, too."

"Yeah, the firm owns the building. Did a complete remodel recently." His voice dropped and his eyes glanced to the side. I'd come to think of that look as the Portsmouth Ocular Evasion. It meant that further inquiry about the Portsmouth Wars would be unwelcome.

Would in fact be met with protestations of ignorance and ultimately with distaste. Some things were Simply Not to Be Talked About these days.

Steve and I spent five minutes catching up, then got to business.

Having heard the news about Leda's disappearance and my relationship with her, he'd thought I might need representation in a criminal matter. He changed gears without a blink when I explained the details of my super-secret employment contract negotiations with the August Association.

"Holy shit," he said, "you're one of *those* Augusts, Jerry?"

"Kind of a shirttail relation, I guess," I said. "But Quincy August is my granduncle, more or less."

"That being the case," he said, "why do you need *me?* Why would you not simply sign the contract and accept what I imagine is Mr. August's largesse?"

"Before I answer that, are you my attorney yet?"

"Little matter of a retainer." He gave me some forms to sign, and I wrote him a check. "Okay, *now* I'm your attorney and therefore bound by attorney-client privilege. So shoot."

"The short answer is that I don't trust Quincy to do the right thing—even by me."

"Ah, well," Steve said, "I wish I could say that your family was unique in that regard. But alas. Okay, now what's the *long* answer to my question?"

"You've heard about my fiancée getting kidnapped right in front of me?" He nodded Yes. "I can't prove it, but I think my uncle is involved in that."

He gave me a skeptical look. "Have you *shared* that suspicion with the police?"

"Are you fuckin' kiddin' me? What do you know about the August Association?"

He shook his head. "Not much," he said, "and none of what I know is good."

"Dark money," I said, as if I understood what that meant.

He nodded. "*Very* dark. Now we move into the realm of speculation. But it does seem to me that a great deal of money is being spent to poison the political discourse in this country." He waved his hand as if to clear the air. "From the little I hear, your uncle's outfit advocates tirelessly *for* the very rich and *against* everyone else."

Not much different from what Max had told me. "Wait'll you see the Association's offices," I said. "Armed security in the lobby. My uncle's personal assistant carries a handgun in the office."

His eyebrows went up a bit. "*Very* unusual around here," he said. "Even if your uncle is big on promoting Second Amendment rights." He hesitated. "Jerry, you've hired me to represent you, and I will do that to the best of my considerable ability. But I'm going to give you my advice right now before I even review that contract for you. You should walk away from the August Association and racewalk away from this deal. In fact, I advise you to move far away from Portsmouth—before you join your fiancée among the ranks of the disappeared."

First Max tells me to run away and now Steve? "Portsmouth is kind of a weird town," I said. "I didn't realize how weird till my family moved away twenty years ago. But it sounds like you know something you're not telling me."

"Have you met his *lawyers?*" Steve said. I said I'd met one of them. He hesitated. "This next bit of speculation is between you and me. I'll deny having said it, okay?"

"Agreed," I said.

"Some law firms will represent just about anyone on just about any side of any issue, as long as the client can pay. Okay, fine, I don't judge. Attorneys have to make a living, and everybody's entitled to the best legal counsel they can afford." He glared at me, although it wasn't me he was angry at. "But there are a few law firms that make it their policy always to be on one side of every issue. They take the side of the rich, bigoted, and privileged against the side of everybody else—and everybody else's civil rights. They do this every time, Jerry, and they never hire Jews. You know what I'm talking about, right? If your uncle's law firm needed a local liaison guy, it wouldn't be *me* they retained. If you were a lawyer, they wouldn't hire *you*, either. Maybe not even if your uncle told 'em to."

Gentiles think I'm a sandy-haired gentile, but Jews often perceive my secret identity, as if I wore a Star of David yarmulke only they can see. The mystery of Jewdar.

"You'll like this story, then," I said. "My aunt asked me to say grace at Thanksgiving dinner, so I said the blessing in Hebrew like my mother taught me. My uncle was ... *perplexed.*"

Steve stared at me for a moment. Then he started to laugh. I laughed along with him. He laughed so hard that he started to cough. Then he couldn't stop coughing. I stopped laughing, worried for him. He fished around in his desk drawer, came up with an inhaler, and took a puff. The coughing subsided just as his secretary quick-knocked on the door and stuck her head in to see if he was okay.

"Don't you die on me," she said. "Your wife says she'll kill me."

"I'm fine," he told her. "Thanks for checking, though." Reassured, the secretary shut the door behind her. He wiped his eyes with a pocket handkerchief, very old-school. "Asthma," he said. "Cold weather makes it worse." He grinned at me. "Dammit, that's the best story I've heard all year, and I can't tell it to anybody."

Steve called the August Association offices, immediately got Quincy's lawyer, and made an appointment for the two of us to review the contract late Tuesday.

As we'd arranged, I met Steve in the parking lot. He'd parked at the very back of the lot, I noticed, far away from the doors and their cameras. The sun was setting earlier every afternoon these days and would continue to do so until the winter solstice.

"Couple of things before we go in," he said. "Beyond the greetings and introductions, I'd like you to let me do all the talking. If you have questions, I'd prefer that we discuss them back at my office. Normal chitchat is okay, but we should assume someone may be watching us and listening to everything we say."

"Is that legal?"

"In the men's room, no. In one of their own conference rooms? They could argue employee safety and security, no expectation of privacy, blah blah blah. So we'll just play it safe: make notes in there, but talk elsewhere."

"How good can a security camera be?" I said, half-kidding. "What if they read our notes over our shoulders?"

Steve looked at me in alarm. "Jesus, I never thought of that. Well, let's scribble illegibly and cryptically, then."

Together, Steve and I ran the security desk gauntlet in the lobby and entered the elevator. Quincy's lawyer met us upstairs, escorted us to a small conference room, gave us copies of the contract, asked if we wanted coffee or soft drinks, said he'd be available to answer any questions, and informed us that he would meet us after we were finished for the day. I found it at least a little reassuring that the lawyer didn't seem to be armed, except with a snotty attitude.

The contract looked fairly standard to Steve. We breezed right through most of it before he started making detailed notes. I made a couple of notes myself. Non-compete clauses I was familiar with, but the Association's stringent confidentiality agreement was completely new to me.

Steve and I were out of there in an hour, telling Quincy's attorney that he'd hear our concerns in due course. I didn't see Uncle Q, although he might have seen me, who knew?

We were back in Steve's office. "That is a very generous contract," he said. "I thought it would be. If you decide you want to take the job, I suggest we go back to your uncle's lawyer and ask for a couple of changes..." He wrote those things down in standard legalese and handed me the sheet of legal paper. I told him those amendments made sense, as far as I understood them. He said he'd have his secretary type up the changes and fax them to the August Association in the morning.

Faxes, ugh. The legal profession kills me with their irrational devotion to low-tech. That, and suspenders.

Steve sat back in his chair and studied me. "Okay, that's my legal advice. My original personal advice still stands. You should hit the road and leave no forwarding address. I'm convinced your uncle's outfit is a bunch of bad people involved in doing bad deeds."

"I can't do that, Steve. Not if I ever want to see Leda again. I'm thinking maybe if I go to work for my uncle, I can find out what happened to her."

"Before it happens to you, you mean?"

I wasn't all alone in this, but I wasn't about to tell Steve about my allies or their, shall we say, unorthodox methods. The man wouldn't even admit why he'd had to repair the foundation of his office building.

22

Mind Games

Aimee and I sat on opposite ends of the infamous cabbage rose couch. I was sitting with my legs folded in front of me and my back wedged into the arm of the couch.

"You know what to do," she said.

I nodded and put my attention on the center of my body's gravity, as she'd shown me while I was learning the basics of, um, elvish conflict resolution. Not far inside me, I watched the light of intention begin to glow. I let my thoughts drift by and go wherever they wanted. It was quite restful, especially given what an angry, anxious man I am.

"Okay..." Aimee said out loud...

... and in my mind I heard words in her voice, *Do you trust me with your thoughts?*

"Yeah, I do," I said out loud, jolting myself out of the receptive state that made it possible to hear her thoughts. I centered myself again and thought back, *I trust you.* I looked up at her and found that our rapport continued unbroken. You have to hold your tongue just right. I smiled. She smiled back.

Ready to meet my husband?

I nodded and thought, *Sure.*

There *he* was in my mind, too. Or rather we were all in a shared mind-space together. My first thought was: *I can't wait to share thoughts with Leda.*

Then I remembered I had to *find* her first.

We can help you with that right now, Jerry, came Daniel's thought.

Can I call you Dan? I thought back with an inner smile. (My outer face was also smiling, but that seemed less important.)

Call me Dan if you like, he thought with an answering smile. *I'm pretty much over all my yuppie affectations.*

I like this guy, I said to Aimee.

I like him too, she said. In the emotion surrounding her thought, I saw how much she missed being physically with him while they were in different worlds. They wanted each other and were not ashamed of it. Elves really *don't* lie.

What Aimee and Daniel asked me to do was to remember everything Quincy had ever said to me, from the party for Phyllis' daughter until the present. I recounted everything I remembered, and the three of us watched those memories unspool. Then we focused on my Other Worldly experiences. The terrifying creature flying above the field. The naked goddess, first in the bushes, and finally on the battlements of the shining city-state.

As I relived these events, I felt-and-saw Daniel's mind darting hither and thither, as if he went further into my experiences than I had when I lived them. I suppose that was entirely possible. I'd still be living happily in ignorant denial if I'd gotten my own way. While he went exploring, Aimee's kind and loving thoughts stayed with me to keep me steady.

Then we turned our attention to my relationship with Leda. No gentleman would willingly share the details of his love life, but Daniel and Aimee assured me there was no choice, no other way forward for us if we were to find where she might have gone. Or been taken.

If it's any comfort, brother, came Aimee's wry thought, *most of my extensive sexual history has been written down for all the world to read.*

If you find this search humiliating, came Daniel's thought, *remember that I once submitted my metal body to be buggered in front of the woman who is now my wife.*

It was a revelation to see in their unguarded minds how much they loved each other. I knew their stories now, of course, but it was still shocking to hear Aimee and Daniel talk casually about their bizarro history the way the rest of us talk about things that happened to us last week at the grocery store.

Oh, by the way, I used to be married to the queen of the underworld who gave me pain to give me pleasure. Did I mention that an Old God turned her into a cyborg because she wanted to live and rule forever?

Oh, by the way, a demonically-possessed seven-foot worm ass-raped me. Did I mention that I was a cyborg at the time?

Jesus Christ! I thought. *Oh wait, you guys have actually* met *him.* They'd made me smile in spite of myself. We were all smiling.

That's the spirit! Aimee thought. *Be strong, this is the last lap,* Daniel thought.

As I relived all the time Leda and I had spent together, my last defenses came down. I started to cry like a little boy. I didn't drop out of mental contact or stop remembering, though. Our first date, our walks, everything we said to each other, our lovemaking. And then Thanksgiving dinner with Quincy and Pepsi, followed by the walk in the cold at Odiorne Point and the assault of heat, sound, and blinding light that had taken Leda away from me.

The three of us went over and over and *over* my memories. I thought I'd lose my mind. Daniel seemed especially fascinated by the vague memory of my fragmentary dream: a woman in my bed, a woman I was meant to think was Leda, but who was not.

Finally, after he'd gleaned everything he could from a dream I now remembered vividly and found profoundly sinister, Daniel's thoughts went ... distant.

Aimee and I sat together in deep, reassuring silence. I hadn't betrayed or sullied my love for Leda by sharing my memories with her and with Daniel. If anything, my love was stronger than ever. And it wasn't like Leda and I had done anything horrible together, quite the opposite.

While his wife and I sat quietly on Earth and he sat somewhere in the next world over, Daniel's mind went a-hunting, first in this world, then in others. I lacked the depth of focus to follow his thoughts wherever he'd taken them. Or perhaps the barrier between me and the Other World was simply my own human defense against anything *numinous.*

Aimee's mind followed after Daniel's wherever it went. That bond was part of what marriage means in the next world over from Earth. Also in her mind like the faintest whisper of whispers were traces of other minds. What I'd read was true. All the minds of those who join the elves are linked, brothers and sisters, indeed. If I strained, I could almost make out words in the shining speech they used among themselves, Elvish, the original human language. The Unfallen Tongue, they called it. It called to something in me. It made me dizzy.

My attention wandered and lost track of Daniel's mind-touch. I opened my eyes. Aimee's eyes opened at the same time. Her face relaxed and she smiled at me.

"Well done, Jerry," she said. "Daniel will be back in touch with us soon—after he recovers."

"*Recovers?* Is he okay?" I hate the idea of anybody sacrificing their life or health for me. I don't think that's just pride. I've always believed that a gentleman tries to help others and not be a burden to anyone.

"He's fine. Or he will be fine shortly, after he spends some healing time alone."

My confusion must have been obvious, because she said, "You know what he did in the last Portsmouth War, right?" I said I did. "As best I understand this and can explain it in English," she continued, "the time he spent out of the body actually *loosened his hold* on his human form."

"So ... he can't ever come back to Earth?"

"Not easily. Also, time flows differently in the next world over than it does here. And who knows what time even means in that Other World where the Old Gods live? My point is that encountering different timestreams can be disorienting. Daniel wants to stay in the body and stay with me, so now he's letting the Healer minister to him."

Aimee had shared her mind with me as I shared mine with her. "You're afraid you'll *lose* him, aren't you?" I said.

She nodded and echoed Peter Brown: "Human love is a good thing, but it's not the *best* thing. Still, being human, we cling to love tightly and grieve it when it goes." By *we* she meant everybody, the people of her world and of mine.

Daniel's thought reverberated in our minds: *I'm back. Did you miss me?* Aimee sent him a wordless thought of love, something like a hug.

My first thought: *Did you find Leda?*

His immediate answer: *She sleeps, brother. The Old Gods, or those who serve them, have cast your Sleeping Beauty into trance, almost into coma, to protect her mind and guard her life.*

They're using her as bait, I thought. *It's me they want.*

Nobody disagreed with me. Gulp.

Daniel proceeded to brief me on what he knew and what he'd intuited, sending me images of what he'd seen. It was better than a PowerPoint business presentation, if only because it was over so quickly.

It took the three of us just a few minutes to decide what I needed do next and when. Gulp, again. With no handsome prince to rescue her, all my Sleeping Beauty had was me.

23

Signing Bonus

Quincy's lawyer made the contract changes Steve and I wanted. The amendments looked minor to me, but what did I know? I think the supercilious Washington dude was surprised I hadn't asked for more money or perks. But Quincy's initial offer was more than generous. I didn't want to play the negotiation game any longer than I had to. Quincy wanted me in the August Association; I found that I needed to be there. On the inside.

Also, my salary and signing bonus now seemed kind of moot. In losing Leda, I'd lost what I really wanted in life. I hadn't lost my attachment to the world, but I'd seen the world's limits. Portsmouth looked like a different place now, both better and worse than I thought when I had to move back here.

I even saw the cemetery across from my house differently. Wherever I breathed my last, whatever world I ended up in, I doubted my body would be laid to rest there by the tidal inlet—or in the little Jewish cemetery on the other side of town.

On Friday at Quincy's building Steve reviewed the revised contract and found it exactly as we'd requested. Mindful that we might be overheard, Steve looked a question at me. I didn't have to read minds to know what he meant: *Are you sure, Jerry?*

I was sure, but not for any reason I'd confided in my lawyer. I just nodded Yes.

Then I signed, Quincy signed, we all shook hands, and Quincy's lawyer darted away with his copy of the contract like I'd just signed it with my own blood and he was carrying it off to the Prince of Darkness like a good little demon. Steve said goodbye and left. I stayed in the office to talk with my uncle.

"I'm glad you decided to join us," Quincy said. "Did you know all your colleagues have signed up with the Association as well?"

In fact I did know that, but what I said was, "I *assumed* they had. Except for Bob, everyone looks very pleased with themselves."

Quincy shrugged. *"Entrepreneurs,"* he said, as if the single word explained everything about Bob. Maybe it was the business equivalent of the *artistic temperament* stereotype. "But come and take a look at the office space we've set aside for you and ... *your staff."*

"Whatever they're working on, you'd like all your IT people under one roof," I said.

"Makes sense, don't you think?" I had to agree. You make better decisions when everybody gets the latest information and everybody talks to everybody else.

We took the elevator down one floor. Quincy said his knees were bothering him. Characteristically, he blamed the continued cold weather, not his age. Q's personal assistant Myra met us at the elevator. She unlocked a set of double doors. As she swung the doors open, I saw the unobtrusive outline of her holster.

What had I gotten myself into? I supposed I'd find out.

There wasn't much to see inside the empty room. We'd have more floor space than we had at the airport office building.

"This looks very nice," I said. "Plenty of room. I should probably bring our hardware guys over to take a look before we plan the move."

Quincy nodded approvingly. "We'll issue everyone ID badges to make the transition easier. Before we finish up here today, Myra will introduce you to our facilities manager."

"While I have you both here," I said, "have you received a ransom call from whoever kidnapped Leda? I'm kind of at my wits' end." That last part was the simple truth.

Quincy and Myra shared what I'm sure they thought was a neutral glance.

"I'm sorry, Jerry," Quincy said. "We haven't heard a thing. I've talked to some of the Association's contacts. No luck there, so I took the liberty of asking our own security folks to make further inquiries with local and federal law enforcement. You don't mind, I hope?"

"I appreciate your help, sir. Beyond trying to implicate me, the local police didn't seem to know where to start looking for Leda."

Quincy put a heavy hand on my shoulder. "We'll find her, Jerry," he said. "*That* is inevitable. Now that you know what *you* want."

24

What About Bob?

Back at the office I mentioned our forthcoming move to Bob. He got upset.

"I don't believe this shit," he said. "God*dammit!*" He slapped the desk with the flat of his hand. There wasn't any paper on it to be disturbed.

"I'm sorry to be the bearer of bad news," I said. "Especially since I didn't know it *was* bad news."

He looked at me with his mouth open. "You don't *know* why I hired you?"

"I assumed it was my natural charm and extensive professional experience. And didn't you recently tell me that you've never *regretted* hiring me?"

"I *did* tell you that," he said. "What I *didn't* tell you is how surprised I was. The August Association basically shoved you down my throat. I figured you'd be a slug."

I sat down in one of Bob's guest chairs before I fell down. "I was ... forced on you?"

He waved his hand. "Okay, okay, I'm exaggerating. What the nice lady said was that *the August Association remembers its friends*. I can take a damn hint. Those are not people a small company should mess with."

"Did this nice lady happen to have one of those husky whiskey-and-cigarette voices?"

"Yeah. Myra something or other, I think."

I nodded; it didn't take long to do the math. "I don't blame you for being pissed," I said. "First you get pressured to hire me. Then my uncle buys your company and pays you a bunch of money to go away. And then he makes *me* managing director so I can run the place. It looks like nepotism all the way."

Bob's no dummy. "Ever wonder why your last employer let you go?"

"I'm certainly wondering *now*," I said. I wasn't actually wondering. Thanks to Aimee and Daniel, I was pretty sure I knew.

For some reason, Quincy had wanted *me*, in particular, to come to work with him. In his building, under his wing. (*Don't think about birds.*) I was pretty sure I knew what would happen next.

25

"Dance at the Gym" from *West Side Story*

Saturday morning I buzzed myself into the Association offices with my shiny new ID card. The weekend security guards, a couple of guys I hadn't seen before, were both armed and alert. Once I showed my ID, they waved me through, figuring I belonged there. The name "August" on the card probably didn't hurt. *Same as it ever was, it's all who you know,* they might have thought.

I didn't expect to see Quincy today, but I had legitimate business reasons for being in the building. I dropped a file folder in the personnel office drop box (the office was locked), the usual forms you have to complete when you change jobs. Ostensibly, I also wanted to take another look at our new office space, make a few sketches, think about who would sit where. Then I'd sit down with my colleagues, excuse me, my new subordinates, to make the final decisions. Ostensibly.

Actually, I wanted to snoop around the building during the weekend. I figured I'd have the place to myself. And security cameras be damned. I worked here now, didn't I?

Also, Daniel had said, or thought, to me: *There's something amiss about your uncle's building. Don't ask me how I know; I can't explain it in English. Body language, demeanor, amount and direction of airborne dust, anomalous heat signatures. Bad vibes, Jerry. The place doesn't smell right. You should check it out. Just be ready to travel.*

All things I had lived through and had entirely overlooked, but which Daniel had perceived at second hand through the eyes of my memory.

Was I ready to travel? I guess. This being a very cold December Saturday, I was wearing hiking boots, cargo pants, a sweater, a light Polar Fleece jacket under a lined leather jacket. I stuffed my hat and gloves into my snazzy leather briefcase-backpack while I rode the elevator up to my new floor. The backpack was a gift from my ex, one she allowed me to keep. Not that I'm bitter or anything. I took off the leather jacket and carried it. Quincy kept his building pretty warm.

Imagine my surprise when Myra met me at the elevator. Had the guards called up to her? Had she seen me on a security camera? Had the ID card reader notified her? She was wearing gym shorts and a serviceable t-shirt, breathing deeply and sweating as if she'd been exercising hard. The lady was solid with serious muscle.

"Morning, Myra," I said.

"Hi, Jerry. I'm surprised to see you here on a Saturday." Was that a tone of skepticism? With Myra it was hard to tell. She had cop's eyes that gazed out upon a guilty world.

I explained about my HR forms and desire to sketch our new offices. She nodded as if that made sense.

"Have you seen the gym yet?" she said. I said I hadn't. "State-of-the art equipment. Your uncle treats his employees *very* well."

She steered us down to the far end the shadowy hallway to where light spilled out of an open door. Besides showing me the gym, I figured she'd also want to show off how much she could bench press or something, so I'd feel properly intimidated or outclassed or outmanned or something. Competitive gym rats can be such assholes. *Do you even lift, bro?*

As we approached the door, I felt something coming, an energetic disturbance which Aimee had prepared me to counter. In the center of myself I also felt a powerful intuition that instead of fighting the oncoming wave, I should let it push me. Time slowed down. I saw dust particles illuminated by the light that shone into the hallway and thought, *amount and direction of airborne dust, anomalous heat signatures.*

Myra sidled up next to me, as if inadvertently. Without pausing, she bent her knees, flexed her muscular legs, and effortlessly hip-checked me into the Other World.

26

The Gateway to the Sun

On Thanksgiving when Leda was taken, I'd reflexively turned away from the bright light and the roaring sound that suddenly filled Odiorne Point. When her hand pulled out of mine, the force spun me around like a top. Blinded and deafened as I'd been, the door to the Other World had slammed shut behind me without my knowing it.

This time I was ready. Well, as ready as you can be for an onslaught of the *numinous* and the *wholly other*. Quick as thought and breath, I centered myself in my physical body like Aimee taught me.

The Other World was still blindingly bright to my squinting naked eyes. I focused my vision, not outside where I couldn't see, but inside myself where I could.

Inside myself I saw opponents surrounding me, mirrored, as we are all reflected and resonant inside one another. I felt the threat as the lights of their energy moved at me.

Without hesitation, I struck, pushed, and pulled as I'd been taught to do, first *here* and then *there*. As long as you stay on your feet and move smoothly, there's a limit to how many people can attack you at once without working against each other. Perhaps my would-be captors expected me to be dazed and compliant; they were unprepared for resistance. Were they armed? I didn't have time to worry about weapons I couldn't see. Inside myself I saw those energy lights fall back from me. I whirled through those half-glimpsed strangers like wind through a field, all movement, no stress or strain.

Then I whipped on my wraparound sunglasses and sprinted off as fast as I could. Wished I was one of those douchenozzles driving a sporty little car with a sticker that said "Oakley Thermonuclear Protection." I ran full-out for maybe ten minutes, then slowed my pace for another twenty. My knees had predictably begun to ache, but it's not like you should stroll away from danger.

As I ran, my eyes adjusted to the light. Even behind sunglasses, I was squinting. The rest of me was sweating, not that it made much difference in the dry heat. I heard my own ragged breath, but no sounds of pursuit. The ground sloped up. I felt gravel underfoot. And then, blessed relief, I entered a patch of shadow. I looked up: natural rock or ruins, I couldn't tell.

I looked back the way I'd come. A wide, packed-dirt road with sandy soil on both sides; I'd run off it and uphill. Nobody was behind me. Hell, nobody was anywhere around me. *The wicked flee when no man pursueth: but the righteous are bold as a lion*, I thought. But when you can't tell who's wicked and who's righteous, distance gives you an edge.

It was possible that my whole arrival in the Other World was an accident, or that I'd hit my head in the August Association's dry sauna and was hallucinating all this. I wasn't betting on either possibility.

Where were my pursuers, though? I saw a small group of people double-timing steadily up the dirt road. *That* was no coincidence. It was too hot to run. I ducked down out of sight, wondering if I'd left obvious tracks in the gravel. The distant sounds faded. The posse, which might or might not have been chasing me, moved on down, moved on down the road. *Safe for the moment*, I thought.

I moved deeper into the shade of the rocks and off the beaten path that wove between them. I sat down on, what else, a rock, and inventoried my backpack briefcase. I opened one of two half-liter bottles of water and took a drink. The water was already warm. It tasted great. In the outside briefcase pocket was a small folding knife. Not much of a weapon, but it was all I had with me; I put it in a pants pocket. Also in the briefcase pocket was a wide-brimmed folding canvas hat I wore to keep the rain off my head; it would keep the sun off my face, too. I stuffed my jacket and sweater into the pack. I must have dropped my leather jacket back on Earth with Myra. Do deserts get cold at night? I was going to find out.

Cautiously, I took my sunglasses off and looked up. The sky looked *wrong.* By which I mean that it was no earthly sky I was used to. Not that I'd ever gone exploring the Negev Desert or anything. I know that people do wander deserts, but people also jump out of perfectly good airplanes for no better reason than the experience.

Still, the sky of the Other World *spoke* to me or *meant* something to me in a way that the blue or cloudy skies of Earth never had. I felt *connected* to that dazzling greenish height, linked by something deep as the bond between my human body and mind. If I hadn't spent hours training with Aimee and Daniel, I might have thought I was having a mystical experience and was on the verge of some insight into the Great Questions.

And what of Daniel and Aimee, you ask? Back on Earth, their minds spoke directly to mine, because I'd given them permission. What about here?

Sitting up straight on that flat rock, I centered myself once again and thought, *Daniel? Aimee?* No answer came. Hmm. I'd lost the connection to those lively, loving, intelligent people. I missed them the way you miss your family. At least those family members who actually like you and mean you well.

I closed my eyes and thought, *Dammit, what do I do now that I'm here? How do I find Leda?* In the center of myself, in the darkness behind my closed eyes, an intuition arrived, fully formed and specific. It swam up from the depths to the surface, like an answer from the fortune-telling Magic 8-Ball:

Wait till late afternoon. Walk that way |^|.

"That way" was perfectly clear to me. It would take me further in the direction I'd already run, as good a direction as any. Whether the idea came from my own common sense or was somehow influenced by my new friends from the next world over, it seemed logical. I had limited water and I seemed to be in a desert or some kind of sun-blasted wasteland. I probably wouldn't be able to see to travel safely after full dark, so I'd travel in the twilight.

I'm coming, Leda, I thought. I had no sense of her presence here in the Other World, but why would I?

It was *hot.* I walked further into the rocks looking for a place to hide, maybe sleep and conserve energy. I saw that what I'd thought were rocks showed repeating patterns of tool marks. A gigantic sculpture garden?

The upright stone had been carved into legs; here and there I saw feet at the tapered end where you'd expect feet to be. Time or war or natural disaster had toppled the upper bodies of the statues; they were mostly covered by sand. "Ozymandias," anybody? *Look on my works, ye mighty, and despair!*

If I remembered it right, Shelley had written the poem about Egypt. I couldn't help wondering if these statues had fallen long before Egypt. Had maybe inspired it.

If that sounds like a flight of fancy, it was how my mind worked here. I didn't feel drunk or stoned the way I had in the field with Quincy at my first Other World contact—and at every contact thereafter. But I didn't feel quite like myself, either.

I found a place where sand had blown into a little hollow in the elbow of a fallen stone arm. Seeing neither snake nor insect nor animal, I lay down in the shady sand with my head pillowed on my backpack. The tide of adrenaline that had helped me escape had ebbed, leaving me shaky and sleepy. I was anxious about sleeping here, but the body has its own imperatives. To my relief, I fell asleep and slept without dreaming.

27

The Subject-Object Dichotomy and the Language of Dreams

Cooler air woke me. The shadows were longer. Time to move ... *that way.* I stood up, brushed myself off, drank less water than I wanted, and hit the trail. It wasn't much of a trail, more of a flattened dirt track with sand blown all over it and piled up in spots, the way dry snow drifts onto a highway. I might have lost the path if it hadn't been side-lit by the sun of the Other World on my left as I hiked ... north. (I decided to call it north, because why not.)

I'd come to know two things I hadn't known when I lay down in the sand. I *knew* I was headed toward the woman I loved. I also *knew* that the Other World encompassed an inexplicable sadness that extended from its molten core to its outer atmosphere. *These are the tears of things*, said the Roman poet Virgil.

Quincy had said that to receive power you had to meet its conditions. Had he embraced the penetrating sadness of the Other World, or had it thrust itself upon him? Had he gazed into the abyss and allowed the abyss to gaze into him?

I had a different relationship to this world than I had to Earth, a closer, scarier relationship, and no idea why that should be so. If I'd come to know something about the Other World, had *it* now come to know something about me? Too late to worry about that. I could have chosen to leave Leda to her fate and run far, far away to the ends of the Earth, but then what would have been left of me? Being who I am, I'd rejected the thought. Betraying someone I loved was the same as betraying myself. A fate worse than death; death can't be helped.

Not on Earth it can't. As far as I know.

So I walked through the gently-rolling country into the twilight, my hat cocked to the left against the glare of the setting sun. On either side of the trail, the sands had drifted over ruins and covered them. Wherever the people of this Other World might be, they didn't live here anymore.

High above me I saw again the alien sky I'd first glimpsed from a Portsmouth field. As the sun set, astonishing throngs of slow-whirling planets and stars filled the darkening heavens. Had the people who once lived in the ruins ascended to become celestial creatures like demigods out of Greek myth? Another of the fanciful thoughts this world seemed to engender. It was profoundly sad, but the Other World was also piercingly beautiful. Perhaps back on Earth the History Channel had a lucrative career waiting for me as a wild-haired *Ancient Aliens* theorist. I'd have to regrow some hair for that one, or maybe shave my head completely, wax my scalp, and cultivate some eccentric don't-take-me-seriously facial hair.

I walked along as fast as I could and still listen to the sounds of the world around me. I hadn't seen any insects or been bothered by them, but I thought I heard them chirring like grasshoppers. Night-flying creatures, birds or bats, whooshed through the darkness in pursuit of the insects. The temperature continued to drop. I fished the jacket out of my pack and walked on, wondering if I'd need the sweater, too, before the night was over.

Way up ahead, I saw firelight illuminating portions of a wall. Human-shaped shadows moved past the light. Was it a village? A settlement? I walked closer slowly then stopped in the road to observe.

What do I do now? I wondered. I had one energy bar and one half-full water bottle left. I really was not prepared for extensive exploration of the Other World.

The only answer that came to me was, *Go talk to people.*

The gift of gab, right? It's no good if you don't use it.

What language did they speak? I suppose we might be reduced to playing charades. Or they might just kill me, not knowing or caring that I was dependent on the kindness of strangers.

I would've stood there dithering awhile longer, but some kids found me. They were just running around in the cool darkness, yelling happily like kids do everywhere. They would have fit right in at Phyllis' house. One little boy almost ran right into me. He looked up, gasped, and darted back toward the fire, shouting, dragging all the other kids in his wake.

Here's the thing about the shouting kid. At first all I heard was the *sound* the words made. But after an interval, the *meaning* of those words filtered into my thoughts: *Dad, Dad, there's a stranger on the road.* Was I just imagining the meaning because it seemed logical?

I walked toward the firelight, slowly, keeping my open hands at my sides. Three adult-size figures walked to meet me. They were all shorter than me. They also looked heavier, but who doesn't? I stood still and waited for them to come to me.

"Hi, I'm Jerry," I said, not knowing what else to say. "I, um, come in peace."

The three approached me cautiously. They stopped maybe six feet away from me.

One man spoke a torrent of words containing what sounded like my name, only pronounced "ZHAY-ray." After a pause, the meaning arrived. I didn't know their language, but, as in dreams, that didn't seem to matter, so I'll render this odd and awkward exchange in English, the only Earth language I actually speak.

"Who is *Jerry* and why has he come to this land?"

That was kind of a long story and I wasn't sure I should tell it to them in detail. What side were they on? How much of it would they even understand? But part of knowing how to talk to people is figuring out what you have in common and building on that.

"A bird as big as a man flew down from the sky where I live. He spoke words I didn't understand. My uncle said he came to *summon* me."

The three men exchanged looks, then looked at me, *peered* at me, actually, in the starlight. The guy who'd spoken first shook his head. Sympathetically?

"*Summoned*, is it? You poor man." There was awe in his tone, though.

"*Lucky* man is more like it," said the second guy.

"Nobody *summoned* to the Shining City ever comes back to this shithole to tell us which it is," said the third.

"The gods do as they please," said the first. "Isn't that what makes them gods?" Then to me, "Come and warm yourself at the fire. Have you eaten?"

28

A Foreigner in an Alien Land

If you can't be good, be lucky. I'd unwittingly done the right thing by giving my hosts my name and telling them what I'd told them. Names were a big deal with these people, I guess. I mean, I didn't know anything about them for sure. Only part of all they said made it through the filter of my own history, culture, and experience. Bottom line, given that I had been *summoned* (the words that communicated that concept had a host of meanings I just couldn't catch) by a creature they regarded as a god, they were responsible for keeping me safe. While doing this, they protected themselves by keeping their own names a secret from me. I'll just call them Larry, Moe, and Curly, even though they looked nothing like the Three Stooges and I mean them no disrespect.

Everybody else in the little village made themselves scarce, leaving me with my three new pals. They wore shirts and pants of rough cloth, not terribly clean, with long hooded robes or burnooses against the cold of night. On their feet were woven sandals of tough plant fiber. They looked to me like standard-issue dark-skinned human beings. I mean, this was another world, right? I guess I was expecting little green men or something. But these guys looked more like Middle Easterners you might see on the nightly news, maybe shooting bullets into the air or burning the American flag. I guess if you live in a desert, you need more melanin than if you live in, say, New Hampshire. If my hosts had firearms, I didn't see them.

The people of this village, I learned, lived by finding precious stones and selling them to gem traders who passed along this side road. Somebody somewhere must grow something worth eating, but our conversation never got that far. It seemed rude to inquire too deeply. What they did eat, and shared with me, was the fruit of some kind of hardy fast-growing bush or dwarf tree, whose wood they also used to make fires. I said Thank You and ate what they offered me. That, it seems, is always the right thing to do in any world.

The fruit was bittersweet: sweet on the tongue, then bitter in the belly. Was it my imagination, or did eating it make me sadder? I was in my right mind, but not in my ordinary mind in the Other World.

The village only existed because of its well. This land had water, but you had to dig deep to find it. Larry showed me how to crank a bucket to the bottom of the shaft, maybe twenty yards down, let it fill, haul it up, and dump the contents into a stone basin so the sand would settle out. He found it funny that I didn't already know this. I found it funny that he'd never seen clear plastic water bottles before. He gaped as I filled mine. I wished I could have given him one, but I didn't dare. I was afraid I'd need both of them before I got where I needed to go.

Which reminded me. "I'm very grateful for your hospitality," I told the three men, "but I don't want to cause you any trouble with ... the authorities. I'm thinking that I should leave your village before dawn." Larry, Moe, and Curly observed me in a silence that changed from courteous to serious. "I was *pushed* into this land by a woman," I said.

"Women push *all of us* into the world, if you think about it," said Larry. We all laughed.

"What I meant to say is that when I arrived here ... *today,* I couldn't see clearly. Some people surrounded me. Because I couldn't see who they were, I was frightened and ran away from them."

My three hosts exchanged looks. "You were *summoned,* but you fled the *[Myrmidons]?*" Moe said. The word I've rendered as *Myrmidons* was another of those complex thought-phrases I had no equivalent for. Part of the thought was *fighters*, part of it was *unquestioning obedience*, and the final part was something about *gender or sexuality* that simply eluded me.

"The woman who shoved me into this land," I continued, "also works for my uncle. She has more muscles than I do." I flexed my right arm and pointed helpfully to my bicep.

"*Myrmidon*," said Curly. Larry and Moe nodded in agreement. How could they know such a thing? Was this some primitive, irrational, or superstitious certainty they used to make sense of their world? Not that I felt superior to them; I simply didn't know what the hell was going on.

"Who is your uncle that one of the gods' own Myrmidons serves him?" asked Larry.

Excellent question. I revised my opinion of these guys upward.

"My uncle is trying to use his wealth to make our land as he wills it to be," I said. "He wants the rich to have power over everything and the poor either to be his slaves or to die." The language of dreams cramped and constrained my more nuanced English into simpler statements these guys could understand. I could see it happening, but was powerless to change it. Frustrating, but way better than charades.

"*Oh!*" said all three men in unison. Their middle-aged faces fell into masks of old sorrow in the light of the dying fire. They understood something I did not. Something bad. They looked at each other, looked at me, then nodded to each other again. It would have been funny, but they were life-and-death serious. They'd come to a decision on behalf of the whole village.

"You should sleep here tonight, Brother Jerry," Curly said. "Tomorrow after the heat of the day, we'll see you on your way. Some things a man has to see for himself." He sounded sorry, not for himself or for his people, but for *me*.

29

A Series of Unfortunate Event Horizons

Late afternoon again. I was back on the sandy dirt track with Larry, Moe, and Curly leading the way. The road still led me *that way*, toward Leda, so I was content to follow along. We didn't have to hike too far before the road passed through more ruins to the right and left. Broken stone pillars told me this was once a city. On the ground lay more half-buried giant figures like I'd seen in the shattered sculpture garden where I'd hidden in the shade. No roof remained in this city. Wind-blown sand scoured the jagged walls of every building, erasing details, leaving everything smooth, colorless, and unidentifiable, covering everything grain by grain.

Narrow columns marked fallen buildings on one side of the road. On the other side, further along, I saw fields of sand with outcrops of rock or wall here and there. I saw a great bowl like a dry lake; the sun glinted off the sand that covered it.

The sadness was stronger here, or I felt it more strongly. I'd been alone all my adult life, even when I was married (*especially* when I was married), but I'd never felt so *forlorn*. To keep myself from crying I said, "What am I looking at?" I knew what it was, though, or my intuition did. What I saw in the Other World was somehow *part of me*.

"*Catastrophe*," Moe said. Larry and Curly nodded. The word

echoed with implicit meaning I could almost grasp.

The same intuition that told me *that way* was the right direction put a series of English words in my mind. I tried to speak the words to take the power out of them.

"War," I tried to say. "Slaughter. Pestilence. Starvation. Murder. Holocaust. *Shoah.*" But what came out of my mouth in the language of dreams instead of *war* was only "Catastrophe." I went on to say, "Catastrophe. Catastrophe. Catastrophe. Catastrophe. Catastrophe. *Catastrophe.*" One word, many meanings, *if it were not so, I would have told you.*

Curly nodded. "Now you know because you've seen for yourself," he said.

"Your land and ours suffer from the same sickness," Larry said.

"When our gods make manifest their power," Moe said, "our people die and our cities fall. This dirt track we walk was once the main road. These ruins were cities. Now the cities are rubble and the people are dead or fled."

Curly put a rough hand on my shoulder to give me such comfort as he could. "If your kinsman seeks power in your country, and a Myrmidon serves him, we know that the gods of the Shining City have prepared more ruin for both our lands."

"Look well," Larry said to me. "What is the meaning of this city?"

"The *Shoah* echoes from this land to mine and back again," I tried to say. But all I managed to do is speak the word *Catastrophe* again.

The Three Stooges nodded. They knew I'd spoken the truth. I found myself walking in the Other World, but living in the shadow of the *Shoah.* Of all the *Shoahs* in human history. How much pointless destruction had sprung from the power of the Old Gods?

Instead of the Stooges, maybe I should call them the Three Wise Men. None of the Jesus movies end happily, though, and all are sadly lacking in slapstick.

I Wonder as I Wander

Before Larry, Moe, and Curly returned to their village, they gave me a woven-fiber sack of hard bread and dried fruit. They also gave me some sort of flexible bladder full of water. I shuddered to think what sort of creature the bladder might have come from, but I also thanked them sincerely. A man really needs water in the desert, and you can quote me on that. When you're thirsty, you don't care if the water jug is clean.

"You've been very kind," I told them. "I'm grateful. I wish I had a way to repay your generosity."

Moe looked at me directly in the fading daylight. "When the gods *summon* a man," he said, "that man has something they need. If you can find a way to keep from giving them what they want, perhaps their power will not manifest. Perhaps lives will be spared. That would be repayment enough."

I nodded. I hadn't told my hosts about Leda; maybe it was time.

"I don't know what the gods *need* from me," I said. "But they stole the woman I was to marry—to bring me here, too."

"This is bad," Larry said. He looked worried.

"*Very* bad," said Moe. He also looked worried.

"It's *end-of-the-age* bad when a bride and groom are summoned together," said Curly. "We should get home and take our families to a place of safety."

"If there *is* such a thing as safety," Moe said. I'd never heard that kind of utter resignation in a human voice. Lucky me.

The three men turned to go.

"Good fortune to you, Jerry," Larry said. "Do your best. No man can do more. I'd suggest you pray to the gods for help, but the gods have done nothing to deserve our prayers."

That was a fair point. I waved goodbye to my friends. They hustled back the way we'd come and disappeared into the night.

The stars and planets above me were bright tonight. No clouds or dust in the upper atmosphere, maybe? My eyes adjusted to the inconstant light, so it was easy to navigate between sand drifts and keep my feet on the dirt road underneath. *I'm walking on another world!* I marveled. This really was *Pee-Wee's Big Adventure*, starring Jerry August as Pee-Wee Herman, the nerd whose bike gets stolen. It would have been quite a different movie if somebody snatched Pee-Wee's girlfriend rather than his bike, I suppose. Say what you will about the predicament I'd been pushed into, it was exciting. Being who I am, I hate most kinds of excitement.

The downside of big adventures, and the reason I'd always avoided them, is that while you're in the midst of one, you don't know if you'll make it out alive. Strictly speaking, it's not an adventure till you're safe in the Explorer's Club sitting in a comfy chair with a stiff drink in your hand telling the story of how you barely survived the Zambezi expedition. And the downside of the Other World, as I'd learned from Larry, Moe, and Curly, was that its power, the power Quincy came here seeking, not only killed its own people, but also killed people on Earth. Not just one or two, either, but millions of them.

As I walked along the dirt track that once was the main road to the Shining City, my intuition, sensitized by contact with the minds of Aimee and Daniel, showed me which random sand-heaped ruins marked the place where Other-World god-power had echoed to Earth. Where exerting power over others had killed those others.

Here Vietnam, and here Cambodia.

There Germany and Poland.

Here Armenia.

Here and there and *there* Africa.

Here China, and here also, with Japan over there.

Here Russia, here Ukraine.

Here the original residents of North America.

There the American Civil War.

Here Roman Judea.

And here the European Black Death.

Over there First World War battles shaded into the Second.

Here Iraq, and here Syria.

On and on it went, as if a whirlwind had sown Earth's bloody past here for the lone and level desert sands to cover. And I walked through it all with my inner ... (knowledge? wisdom?) pointing out the facts in the unemphatic monotone of a bored tour guide. The Other World was sad because it was the lever that moved so much murderous human history. My feeling of special relationship to this world was now revealed to include a special relationship to pandemic and slaughter. I wanted to scream.

If I dug deep into the ruins like an archaeologist, what would I find? Swastikas? Hammers and sickles? Crosses and crucifixes? Stars and crescents? Flags of many nations, red with blood? Lovingly rendered murals of mass slaughter? Bas-relief sculptures emerging from flat stone, coming to illusory life in the world like Pygmalion's Galatea?

But *I* wasn't responsible for any of that, was I?

Feebly, I tried to blame the elves for all this bad old news, but they weren't even the messengers. The elves weren't Santa's little helpers. They weren't fairy tale beings who'd made shoes for the shoemaker. They weren't even the separate, immortal race Tolkien described. Those we miscalled *elves* were just human beings who looked unflinchingly into human nature and tried to help the rest of us. Aimee and Daniel had found a better way to live. Rejecting power over others, they sought power over themselves. The power that sustained and guided them had induced a kind of intuitive magnetic field in me.

> Now I knew
> What I knew.
> What should I do?
> What could I do?

A collection of shadows detached themselves from a shadowed pile of fallen stone pillars. The shadows arrayed themselves across the road, blocking my path. And what was that *wsshh* sound? Did I see the shadows of drawn knives?

"You wouldn't happen be Myrmidons, would you?" I called to them.

31

Tomorrow Shall Be My Dancing Day

One of the shadows stepped forward.

"Myrmidons, indeed! Would you be Jerome August?" said a contralto voice. A woman? It took me a moment to grasp who *ZhayROOM OwGOOST* might be.

"That depends," I said. "Are you planning to kill me?" Once again, I stood with empty hands open at my sides, hoping to demonstrate my harmlessness. I didn't know what I could do against six long knives, but I wasn't planning to die without a fight.

The forward shadow moved toward me at a deliberate pace. I saw a fluid cross-body movement and heard a blade being sheathed. "On the contrary. Our orders are to *protect* you, even at the cost of our own lives. So our god, blessed be he, has decreed by *summoning* you." On the Myrmidon's lips, the word I've rendered as *summoning* carried a lot of spiritual weight in the language of dreams. *Religious calling* or *sacred task* can only suggest how seriously she took the whole business. Having a personal relationship with the Old Gods of the Other World was a hell of a lot more personal and concrete than any Earthly relationship with Jesus. No disrespect intended.

"Call me Jerry," I said.

"You may call me *Squad Leader*," said the woman. A note of pride crept into her voice. "It is proper to address my squaddies as *Trooper.*" It seemed that names and titles were a big deal to all the people of the Other World I'd met thus far. They knew mine, but I was not to know theirs. Okay, fine.

She came within polite conversational range and in the starlight I saw that she was perhaps an inch shorter than me, but heavier. Her squad arrayed themselves around so they could get a good look at me. As far as I could see out of the sides of my eyes, they were all women, all built as solidly as Myra. Huh.

"I'm curious, Squad Leader. How did you find me?"

She laughed. "I'd like to say it was skill, but it was only good fortune. Our god, blessed be he, dispatched hundreds of us to search all roads leading to and from the [*Nexus*]."

The word my mind reported in English as *Nexus* also came laden with spiritual freight.

"*The Nexus?*" I said.

Planets trailing incandescent gas whirled above us through the high heavens. The Squad Leader peered at me curiously through the starshadows. Her face was about six inches from mine. Other World people stood closer to each other in conversation than most Americans do.

"A *Nexus* is a sacred doorway between our land and yours," she said. "There are several. Do you not know this?"

I decided on a partial truth. "I was blinded and deafened when I first arrived in your land. I was immediately surrounded by people I couldn't see. I was so frightened I ran away from them."

Hostile murmuring came from the troopers. Did they think I was lying and showing them disrespect? Maybe it was like lying to the police. Not that I'd know anything about that.

The Squad Leader sidled further into my personal space, drew her knife, and held the blade to my carotid artery. With each beat of my heart, the thin skin of my neck gently touched the steel. I stood still. This made me a little nervous, but my inner vision showed no threat emanating from her. Besides, where in the Other World would I go but where she had been ordered to take me?

"We were *told*," she growled, "that you wove your way at speed through the drawn knives of six Myrmidons. By some magic, they laid neither hand nor foot nor blade upon you—as you knocked them to the ground, stunned but uninjured."

"That all seems a bit unlikely even to me," I said mildly, "and I was *there*. As you can see, I'm a man of peace."

The Squad Leader sheathed her blade again with the smoothness of constant practice. She laughed once, at least I assumed it was a laugh; it sounded more like a grunt. "*Umph!* I had my blade to your throat, could have killed you with a flick of it, but you were not afraid. Whoever you are, I very much doubt you're a man of peace."

I looked at the woman directly. "Why fear human warriors when the gods kill us for their sport?" I said.

The Squad Leader looked away from me, unable to meet my gaze even in the inconstant shadows. She was about to dodge my question.

"I know little about the things of the spirit," she said in the language of dreams. *Don't give a shit about that nonsense*, is what she meant, probably what that evasion always means. She'd unknowingly stuck the blade of irony into my heart. There'd be no more evasions for me, not here in this world where *the things of the spirit* became matters of survival.

32

He Hastens and Chastens His Will to Make Known

The squad led me back overland, retracing the way they'd come. We left the path where they'd found me and headed for the main road. I noticed they didn't talk much among themselves, not that I know much about small unit military discipline and tactics. The Myrmidons talked less than most of the men I knew and a lot less than all the women I'd ever known. I draw no conclusions from any of that.

Now that I'd passed their leader's little test (and she'd failed mine), their manner toward me was respectful, reserved, even solicitous. Interestingly, the Myrmidons seemed to have much better night vision than I did. Whenever I was about to put a foot wrong, one or another of the women would grab my arm and firmly steer me back onto a path my eyes could hardly see. I watched how and where they moved through the low dunes and high ruins and tried to walk as they did.

After maybe three hours of this broken-field hiking, I was relieved when the dunes opened up and I felt hard, smooth dirt under my boots. I was also relieved when the Squad Leader called for a rest stop. It was exhausting not quite being able to see the ground under my feet, but I was too stubborn to ask for a break. Call me sexist if you must.

"I'll be right back," I said as I walked behind a sand-covered head high wall. "Just need to take a leak." The Myrmidons all giggled at that; they were full of surprises. One of the women followed me at a distance to be sure I didn't make a run for it. She pretended not to be watching while I relieved myself. I had my back mostly to her, but I still had to think about the Red Sox to persuade my bashful bladder to empty. There wasn't a lot in it. All this hiking was dry work. I really could have used a shower, but water was only for drinking in these parts. Being who I am, I washed my hands with sand, then brushed them off on my pants. I wandered back and sat down among my escort, trailed by my minder, who whispered something to her leader.

Escaping the Myrmidons would've been out of the question. I was even more tired than I'd thought. I could have fallen asleep right there at the side of the main road to the Shining City, but our fearless leader wanted to make progress before the sun came up and we had to take shelter. The squad got to their feet as ordered, without grumbling. I wanted to bitch, but didn't, once again shamed into silence. Amusing to learn that I could have been a good soldier. At least I had endurance and the ability to keep my mouth shut.

High above us, my eyes caught a flash of white streaking across the sky. Surely not an aircraft. A comet? In a sky so filled with wonders, I didn't know what to expect. But as it flew away, I heard a distant cry, not quite human, but not fully avian, either. Very different from the red-tailed hawks who nested in the pine tree in the frozen marsh where I'd declined a summons to the Other World. It was the wildest, saddest triumphal call I could have imagined from an intelligent being. It pierced my mind as if it came, not from the heavens, but from inside me.

My intuition presented me with a fact I had no way of knowing: *I have been seen.*

The troops all bowed their heads. "Our god, blessed be he, is pleased with us," said one. The others nodded solemnly.

"He is pleased that we bring Jerome August, whom he has summoned, into his sacred presence," said the Squad Leader.

I didn't know whether to be pleased or not. That would depend on whether Leda was okay—and whether I could wake her up and take her home with me.

Before the sun cleared the horizon, we found another garden of fallen columns that offered shade where we could rest. Thank God. The Other World seemed to have been big on tall buildings. Which is kind of stupid if you think about it. Why build *up* when you've got a whole planet to build on horizontally? I assumed whatever land mass we were on was bigger than Manhattan Island. There's no accounting for an autocrat's architectural whims, I suppose. Especially if that autocrat is worshiped as a god.

The Squad Leader assigned sentries. I found myself some soft sand, grateful to be sitting down. The Myrmidons shared some hard bread and a water skin around, like school kids swapping bag lunches. I offered them some of what the villagers had given me. We all thanked each other and ate and drank with pleasure. *God, I miss Leda*, I thought. She would have enjoyed meeting these people. She would have loved sitting here next to me. Intuition formed a message: *Soon*. I found the word comforting. I really needed comfort, wherever it came from.

My comfort was short-lived. The Squad Leader turned to me and said in a normal, conversational tone, "My squaddie tells me you have a penis. Are you a man?"

How many choices are there? I thought. I managed not to choke on the water I was sipping, swallowed it, and said, "Yes, I am. Why do you ask?"

The Squad Leader shrugged. "The way you fought at the Nexus. The report we had of that made me think you might be Myrmidon, like all our finest warriors."

I struggled with the gender math. It was like my third semester of calculus when I found myself lost inside the Cloud of Unknowing. "I mean no disrespect," I said, "but I thought you and your troopers were women."

The Squad Leader shrugged off her burnoose and flexed the muscles in both arms. Very impressive, like Myra's musculature. "What *woman* has thews like this?" she said, as if I'd asked a stupid question. "Myrmidons have almost everything a man has—and almost everything a woman has, except the curse of menses and of bearing children."

I nodded as if I understood, although I didn't, not really. "Forgive my ignorance," I said, "but *all* of you? All Myrmidons are both male *and* female?"

She laughed. "Would you like me to show you my *sword*? Or would you rather see my *scabbard?*" Something flirtatious in her tone suggested she would find that sort of dalliance not entirely unwelcome.

Not my sort of thing, though, so I guess the joke was on me. I laughed, too. "You're very kind, Squad Leader, but I am ... *spoken for*. Perhaps you know the lady who is to marry me? I'm told your god has also summoned *her* to his Shining City."

That certainly threw cold water on the conversation. "I have heard this story," said the Squad Leader, "but I do not know your *lady*. In any event, it's now time to *sleep*." She stalked off to find a place to bed down. The other troopers gave me the stink eye and did likewise.

Had I hurt her feelings? Should I continue thinking of her *as* "her"? On the other hand, hadn't Myrmidons kidnapped Leda? Maybe they *deserved* hurt feelings.

3 3

I Am a Gentleman in a Dustcoat Trying

I have not said what the Myrmidons looked like. Now that I'd seen them in daylight, I saw nothing that contradicted what I'd told the Squad Leader. To my eye they still looked like women. Possibly American or European women of Middle Eastern descent, possibly lesbian, possibly just big, strong, athletic farm gals, but still. All six Myrmidons wore their hair short by the standards of most Caucasian Earth women, but still longer than mine. They might have cut their hair even shorter if they'd had very curly hair like African women, not that I was any expert. Muscular though they all were, they still had more hips than most men and what looked like breasts under the light woven armor that covered them from neck to mid-thigh. Even a gentleman notices these things. Under the armor, they wore loose sleeveless shirts and trousers of what looked like undyed cloth. They wore light-colored burnooses with their knife sheaths tied on the outside, at the waist for easy access.

As we hiked along the main road, the ruins and sands gave way to fields and farms and small villages. The climate became slightly more humid. Had we been climbing a very slight grade? I decided it was possible that we'd gained altitude over the last few days. I hurt all over, my legs no more than the rest of me. Not that I would have thought of complaining when nobody else did.

The Squad Leader continued giving me the silent treatment. She took the point and left me near the back of our little column, so she wouldn't have to talk to me. I put up with that for a day or so before broaching the subject with one of the troops.

"I seem to have offended your boss, Trooper," I said. "That was not my intention."

She looked at me, startled, as if a statue had spoken. "Ah," she finally said, "how could *you* know our ways? You're from another land where everything is different. No, you said nothing to offend. Marriage is a sore subject with Myrmidons, though."

"May I ask why?"

She looked at me. "I mean *you* no offense, Jerry," she said, "but talking to you is like talking to a child."

Had she been talking to my ex? "You're not the first ... person to tell me that, Trooper," I said. I almost said "woman." I'm a little slow sometimes, but rarely completely stupid.

She laughed. "Since you really seem not to know this, understand that Myrmidons neither marry nor are given in marriage. Our god and goddess, blessed be they, *touch* us in our mothers' wombs and make us warriors who can take comfort with each other, with men, or with women. But we are *married* only to the gods, and that for our whole lives. We have good lives. We have enough to eat. We have the honor of fighting for our gods. Marriage and childbirth are denied us, but not children. When a child is born Myrmidon, her parents bring her to live with us to learn our ways."

The phrase I've rendered as *take comfort* actually meant *have sex* in the Other World. The language of dreams was less clinical than English, but more accurate in human terms. I considered asking her *what went where* when comfort was taken, but I didn't really want to hear the answer. Also, the question would have been both stupid and rude. Sometimes a gentleman has to figure things out for himself.

"I thank you for educating me, Trooper," I said.

She threw a strong arm around me and gave me a brief comradely hug. "You seem a good man," she said. "Humility is as essential as courage in a warrior. The men of our land, by and large, are as headstrong as our women are spineless."

"The men and women of my land are rather a mixed lot," I said. Talk about understatement.

34

I Am a Lady Young in Beauty Waiting

As we hiked, the land grew green and lush on both sides of the road. Wells and settlements were closer together now. The road felt smoother under my feet; perhaps it was watered to control the dust and packed down by cart wheels and by many passing feet. Ordinary citizens stepped to the roadside when they saw a squad of Myrmidons coming. They gawked at me. I wondered if I'd ever get used to being gawked at.

I could tell that we were climbing now. The incline steepened up. The days were cool enough that we could hike during the day and only had to lay up for the hours around high noon.

The Myrmidons, and especially the Squad Leader, began trying to march me into the ground, to see how far and fast I could hike before I begged for a rest. They failed, not because of any great strength or virtue of mine, but because hiking boots are better for hiking than battle sandals. And maybe also because my lean muscles were more efficient than their thick muscles. It was all an accident of birth.

I finally got sick of the pissing contest and exerted myself enough to jog up to the front of the column where the Squad Leader was sweating away setting a blistering pace. She looked at me in frustration as I fell into stride with her. She was breathing harder than I was.

"Please allow me to apologize for whatever I may have ignorantly said or done that caused offense," I said. "My land and yours have different customs." No kidding.

She kept walking, glared at me, and remained silent. Well, except for her heavy breathing. I was afraid we were about to play a round of the "Oh, Nothing" mind-reading game some women seem to enjoy so much: "What's wrong, dearest? *Oh, nothing. (Sigh).*"

The Squad Leader slowed her pace, turned to her troops, and ordered them to fall out at the roadside to rest. She and I sat together in silence for a while (on *grass!*) in the shade of a field of some densely-planted crop. It was very, very *green*, whatever it was.

"I took a man as a lover once," she said without preamble. "I loved him with all my heart and with all my parts." She made a graceful gesture to indicate the area below her waist. "And I believe he loved me the same way."

"Love's about more than just the parts, isn't it?" I said, thinking of Leda and me.

She nodded and smiled sadly. "You *do* understand, then. Most men would not. Most ordinary men and women find Myrmidons ... *bizarre.* Although it is our own god and goddess who make us as we are." Another pause. "So perhaps you will understand something of how I felt when my lover left me to marry a woman. Because, as he said, he wanted to father *children.*" She spat out the last word, her pain turning into anger.

I put my hand on her shoulder, hoping to comfort her. "I once had a wife who left me for another woman," I said. "It hurt that she didn't want what I had to give her."

Interested, she looked at me. "And what of your children?"

I shook my head. "We had no children."

"How not?" She sounded like such a thing was impossible to believe.

I shrugged, not wanting to talk about birth control. Or about how grateful I was *not* to have had kids with someone beautiful, intelligent, and ambitious who didn't like men in general and didn't love *me* in particular. Who knew what other taboos the Other World and the

Myrmidons had lying in wait for me to violate?

"It *cannot* be that you are sterile," she continued, "or the god, blessed be he, would not have summoned you—or your bride-to-be—to the Shining City."

I didn't like the sound of that. "I'm sorry, but I don't understand."

It was the Squad Leader's turn to shrug. "Who understands the gods? They do with us as they will."

I remembered how worried Larry, Moe, and Curly had been when I told them about Leda. "Has your god summoned us to witness the *end of the age*, Squad Leader?" My tone was light, as befits a discussion of apocalyptic superstition.

But the look she directed at me was pure pity. "Ah, Jerome. Not to *witness* the end, I fear, but to *engender* it."

"*That* comes as something of a surprise," I said as mildly as I could. "Are we talking about my death?"

"Not death, but *change*," she said. "It is a great honor that you and your bride thus be called up, that the bodily life of our god and of the goddess may continue in this world. When this happens, a new age begins for all who live in this land. It is nothing to fear."

"I appreciate the reassurance," I said.

The Squad Leader may have detected my sarcasm. She grabbed my shoulder. "Everyone dies," she said, sounding like Uncle Quincy. "I would be content to die in battle, a death with honor. But I would be more grateful if I were *called up*, as Myrmidons often are in between one age and the next, so that my life might continue as part of the god's and goddess' sacred marriage."

"That is one of the things of the spirit about which *I* know nothing." I said it while wearing my best poker face, but I don't think I fooled her.

⚓ 3 5 ⚓

You Were Expecting Maybe the Emerald City?

The Shining City sat atop a hill, just as Ronald Reagan had pictured it. It wasn't much of a hill, but it really was one hell of a city. I barely managed not to hang back gaping, gawping, or goggling as the Myrmidons briskly escorted me through the wide-open gates. The reason for my wonderment was not so much the city itself, splendid though it was, but the fact that *it looked exactly like the vision I'd had of it* when I was skating on that frozen pond near the Atlantic. The city, or the powers behind it, had reached out from the Other World to Earth. And now here I was in the flesh. *Who you gonna believe, me or your own eyes?* Seeing isn't always believing.

Jesus Christ, I thought, *what kind of universe* is *this? Or is it a multiverse?* My thoughts turned hazy and began drifting like smoke, a symptom that had been muted for most of my time in the Other World. On the metal-roofed battlements above us pennants of the winged god snapped in the hot wind. I saw no sign of the goddess with the Archaic smile, but with sun glare dazzling on all that window glass above us, she could have been watching my approach unobserved. I kept my own eyes open.

The Squad Leader exchanged greetings with the Myrmidon sentries at the gate. They needed no passwords. Myrmidons all looked enough alike to be related. I wondered if they all knew each other. I wondered a lot of things. Like: Who are their enemies that they need battlements? And: *Where is Leda?*

The inner voice I'd identified as my own intuition spoke up: *Center yourself.* That's always good advice. The ensuing calm felt better than anxious runaway thoughts.

Inside the walls, the city went on and on, and up and up. I'd been expecting something squalid and medieval, but everything looked clean. Maybe not Earth-modern, but a triumph of city planning. I saw that the citizens moved goods around the smooth roads of the Shining City on wheeled carts. I smelled that they cooked and baked with charcoal fires. What I did *not* smell, if you'll forgive the vulgarity, was *sewage,* hallmark of the developing world and the unmitigated shame of corrupt Earth governments. Somebody even cleaned up after the horses. The Shining City smelled fresh and looked well cared for.

The Myrmidons I understood to constitute a class unto themselves, obedient only to the gods and their chain of command. I saw that the city contained both commoners (who dressed in utilitarian work clothes more like the ragged villagers I'd first met) and nobles (who wore white robes decorated with elaborate designs). And everyone, highborn and low, turned to their neighbors when they caught sight of me in my odd Earth attire and whispered, *The gods have summoned him.* Whether this was bad news to them as it had been for Larry, Moe, and Curly, was hard for me to discern. Maybe events that were mere ripples in the Shining City created havoc out in the desert provinces. Any resemblance to the District of Columbia was probably just coincidence. After all, there was *no* distinction between religion and politics in the Other World.

All roads in the Shining City led to the gods' temple or palace at the center. The language of dreams had one phrase that covered both concepts, something like *godhouse,* but it carried a lot of spiritual baggage I couldn't unpack. I mean, the people here didn't go to an empty church to worship some deity they couldn't see. Here, the gods dwelled among them in the flesh in a splendid mansion and the people served those gods and did as their gods directed. Which all would have been fine if their gods didn't use their power to inflict catastrophe on Earth—disaster which redounded to the detriment of the Other World where they lived.

The palace of the gods sat at the top of a wide stone stairway. I couldn't help being reminded of the steps that led to the U.S. Capitol Building in Washington, although the two buildings had nothing else in common. The palace looked like a step pyramid of stone built around a shiny pearlescent tower of metal.

At the bottom of the stairs, the Squad Leader thanked her troops and ordered them back to their barracks. I thanked them, too, God knows why. *Noblesse oblige?* But we'd hiked a long way together and the Myrmidons had kept me safe, God knows from what. Manners don't cost anything, my father always told me. So we all smiled shyly and waved goodbye and they went on their way. The Squad Leader and I climbed the long stairway to the entrance of the palace.

At the top of the stairway, two Myrmidons stood guard on either side of the palace door.

The Squad Leader exchanged nods with the sentries. I'd never seen Myrmidons salute or engage in any elaborate military courtesies. On the other hand, I'd also never seen them question an order. She indicated me with a forceful gesture. "This is Jerome August, whom the god, blessed be he, has summoned."

The sentries nodded again as if we were expected. One of them opened the palace door while the other kept an eye on me.

I took a look around me from the top of the stairway. At the end of one long, straight boulevard, I saw what had to be an aqueduct. It was massive and tall, but still only entered the city halfway up the high city wall. I saw another building, nearly as tall as the palace, but windowless; the aqueduct led into that structure, but no further. A water tower?

I turned back as someone came out the now opened door. Someone I recognized, who now wore the uniform and armor of a Myrmidon.

I couldn't help grinning. "Hello, Myra," I said.

362

Hear the Spectral Singing of the Moon

Myra didn't smile. "You know, of course, that my name is not *Myra* or anything that even sounds like that?" she said. "Your uncle *gives* people names when he can't remember their real ones. Since I am captain of the palace guard, you should address me as *Captain*."

Message received. I was on *her* turf now. "I'm always happy to learn new things, Captain," I said. "Did you learn a lot during your time in ... *my* land?" I tried to say *Earth*, but the language of dreams only rendered that word as *dirt/soil/land*. Fair enough.

"I went where I was ordered to go and did as I was told," Myra said. She sounded sulky and defensive. Even with what I'd learned about the Myrmidons, I couldn't help thinking of her as Myra. I also couldn't help thinking of her as *her*, even though I understood that Myrmidons were born with both a penis and a vagina. That limitation in my thinking was abetted by the fact that neither English nor the language of dreams had an intersex pronoun. I wondered if she'd learned anything on Earth that helped her make sense of her part of the human predicament.

"You were ordered to bring me here?" I said.

"You were *summoned*, but would not obey," she said. "I just gave you a little *encouragement*." She grinned and mimed a hip check. Subtle.

"Well, thanks for that," I said. "I've met some lovely people since I

179

came to your land. I've seen things I never expected to see, things I had no idea even existed." I spoke mildly and factually. *Hiroshima mon amour*, I thought, remembering all the god-smitten ruins I'd walked through. "By the way, have you seen my very good friend Leda Clayton?"

Myra shrugged. "She is here. You will see her in due course. In the meantime, perhaps you'd like a bath and some clean clothes." Not a question, but an order: You people *will* get clean and you *will* like it. I thought of Gunnery Sergeant Hartman in *Full Metal Jacket*. Myra could have eaten the actor R. Lee Ermey for lunch and still had room for tiramisu.

"You're very kind," I said. "That sounds wonderful..." I paused. "...*Captain*," I finally added. Being a gentleman doesn't mean I can't be a passive-aggressive dick.

Myra hustled the Squad Leader and me into the palace and turned us over to the household staff, young women all dressed in white. The Squad Leader remained respectfully silent while Myra and I were talking, although she followed our conversation with great interest. "Make yourself worthy for the god, blessed be he, to look upon, Squad Leader," Myra said. "And keep an eye on Jerome August. See that no harm comes to him—or *from* him."

The Squad Leader bowed her head in obedience. Myra left us with the servants, stalking off toward the center of the palace. I bet there was a stairway in the central tower. The god could fly, but his servitors still had to walk.

The servant girls led me to the guest quarters, provided me with drinking water and bittersweet fruit. One girl shyly pointed out the sanitary facilities, a stone Roman-style toilet, flushed by flowing water beneath. It wasn't great by Earth standards, but it was better than digging holes in the desert or in some farmer's field like I'd been doing for weeks. The bath turned out to be a shower, really a head-high spigot in the wall with a narrow opening that sprayed warmish water all over me when I turned a lever. An amorphous lump in one shower wall niche turned out to be mildly-scented soap. The palace was an odd mixture of high-tech and low-tech. But on the other hand: flying god.

It was good to be clean, that was for sure. It took me a while and a bit of scrubbing before I got all the dirt and sand off. My hair was longer than I liked it, but I was more concerned about all the beard I could feel on my face. It didn't itch like it had while it was first growing out back in the desert, but I really wanted a shave.

Imagine my surprise when one of the servant girls handed me a towel and offered to brush my teeth and shave me. I didn't see any mirrors, so I said Yes. I sat on a stool while the girl in the short white dress carefully and gently cleaned my teeth with an odd-looking little brush on a stick. She did this more thoroughly than I'd been able to do on the road. Then she carefully and gently shaved off my beard with a razor-edged knife. Gulp. She did a great job. At least I didn't feel any blood trickling down my cheeks. She applied some scented balm to my skin. It all felt very nice, although I don't much like being waited on hand and foot.

Once those things were done, the servant girl stuck around, looking shy and embarrassed.

"Yes?" I said quietly.

She couldn't meet my eyes; this was hard for her. "Would Sir like his man-hair shaved?"

"Oh! No, thank you. That's not the custom in my land," I said. I suppose that wasn't entirely true, but it was true enough of me. And whose pubes were they, anyway?

Even as dark as her skin was, I could tell the servant girl was blushing. She still couldn't meet my eyes. How old was she, anyway? Seventeen? Eighteen? "Does Sir wish to take comfort with me?" she said. Her last words were almost inaudible.

That was just about the saddest thing I'd ever heard. I thought of condemned men being offered hearty meals. But it wasn't my possibly-condemned self I was sad for.

I spoke gently. "Dear girl, you're very beautiful and I've been without comfort for a long time. But I'm spoken for. The Captain tells me that my bride-to-be is here in the palace."

The kid looked profoundly relieved. "If there's nothing else, then?" she said. I said there wasn't, but hadn't the Captain said something about some clean clothes? The girl, still blushing furiously, pointed to a neat white pile of clothing on a woven sleeping mat in the corner of my little guest room. Then she skedaddled before I could change my mind and order her to lie down with me.

I'd just dropped the damp towel on the stone floor and was sorting through the clean clothes trying to figure out how to go about putting them on when the Squad Leader walked into my room fresh from the shower. Naked.

Myrmidons, it seemed, were not at all body shy. Clothed and armored or stripped bare, they were as their gods had made them. Were in fact in a special relationship with them. *Married* to them in some way, the trooper had told me during our long hike out of the desert.

"Getting along all right, Jerry?" said the Squad Leader, looking me up and down with frank curiosity.

"Yes, thanks," I said, maintaining eye contact with great resolve. "Except that this clothing baffles me."

She laughed. "Believe me, I understand. Myrmidons wear battle trousers everywhere but the palace. Here, let me show you..." What I ended up wearing was a kind of calf-length robe secured by a belt tied around my waist. There was nothing intuitively obvious about it. I wasn't even sure I could replicate what the Squad Leader had done to help me put the damn thing on. Apparently people ran around the palace of the gods without undergarments. At least the Shining City had a warm climate. I managed to put the new sandals on unaided.

The Squad Leader, still naked, looked at me sadly, but with approval. "You are worthy for the god to look upon, blessed be he," she said. "Are you ready to be changed?"

Be changed sounded a lot like *die* to me. "Who ever is?" I said. Was this to be my last day in the Other World, so far from Earth? I hadn't considered the possibility. *Not today*, said my intuition. Or was that my own wishful thinking?

"I heard you send the pretty little servant away," she said. "Was the girl not to your taste?"

"It seems ill-bred to take comfort with a stranger when Leda, my bride-to-be, is here in the palace. Speaking as a man of my own land, that is."

The Squad Leader looked even sadder. "You understand that she whom you were to wed is now the god's, do you not? You and she will not be allowed to take comfort with each other, not in the usual way of a man with a maid. Would you like me to call the servant girl back for you?"

"Really, that won't be necessary," I said. At the moment, sex was the last thing on my mind.

The Squad Leader looked at me with new interest. "I find loyalty *very* appealing," she said. My peripheral vision told me that she was not exaggerating. "Do you find me even a little attractive?" She stood with her legs apart and held her arms out to the side. Uh-oh.

I finally gave up and looked her up and down to satisfy my curiosity. Yup, muscular torso with small, firm breasts, now-erect phallus instead of clitoris at the top of moist, hairless vulva with prominent labia. Full lips, dark eyes with long eyelashes and dramatic eyebrows, short, thick hair still wet from the bath. She was very beautiful, abstractly considered, setting aside all my usual expectations for naked human bodies. Something for everyone. Everyone but me. I grinned at her. "Besides being more of a woman than me, Squad Leader, I see you're also more of a man."

That made her laugh. "Ah, Jerry, you'd be more than enough man for me. But as you say, love's not about the parts, is it?" She punched me gently in the shoulder and went off to dress, the muscles in her back rippling as she padded away.

Jesus, finally.

37

The Lost Bride and Groom

A thick sleeping mat on the stone floor seemed sinfully luxurious to me. Not to mention the feeling of being clean and shaved again. I hadn't been dozing long when Myra and the Squad Leader came in and woke me up. Oh, well. The three of us made our way through high-ceilinged corridors to the stairway of the palace's central tower. Outside the stairwell, the palace was built of massive blocks of stone and thick timbers. I hadn't seen any forests in my travels, but that didn't mean there weren't any—or that there had never been any in the past.

The spiral staircase felt and looked like metal, as did the tower. From the plaza outside the palace, the central tower seemed to be all of a piece. Inside the tower I saw that the structure was built in sections, like pipes with flanges on the inside. The thick flanges were held together with big honkin' bolts that screwed into insert nuts at the bottom. A screw, I recalled from high school, is just an inclined plane wrapped around an axis: technology known since the ancient world on Earth. Thus endeth the physics lesson.

"Who built this tower?" I asked Myra. We were climbing the narrow stairs of the spiral staircase in single file. There were doors out of the stairwell that led to the upper floors of the palace, then there was a long interval of tower with no doors at all.

She stopped to catch her breath and looked back at me. "The men of old had arts of metalsmithing which are now lost to us," she said.

"I'm surprised the gods let that happen," I said mildly.

"The world changes around us always," Myra said. "Only the gods, blessed be they, do not change."

"Well, except that to remain changeless, the gods seem to *require* something from the rest of you." *And something from Leda and me*, I thought.

Myra didn't respond to that and resumed climbing.

Each step up made me feel stranger than the last. It wasn't just the effort of the climb. Something familiar was happening. My thoughts floated and drifted. I made the effort to center myself and watch the disconnection of my ordinary mind. I would simply have passed out if Daniel and Aimee hadn't team-taught me Mind and Body 101.

The Other World is not a dream, I thought, *but it's* like *a dream. You're in it and it's in you. There's no way to figure it out, you just have to find your way through.* The closer we climbed to the top of the tower, the further away my ordinary mind drifted, but the clearer I heard the voice of my own intuition, a voice that had been amplified by the touch of other, wiser minds back on Earth. The shining minds of my friends.

I'd lost all sense of duration by the time we reached the top of the tower. My body continued to work while I (whoever *I* was) observed the incomprehensible world (that I was part of) from a cloud of silent unknowing. In me, the unfathomable world attained consciousness and found itself of only passing interest. My vision had narrowed to a shaft of brightness which revealed only what was directly in front of my face.

The two Myrmidons exchanged a look. "He's still conscious," Myra said. "Those who are summoned *always* collapse from proximity to the gods."

The Squad Leader gave me a sad, affectionate glance. "Jerome August is an unusual man. A good man with a warrior's heart."

Myra grunted. "Whatever he is, the gods, blessed be they, have summoned him. Let's do our duty, then."

Each soldier took one of my arms. I didn't resist as they led me through a doorway out of the stairwell. I found myself upon on one of the walled parapets from which the goddess had summoned—and almost drowned me. On the opposite side of the battlement, two biers or altars sat side by side, covered with rich tapestries. One was empty, but on the second lay the woman I'd come so far to find.

Leda.

Mysteriously dulled though my thoughts and emotions had become in this place, my heart still sped up a bit and my breathing quickened when I saw her. Neither of my escorts would have noticed.

I could hardly move of my own volition. I could hardly see. What could I *do* that would save us both? Leda's eyes were closed, her breathing was regular but very slow. As Daniel had seen, Leda was a long way from the waking world. And I wasn't quite myself today, was I? I didn't think I could fight my way out of here.

You have to find your way through. That intuition again.

When you can't move easily and can't think straight, what remains? Within my own echoing center, from the mind-space where I'd encountered Aimee and Daniel, I reached deeper into my mind, groping inward toward Leda's.

Leda?

A sense of swirling silence and rising half-thoughts, until I heard: *Jerry? What ... how...?*

Keep your eyes closed and breathe slowly, babe. There's a way out of this. We just have to find it.

A sense of peace from Leda, a smiling mental embrace. *Never leave me, again, okay?*

There might have been tears on my cheeks. In my benumbed condition, it was hard to tell. *We're in this together, kid,* I thought back.

With my slowed, intoxicated responses and spotty, unreliable tunnel vision, I'd missed the fact that there were other people here on the parapet besides me and my escorts. I moved my head, gazing vaguely around and saw the rest of the Squad Leader's Myrmidons, now dressed in white for honor guard duty in the palace of their gods. I saw a handful of servant girls and boys.

And in a richly-cushioned chair sat my Uncle Quincy dressed in white as an Other World noble. I was not at all shocked to see him. In fairness, I was pretty much beyond shock by then. Seated next to Quincy in her own chair was my Aunt Pepsi. Apparently she was an aristocrat in this world as well. I may have goggled at the two of them, so far from New Hampshire.

Quincy's face held nothing but contempt. "Hello, *Jewboy*," he said. "How do you like the Other World?" He wasn't expecting an answer.

"Quincy, don't be *vulgar!*" Pepsi said. She didn't expect a response, either.

38

Fancy Meeting You Here

Sacrifice is bullshit. Elf or Earthling, we do what we signed up for, as best we can. And then we live with the consequences.

- (Jean-Paul Herold)

It dawned on me—slowly—that I'd heard Quincy and Pepsi speak (and understood them) in *English*. Leda and I had also shared thoughts in our native language. Directly, without any language-of-dreams filtering, as far as I could tell. I mean, given that I was in a kind of fugue state, separated as if by gauze curtains from the Jerry August of yore. One present moment succeeded another. I was fully present in each one, but all thought of moments past and future was on the other side of the gauze curtains.

"Curtains" is a way of describing what lay just outside my narrow-focused perception. It wasn't just a metaphor. Waves or curtains of light also emanated from, surrounded, and flowed into Quincy and Pepsi. Inside those light curtains my aunt and uncle looked, not young, but *ageless*. They observed me, Leda, and the world around them with stoic

189

detachment. The servants simply awaited orders, resigned to whatever might happen. The Myrmidons looked nervous and alert.

Something was coming. I could feel it. We could all feel it, this sense of imminent arrival. The curtains of light around Quincy and Pepsi brightened and swirled faster. Again I heard the sound of rivers that met each other and the roaring violence in which they rushed to the sea, and the sea to them. But *what* rivers and *what* sea? I knew I'd heard that sound before, but where? Not that it mattered. If you want power, you meet its conditions: Quincy and Pepsi had done exactly that. They turned their faces up to the sky. I could hardly see my aunt and uncle now inside thick bands of aurora-colored light.

Power itself was coming, was almost here. Was also *immanent* because here in the Other World it was always present.

I looked up, too, thoughtless and wordless as a bull led to the altar of Mithras to shed his blood. The only thought in my head was a fully-formed intuition:

> *You want power? Pay its price:*
> *Old Gods require sacrifice.*

Swell, my own intuition was making fun of me. Not that I was able to take umbrage. The rhyme fastened itself to my mind and refused to float away, while every useful thought passed through and evaporated.

Descending an invisible stairway in the air above us strode two human-shaped figures vast as thunderheads. Crystallizing from the essence of earth and sky, they approached the parapet below them at an unhurried pace. Was it not *their* world? Did they not have all the *time* in that world? Their bodies condensed as they came down, still larger than human. Or perhaps their size was only the effect on my sensorium of the overwhelming energy crackling around and through them.

Energy that seemed also to come from and to enwrap Quincy and Pepsi.

The god who was both man and bird spread out his arms and his mighty wings. Wings that grew from his broad and sinewy back extended past his fingertips like the sails of a ship. The wings were attached to the backs of his arms and forearms. In the shelter of the god's broad left wing the goddess extended both her arms as if to embrace all of us who awaited her advent here atop the tower of her palace. She smiled her Archaic smile: *all is understood, all is blessed.* The god smiled from the depths of his eternal strength and power: *let all things be as I will.* Both god and goddess wore garments of shining white which left their strong arms free.

With her eyes shut and her mind touching mine, Leda saw what I saw through my eyes. I felt her wonder at this vision along with my own.

Jerry, came Leda's thought, *whoever they are, I'm pretty sure they just want to fuck with us. And not in a good way.*

The touch of her mind and the sting of her wit brought me closer to myself. *Leda* was why I'd come here. She was who I'd come here *for.* Whatever mystical attraction the Other World and its gods might have had for me, it was Leda I loved. I told her that mind-to-mind. *There's something very wrong in this world—and Quincy and Pepsi are right in the middle of it,* I thought. I sent her thought pictures of the Other-World ruins where catastrophe after catastrophe had echoed to Earth, generating unnatural disasters in both worlds. One Apocalypse, many Horsemen, no waiting. End of the age, indeed.

This whole ceremony was choreographed, as if the servants and the Myrmidons had assisted with it before. At a signal I didn't see (the god and goddess continued to descend to us), servant girls removed Leda's robe leaving her naked atop the altar. I felt her sudden surge of fear as I felt my own, felt her grow calmer as I reassured her by calming myself. The Squad Leader gently removed the robe she'd helped me put on. "I'm so sorry," she whispered, and I saw how deeply she meant it. The world and she herself were as the gods had made them. What choice did she have but to obey? Myra and the Squad Leader led me to the altar next to Leda's and laid me down upon it. Still dazed, I didn't resist.

Also, intuition urged me to go along with the program for now. That same sense of *direction* had been with me since Myra first pushed me into the Other World.

We'll be okay, I thought to Leda.

I dunno, Jerry, Leda thought back. *I'd rather we slept with Beth and Janjan than any of these people.*

I saw her point. When I wasn't looking, Quincy had positioned himself next to Leda. I found that Pepsi was now standing next to me. I didn't like the way they were looking at us.

Quincy stared at Leda *hungrily.* She was so beautiful. But he had no right to her; she was her own woman. She had given herself freely only to me, and I to her.

And I didn't like the hungry way my aunt looked me up and down. I was her *grandnephew,* for God's sake. Whatever station in life Pepsi had been born to, it was clear she was no lady.

39

The Protocols of the Elders of Zion

I struggled to speak, fought my way through the curtains of confusion surrounding me. As I got the first few words out, the gods paused above us in their descent. I didn't have time to think about supernatural beings. I had things to discuss with Uncle Q.

"So ... who ... *was* ... your *lost love*, Quincy? Or were you just lying to me about your dream?"

Quincy blinked at me across Leda's naked body, surprised that I'd spoken. I was surprised myself. He looked up at the hovering gods, then smiled at Pepsi. It was almost the saddest smile I'd ever seen. "If you live long enough, you turn into someone else—and so does whoever you love. I dreamed of Pepsi as she was when we were young and still wanted each other. *She's* my lost love, and I suppose I'm hers." Pepsi was gazing raptly at my modest unit like she had big plans for it. She didn't see Quincy's smile or register his words.

I looked up at the god who was also a bird. The god looked down at me with great interest. His image would not stay still in my mind's eye. (A confluence as of mighty rivers of light.) My physical eyes did their best to reflect what was above me, but this creature who hovered in the air was beyond their grasp.

"Why did you want me to come to this world?" I asked. I thought I knew, but I needed to hear him say it. "I mean, why *me?*"

Quincy used his right hand to tick off reasons on the fingers of his left. If there's a definitive old-guy rhetorical gesture, that has to be it. "Divorced. No children. Highly portable profession. So I brought you to Portsmouth." He paused, considering how forthcoming to be, and finally shrugged and ticked the final finger. "And you're a Jew. The perfect sacrifice. So I brought you here."

Pepsi concluded her visual inventory of my midsection. "I don't know, Quincy," she said. "He appears to be *deliciously* uncircumcised." She and the goddess in the air shared a lubricious smile.

"My mother wasn't at all religious," I said, by way of explanation, although none had been requested and none was deserved. "But *'sacrifice'*?"

Quincy shrugged again. "Abraham and Isaac. It's all in the *Hebrew* part of the Bible." He spoke the word *Hebrew* with contempt. Payback for my Thanksgiving blessing.

The god-intoxication began letting go of my body as my mind got up to normal speed, but I still needed to play for time. Would the gods complete their descent if I stopped talking? And then what? "Okay, fine, that sort of explains why you wanted me, Quincy," I said. "But why bring *Leda* here? She was raised Episcopalian."

"It became clear you wouldn't come here of your own accord," Quincy said. "But just take his little *shiksa* away from the Jew and observe how the universe aligns itself around those who meet the conditions of its power!" He held up one bare, meaty arm up to the shining being whose power he sought. He held his other hand out horizontally over Leda's loins. (Her eyes moved beneath the lids.) "*Archetypes*, Jewboy! Read your Jung. Read Yeats. Has it escaped your attention that our god is also a *swan*? It seemed perfectly fitting to bring him his *Leda*."

That sounded like confirmation of Leda's intuition that some sort of rape was on the agenda. "So what's the plan now that you've got us here?" Inside myself I watched all the human energy centers light up like traffic signals, blink blink blink, as I centered myself in the breath.

Quincy now held up both arms to both gods in the *Orans* gesture I'd made at Thanksgiving dinner. Unlike me, he wasn't being ironic. "The god and goddess who have kept Pepsi and me alive in perfect health for so many years, and who have showered us with the blessings of wealth, now ask that the debt to them be paid—either with the sacrifice of our lives or with the lives of others."

"You know what happens if you do this, right?" I said. "People die in this world and on Earth. Thousands of people. *Millions* of people, Quincy." I found myself speaking not just to Quincy who stood on the other side of Leda, but also to the winged god above me. On the face of the god, if I am any judge of human expressions, was a look of *approval.* This approval was mirrored in the face of the smiling goddess like a blessing as she gazed upon Leda from the middle of the air. As if she felt that gaze upon her, Leda opened her eyes.

Oh, Jerry... she thought as she, I, the god, and the goddess beheld one another for the first time. It was a thought full of meaning that went far beyond the words.

I know, Leda, I thought back. To look into the faces of the god and goddess awakened some unsuspected knowledge in us. It wasn't power coming into us from outside. My love and I shared in some wisdom or direction that came from deep within. From the mind-space where my mind had met with the minds Aimee and Daniel Ryun. Where their minds had touched mine. It felt very much like walking into a room in your own house you'd somehow never seen before.

Speaking of archetypes. The one Leda and I had been press-ganged into got back under way as the god and goddess resumed their descent, obviously intending to walk among us. Or into us.

The god-induced anesthesia had worn off. I was fully awake and alert and able to be scared again. "So what happens when Leda and I die here, Quincy?"

But it wasn't Quincy who answered me.

"Quincy and I get your *lives*, stupid boy," said Aunt Pepsi. "We get your beautiful young *bodies*. You get our ugly old ones—just for an instant, until the god and goddess *assimilate* you. So you'll suffer none of the indignities of old age as we've had to do."

I must have looked as baffled by that as I felt.

"Your aunt and I *go on* in your bodies, Jerry," Quincy said. "You and Leda are *called up*. You become *one flesh* with the gods."

"*Numinous?*" I said, remembering what he'd said to me on Thanksgiving. "*Wholly other?*"

"Sure, Hymie," said Quincy. "It's all in *The Idea of the Holy*. Or was it *Moses and Monotheism*?"

Terrified Vague Fingers

Words I know
Are vain unless they mean, Imagine Beast-
Wings, the power to choose what that love yields.

- (Robert G. Tucker, "Imagine Beast-Wings")

Even if I'd been inclined to think about mythology, psychology, and comparative religion (I wasn't), there was no time. The god hovered right above Leda where she lay naked upon his altar. He smiled, well pleased with her, as what male creature would not be.

I saw the goddess in the air right above her altar and above me. Her Archaic smile was entirely for me and for no one else. It was me she wanted. The smile said that to give her what she most desired would be bliss for me.

In his best parade ground voice, Quincy barked an order to Myra and her Myrmidons: "*Hold them*, you people!" I heard him in English, but the Myrmidons who rushed to obey must have heard his words in the language of dreams. Interesting. What Other-World power had Quincy arrogated to himself that the gods' own servants did what he told them?

Myra and three others held Leda. Myra's face was set and grim. The Squad Leader and another three soldiers held me. The Squad Leader's face was sorrowful. She held my arm down with one strong hand and patted my shoulder with the other, either to comfort me or to comfort herself.

Neither Leda nor I resisted. Our minds were still joined. It was a great comfort to say and hear *I love you* and know it for the truth. All the energy centers in Leda's subtle body blazed with light in harmony with all the settlements of light in mine. I guided her, as Aimee had guided me, through the stations of the breath. This time it was quite different.

Will you have me? *I will.* Do you take me? *I do.*

Married in mind in full freedom of the will, our separated bodies entered the synagogue of desire. I felt her arousal as my own and she felt mine. *Jerry, how...?* she thought as her thoughts journeyed on to the sea of love where the thoughts of lovers sport and swim in the warm waves. I thought back, *We can't fight our way out of this world. If there's a way out, it's here inside us...* Then my thoughts followed hers and the invisible flames of our energy twined, deeply rooted in the belly as the body is rooted in the world.

Close above us now, the god and goddess shared a long glance. Being what they were (more than human?), they saw past the solid flesh of our separate bodies into the original mind energy in which Leda and I were joined. That more-than-personal power was perhaps the kingdom which adjoined their own. *I saw them see us as we truly were.* There's little comfort in being understood by the incomprehensible.

That's what the shining beings saw. But all Quincy and Pepsi saw—and lusted after—were Leda's body and mine.

"*Help us up*, you people!" Quincy bellowed. A rugby scrum commenced between the Myrmidons holding me down and the servants helping Pepsi climb atop the altar—and atop me. Next to the adjoining altar a dance-fight broke out between the Myrmidons holding Leda still and the servants trying to help Quincy off with his robe and up onto Leda.

I really really *really* did not want my octogenarian aunt to rape me. My eyes were mostly closed, not that it mattered. Like Leda's, my spirit saw everything that was happening around me—and what was about to happen to both of us. I really really *really* did not want my octogenarian uncle to rape the woman I loved.

Our bodies followed our minds, though, like the faithful servants they were. With each breath, Leda and I walked together through the gauze curtain of another inner orgasm, and our physical arousal was there for anyone to see.

Quincy and Pepsi thought our obvious desire was all for them, perhaps induced by the god and goddess. Thought *Leda and I* were all for them. Were they not *entitled* to live forever and take whatever they wanted from anyone who struck their fancy? What else are gods *for*, but to keep the world from changing for those few mortals who *deserve* all the world's fruits?

Deep in love, deep in desire with Leda and with no one else, I sensed every little pulse and every bright flash of energy in ourselves and in the world around us. The Other World which was in some measure one with us and we with it. My eyes flickered open. (I felt Leda's eyes open, too, although I couldn't see her face.)

Above me on the altar was Pepsi. She not yet taken me inside her. Her face looked decades younger in the light of the goddess who surrounded her. I saw the beautiful young woman she had been when young Quincy first loved and married her. There is no better way to say this:

She *became* the goddess. Or: the goddess entered into my aunt and *became her*.

I felt Leda's shock as she saw the same thing happening to Quincy above her as he became one with the god.

Hold to me, beloved, I thought, and Leda held to me. We breathed together. Another orgasm came effortlessly to us and through us, a vast, slow wave from the sea of love.

Above her now Leda saw only a winged naked godlike being whose face held traces of Quincy's. My uncle's body was taken up, transformed, and transfigured. The god's neck somehow lengthened itself. Atop that too-long swanlike neck, his head swayed. His full lips pursed like a beak.

Above me now I saw only a naked goddess whose face held traces of Pepsi's. My aunt's body had been subsumed by a higher power.

The gods had become flesh. Now they hungered for the things of the flesh: adoration of their persons, children of the body, and for bodies of their worshipers to be burned to feed the sacred fire.

41

The Feathered Glory

For the living know that they shall die: but the dead know not any thing, neither have they any more a reward; for the memory of them is forgotten. Also their love, and their hatred, and their envy, is now perished; neither have they any more a portion for ever in any thing that is done under the sun.

- (Ecclesiastes)

High above the tower in the cloudless blue-green sky of Other-World day, all the stars and planets spun and leaped as if in celebration. Our human bodies, I'm told, are made of atoms that once lived in the hearts of stars. So therefore we are the universe we see around us and it is us. Long ago on Earth Quincy had said to me: *We see the Other World and those who live there, not as they are, but as we are.* He didn't tell me that those who see us do so not as *we* are, but as *they* are. And so the merry dance of beings great and small, and of minds and bodies heavenly and human, continues for all eternity, as one part is caught up into another again and yet again. No one ever asks Why.

As the god and goddess of the Other World saw it, what Quincy and Pepsi were about to do to Leda and me under divine auspices was as natural and inevitable as the nitrogen cycle. Of course at the end of this, the Old Gods would still be there and Leda and I would not. Omelets require eggs. The fruit of this sacred marriage between Leda and the swan-god would be a supernal child. A twenty-first century Helen, perhaps, to spark a Trojan War for a new age. Not with swords and spears this time, but with modern weapons.

And I wondered: Had the gods of the Other World become displeased with the Earth, like the mythical gods of Olympus? Did they even know about the heroes who'd saved our world three times since the 1980s? Had the elves, without intending to, somehow frustrated the Old Gods' designs by winning the Portsmouth wars? Or were the elves simply irrelevant to these Other World immortals—along with Earth and its people?

Except for the elves, all creatures struggle to survive and to reproduce. The gods embodied the template of that drive; thus it had always been, thus it should always be. To survive in the body, the Old Gods needed worship in the form of periodic sacrifices. The society that had grown up around them, nobles, commoners, Myrmidons, served the god and goddess perfectly. Why should Quincy and Pepsi *not* be preserved in new human bodies to spread the worship—the devotion and the burnt offerings—from the Other World to Earth?

So with one penetrating impersonal glance, the god and goddess gazed into Leda and into me. And we gazed into them; their desires and designs had never been a secret. We saw that as a practical matter, the genetic material would pass from me, though the goddess, to the god. Then inevitably altered by this divine passage, my sperm would fertilize Leda's ovum. The egg, thus fertilized, would be drawn up and changed again by the god and returned to the goddess to mature in her divine womb as they coupled in the heavens.

Once the Divine Child was born a timeless instant later, Quincy and Pepsi, now distilled out of the sky god and the earth goddess, reborn in the young bodies they had stolen from Leda and me, would return to

Earth to raise the demigoddess as their daughter.

Then in the gods' good time, there would again be war and sacrifice. The worship of the Old Gods—and ultimately the gods themselves—would return to Earth. The few human beings who were rich and powerful would reshape the rule of every land and would bend the poor powerless masses to their will. That Earth had long ago embarked upon a better way, however imperfectly, meant nothing to the god and goddess—or to Quincy and Pepsi, caught up as they were in the immanence of divine being. Where their desires matched those of the gods, my aunt and uncle partook of the gods' nature. But the gods also took on the ... *coloration* of Quincy and Pepsi.

All this Leda and I saw in the god and goddess who had raised up and incorporated my aunt and uncle. It was incomprehensible. It was undeniable. We simply had to accept this impossible knowledge as we accepted the Other World we found ourselves in.

But we were in the midst of a sacred marriage, weren't we? The *hieros gamos* fertility ritual you may have seen symbolically and solemnly enacted in the movie *Eyes Wide Shut.* The reality was far more mysterious and frightening for Leda and me, its intended victims.

Well, until reality and anatomy turned the whole production into a metaphysical Three Stooges movie. Nyuck nyuck nyuck.

The goddess lowered her wet and desire-swollen pudenda upon mine, or tried to. The hot and long-sought connection became a game of Just the Tip, something I had always believed to be only an urban legend. What *she* had would not accommodate what *I* had. I had no idea why.

Deep in my mind and Leda's, inside our real connection, waves of inner orgasm broke and broke on the shore of the sea of love. What was being inflicted on our bodies, while horrible, seemed mercifully irrelevant.

What the goddess wanted of me she could not take; I would not give it to her. Frustrated, she began to hurt herself upon me. In the process, she hurt me. Male anatomy has a way of shutting down pain in that area.

The god, hovering between Leda's parted thighs, spread his wings. I saw through Leda's eyes that what he proposed to introduce into her was no mere human phallus, but something more like a giant, hideous corkscrew duck penis. Nobody ever talks about what the mythical Swan who was actually the mythical god Zeus brought to his picnic with the mythical woman Leda. It was scary. It was disgusting.

It was fucking hilarious. Naturally I thought it was funnier than Leda did.

The bird god and the bird goddess had something like bird genitalia.

But human anatomy ain't perfect either. The goddess managed to siphon up a few drops of my involuntary pre-ejaculate into her inner spiral. That wasn't anything like all she wanted, but it seemed to be all she needed. The ectoplasm thus extracted she passed to the swan god with a touch of her shining hand.

Then things got even weirder. On its way to the ovary, the god's horrible swan member managed to penetrate poor Leda all the way up her cervix and into her uterus...

...where Leda's copper IUD penetrated the rapist god's nasty, spiral bird penis and wounded it. From the divine being's mouth came the unmistakable voice of Quincy August.

"Ow, fuck!" screamed my uncle in American English. "Ow! Fuck! Owfuck, *OWFUCK!*"

Insulted and injured, the offending organ snapped back like a tape measure into the body of the naked god. No human egg, no divine child. Score: fifteen/love.

"Look what you've done, you damned dirty *whore!*" Quincy screamed at Leda out of the god's face. Human or god, he was no gentleman. Being a lady, Leda didn't laugh at him.

I was tempted to make a *misconception* joke, but it seemed wiser for us simply to make our way to the exit.

42

Conway Twitty Sings "Walk Me to the Door"

Step by dignified, unhurried step, the swan god and the goddess his mate retreated up into the dancing blue sky, taking my aunt and uncle with them. They grew larger and more diffuse as they climbed their invisible stairway. They ascended gracefully backwards, perhaps to keep a wary eye on us mortals. The divine countenances were full of Quincy's and Pepsi's sorrow.

We've disappointed them, I thought to Leda. We shared an inner smile.

And not in a good way, she thought back. *Well, it wasn't good for them, was it? Um ... what now?*

These Myrmidons holding us down? I'm gonna try to persuade them that the gods have somehow called up Jerry and Leda—and swapped Quincy and Pepsi into our bodies

What about the gods? Leda thought.

Well, maybe they're flying around up in the sky trying to cook a baby up out of a couple of my sperm cells. How the hell do I know? Point is, you and I are the only ones with a clue about what just happened—and what didn't happen. Just follow my lead, okay?

Okay, she thought with a lascivious inner grin. *And if you ever have to leave my side again, never leave my thoughts. I'm still shaking from all the inner sex we had—and the gods didn't.*

Yeah, me too, I thought.

The Myrmidons still stood around us on the two altars. Nobody had given them new orders. All their attention was focused on the dwindling figures of their gods above. They weren't holding us tightly because they hadn't had to.

Prompted either by intuition or by my own knowledge of people, I took a chance. I opened my eyes fully, looked the Squad Leader right in the eye, grinned and winked at her. She understood what I meant, grinned back at me and darted a glance over at Leda. I nodded: *We're still ourselves. The age hasn't ended.*

I held my body like Quincy did and used the inner energy to impersonate my uncle's command voice. "*Help us down from here*, you people!" I shouted in classic Quincy fashion. Suppressing her grin, the Squad Leader began helping me sit up. Her troopers obeyed without question and helped me sit up on the altar. "Don't just *stand* there *goggling*, Myra," I blustered, "help Pepsi up!"

Myra did as I'd told her. She looked too shocked to question the order.

"*Thank* you DEE-yah," Leda said to Myra. I wasn't sure the gracious Aunt Pepsi New Hampshire accent would translate into the language of dreams, but I still wanted to laugh for joy.

"Get us some *clothes*, for the sake of the gods!" I shouted. "Have you no sense of *decency?*" When impersonating Quincy, it was almost impossible to lay it on too thick. Servants and Myrmidons rushed to drape us in clean robes. Had the two naked people before them not been touched by the gods? Were we not radiant with the divine afflatus?

"Myra, organize an escort and get Pepsi and me back to the Nexus," I ordered. "I have urgent business back in my own land."

Puzzled, Myra looked at me.

I leaned toward her confidentially, Quincy style. "Business on behalf of the god and goddess, blessed be their hidden names," I said in a low voice.

Myra's eyes got big and she bowed her head to me, a crisp soldier's bow like a salute.

After all that drama in the palace of the gods, the long trip to the Nexus was almost a walk in the park. Well, except that Leda and I had to be on our guard the whole time, awake and asleep. Instead of hiking, we rode like nobles in a horse-drawn cart, shaded from the sun, while our Myrmidon escorts hiked along beside us. Once we reached serious desert, we were again limited to travel during the cooler hours of the day.

Fortunately for our sanity, Leda and I were able to explore our mental connection. Leda had been carried unconscious to the Shining City and kept comatose almost until I showed up. All the sadness that seeped out of the Other World ruins and the catastrophic history that mirrored so many, many Earth disasters, known and unknown, had troubled Leda's twilight sleep in this world, but had not entered her conscious mind. Until now.

She wanted to weep, but could not. I wanted to hold her in my arms and console her, but could only do so in our shared thoughts. We were impersonating Quincy and Pepsi who were, shall we say, *restrained* in their public displays of affection.

She thought, *This is where it comes from?* She meant war, pestilence, famine, genocide, the whole horror show.

I thought, *A lot of it, I guess. This is where it starts. It ends up on Earth, then blows back here and destroys the source. Every time an Other-World age ends, people die on both worlds.*

She thought, *What can we do about that?*

I don't know, either, I thought, *but we have friends who understand this stuff, right?*

For now, that would have to be enough.

The trip was nerve-wracking for another reason. Myra was no fool. She couldn't help wondering how Leda and I could really still be her employers. The Squad Leader was no fool, either. She knew who we were, but kept her own counsel with a soldier's discipline.

The Myrmidons brought our horse cart to a halt at the bottom of a hill like so many others we'd descended. I looked back up the way we'd come. I vaguely remembered running, panicked and half-blind, up that hill, off the road, and into the forest of buried columns.

The Nexus connecting the Other World to Quincy's Earth office building was inside a ruined stone building, perhaps an ancient temple. Myrmidons assigned to the temple kept it clean and free of sand. Otherwise the place would soon look like every other ruin in the Other World. I suspected you had to do something pretty bad to be ordered to temple-sweeping duty out here in the desert.

How did I know we'd reached the Nexus? Just below the threshold of my physical hearing, the ears of my mind picked up the precursors of rushing currents like mighty rivers. And there was a light inside the building that was, not brighter than the pitiless Other-World sun, but shining on a different frequency. My rational mind found that silly. But on the other hand: *not Earth*.

During the endless days of the trip here, Leda and I outlined a plan of action. Who knew how well it would work in practice? Some things in life are like computer code. You try to do things right, one step at a time, and see what happens.

Of course in the IT world, nobody dies during beta testing, but still.

In the lengthening shadows, Leda and I climbed off the cart and shook out the kinks in our bodies. Leda patted the horse goodbye. We didn't know the horse's real name, either.

"Here's what I want you to do, Myra," I said in my best Quincy-style oblivious-rich-guy bellow. "The Squad Leader's coming back with us. Brief her on how to pass through this Nexus-thing of yours. It wouldn't hurt if you reminded Pepsi what to do—poor lady's had a dreadful shock here in your land. What with one thing and another."

The Squad Leader made the classic *Who Me?* Face. But orders were to be obeyed, coming as they did from the gods themselves through their human representatives and the Myrmidon chain of command.

Myra did *not* like that order. Was she not Captain of the Guard? "Perhaps Sir has forgotten the *language problem* in his land?"

I waved that away with the arrogance of the very rich. Other people's problems were by definition not serious to Quincy. "You'll teach her yourself," I said. "And of course, your clothes will fit her, will they not?" Myra had to agree that she and the Squad Leader were pretty close in size. "We'll need more sandals on the ground back in Portsmouth—who better than one of you Myrmidons? All right, then!" I plowed on, Teddy Roosevelt fashion. "Let the briefing begin! We've got business to do ... over there!"

Cowed by my apparent absolute and entitled certainty, Myra explained to Leda and the Squad Leader (and of course to me), "It's quite simple. We walk into the Nexus in single file. You close your eyes. When you feel the light and the heat and the wind, *breathe out.* The next breath you take, you'll be breathing the air of the other land. You may feel like stopping to look around, but do *NOT* stop moving. *Keep walking* and all will be well."

Was Myra quoting that song by Peter Gabriel or the one by The Killers? Anyway, those seemed like reasonable instructions. What I wanted to say was, *Important safety tip. Thanks, Egon*, but instead, "*Pepsi*," I bellowed to Leda, "you got all that?" She controlled the urge to grin at me and just nodded. "Squad Leader, any questions?" The Squad Leader looked understandably frightened, but bravely shook her head No.

"Right," I said, "let's go! You first, Myra, then we'll follow."

432

Much Wisdom, Much Grief, No Waiting

For in much wisdom is much grief: and he that increaseth knowledge increaseth sorrow.

- (*Ecclesiastes*)

So Myra would go back to Earth first, then the Squad Leader. Leda and I disagreed about who'd be next. She wanted *me* to go first to be sure she wouldn't be kidnapped again. I argued that *she* was more likely to be pulled back out of the Nexus into the Other World than to be kidnapped on Earth before I could get there. The Myrmidons traveling with us would protect both of us, each for her own reasons.

I see your point, she thought, *so you win this debate. But the next time we, um, take comfort together, I get to be on top.*

I pretended to hate the idea. *Fine, whatever*, I sulked. Behind our serious faces, we smiled.

The four of us walked cautiously into the ruined temple. Sand that the Myrmidons hadn't managed to sweep away crunched under my boots. (That morning I'd put my none-too-clean Earth clothes back on. Leda wore her Thanksgiving outfit and the demure shoes with the mysteriously-named kitten heels.) I couldn't see much of the floor or of the columns on the opposite side of the living-room-sized space because of the swirling ribbons of pale light that filled the temple. The sound of the energies that filled the Nexus filled our minds.

I shared another thought with Leda. The *feeling* of the Nexus was exactly like what I'd felt when the god and goddess approached their altars in the temple tower. The *look* of the swirling lights was like nothing so much as the swirling of the stars and planets in the spectacular night sky of the Other World. To look into a ceaseless confluence as of mighty rivers and hear the roar of an ocean of stars was in some measure the same as looking into my own unquiet mind in a quiet room.

Something I would never have noticed before Aimee and Daniel's minds smote upon mine as they taught me. Self not different from world. World not different from self.

Here in this temple we're seeing the flawless impersonal power of the gods of this world, I thought to Leda. *We saw their personal power back in the Shining City, and it's just as fallible as their human subjects.*

She thought back, *I'm scared shitless, and you wanna talk theology?*

Myra walked unhesitatingly into the vortex and disappeared. The Squad Leader looked at me beseechingly. I shouted, "You go ahead. We'll be right behind you!" She couldn't hear me over the thunder of the Nexus, but she understood my shooing gesture. The Squad Leader nodded to me, *I trust you,* squared her shoulders like the warrior she was, and followed Myra into the light and the heat.

I'm scared, too, my love, I thought to Leda. *But we can't stay here, can we? You go first. And just keep walking, okay? Much as I like being one with you, I don't want us to explode together—in the bad way, I mean.*

Total protonic reversal? That would be bad, she thought. She loved *Ghostbusters* as much as I did. *Okay, here I go.*

And off she went. What a gal.

I counted to ten, perhaps the longest ten seconds of my entire life. Then I walked into the Nexus and exhaled.

Just as Myra had said, I passed into the whirlpool unharmed, with a sense of being buffeted by winds or waters whose crosscurrents canceled each other out. As instructed, I just kept walking forward, putting one foot in front of the other again and again. When I inhaled, I found myself *pushed* out into the cold, low-lit hallway of the August Association's office building. It felt just like stepping off a carousel.

Nighttime in Portsmouth. *Cold*, even indoors.

It wasn't just the ambient temperature that was different here. I felt a difference inside myself. The intuitive guidance that had helped me find my way through the Other World was shocked once again by the familiar touch of another mind—a mind that wasn't Leda's.

I had no time to think about anything. I was so filled with adrenaline that I almost reacted to my arrival on Earth in my own style, not in Quincy's. I sent Leda a warning thought when I saw her heading toward me to hug me. Instead of a hug, she reached out and patted my shoulder the way Pepsi would have done. I smiled at her. Smart girl.

If Leda and I had any false notes in our performance, Myra was too preoccupied by the Squad Leader's panic to notice. The language of dreams simply didn't work on Earth, so nothing but nonsense came out of the poor Myrmidon's mouth. It must have been like what happens to a stroke victim. Her thoughts were cogent, but her language center was offline.

The Squad Leader was of course sworn to obey her Captain, but she'd come to trust me for whatever reasons one person trusts another. I stepped in and put one hand on her muscular shoulder. I pointed to myself. "Jerry August," I said. I pointed to the Squad Leader and said "Mary!" Then to Quincy's assistant, "Myra, remind me what last name you use on Earth?"

"*Breck*," said Myra. She suspected Quincy had played some sort of joke on her. She couldn't have known that he'd named her after the transwoman in Gore Vidal's dated, nasty satire *Myra Breckinridge*. Q seemed to despise everyone, even the people he relied on.

"Of course, of course," I said, playing absentminded old Quincy, too self-involved to bother to remember the servants' last names. "Well, you two look enough alike to be sisters. How about if you're Mary *Breck*?" I said to the Squad Leader. I pointed to her and looked a question at her.

"Mary?" said the Squad Leader.

"Yes!" I said. Then I pointed to myself.

"Jerry?" she said. She still pronounced it ZHAY-ray, but hey.

Myra looked confused and hostile. Uh-oh. "I thought your first name was *Quincy*, Mr. August," she said.

"Of *course* it is," I said, "but I don't look quite the same as I used to, do I? Just a tad *younger*, perhaps?"

"Thanks to the god and goddess, blessed be they," Myra said automatically.

"Well, then," I plowed ahead, "in this world where all devotion to the god and goddess has died out, no one will understand the miracle of our transformation."

"So for the immediate future, dear, Mr. August will have to *pretend* to be his nephew Jerry," Leda explained to Myra, like a gracious aristocrat spelling things out for the dull-witted help. "And I will have to *pretend* to be his nephew's fiancée Leda." She wrinkled her nose at the indignity.

"Just until the lawyers get all the *legalities* sorted out," I said, waving a hand at the utter triviality of such concerns. "In fact, Mrs. August and I will have to tread carefully in order not to be imprisoned."

Myra put a hand on the hilt of her fighting knife. "I would kill anyone who tried to arrest you."

Leda patted Myra on the shoulder to reassure her the way an adult pats a child. "I *know* you would, dear. No one could ask for a more loyal assistant than you."

"Pepsi's absolutely right. We're lucky to have you, Myra," I said.

44

Ylvis Sings "What Does the Fox Say?"

We walked down the Association's hallway. I saw that the doors to the new office space were ajar. I stepped in and flipped on the lights: still vacant. Nothing had changed since the day I left. In my absence—and Quincy's—no interior construction had been done. Nobody had moved in yet. Huh.

Someone had thoughtfully hung my leather jacket on a hook in the entryway.

"Jerry's jacket?" I said. Myra nodded Yes.

I put the jacket on. In one pocket I found my cell phone (dead battery). In another pocket were my car and house keys (no batteries required).

Myra kept several changes of work and gym clothes in her locked office closet. The two Myrmidons cleaned up and changed while we waited. Myra briskly marched the four of us past the security desk. The sleepy guard was about to ask who we all were, but Myra showed him her war face. *Nothing to see here, minion.*

As directed, Myra reluctantly drove herself and the Squad Leader— excuse me, *Mary*—back to Quincy's house in Quincy's Mercedes. I watched the tail lights leave the parking lot.

I unlocked my car and opened Leda's door for her. I'd almost expected to find the car gone, towed away as evidence, or bedecked with crime scene tape. But nobody had reported me missing, one of those good news/bad news things. After a scary bit of slow, unpromising cranking in the winter cold, the engine started up. Whew.

We batted thoughts back and forth as I drove north on Route 1.

Everything looks familiar, but it's like everything has changed.

Yeah, Earth feels cold to me, and it's not just the temperature. I turned the car's heat up high.

It's like we were part of the Other World. Earth is just a place where we happen to be. We can hardly see the stars—and they have nothing to do with us.

Car headlights dazzled my eyes until I remembered to look away from them. I felt deeply fatigued, frightened, and depressed. *I don't understand anything. Nothing feels right.*

At last we were back where we wanted to be. We were driving home together. We'd waded into a sea of troubles; the question was how to take arms against them. We'd acquired some wisdom in the Other World, but how could it help us here on Earth? Consider:

The authorities believed Leda was missing. Like her friends and family, they thought some harm had come to her. Unlike her friends and family, they suspected me of complicity in her kidnapping.

Did Jerry August and Leda Clayton still have jobs? We'd been gone for weeks.

Leda and I were masquerading as Quincy and Pepsi August. Initially, we only had to do this for Myra's benefit. But Quincy had surely left word that he and my aunt were going away for an indeterminate time and might return looking a little, well, different. Perhaps more like his scapegrace nephew and his nephew's girlfriend? The things plastic surgeons can do these days!

And who would Quincy have left word with? Secretary? Facilities manager? Lawyers?

Certainly the lawyers.

Other allies, operatives, and functionaries of the August Association?

And what instructions might Quincy have left? Passwords? Countersigns? Codes? Combinations?

How much did Myra know? How much could we find out from her without giving ourselves away?

My intuition, as strong as it was in the Other World, told me this mess wasn't anywhere near over. My mind kept running into walls. Stupid reality. If *reality* was the right word for the rabbit hole we were trying to climb out of.

Oh, and: there were real, live people back in the Other World for whom Leda and I now felt some responsibility. If we could find a way to help their world, we could end the cycle of mutually-assured catastrophes with Earth.

It looked like the god and goddess had absorbed Quincy and Pepsi, but what if it was the other way around? If the gods did not exist, would it be necessary to invent—and modify—them? I didn't like thinking about what would happen if my aunt and uncle acquired godlike powers.

At least tonight Leda and I could go back to my house and be alone. At least we could figure out what to do tomorrow and all the tomorrows to come. At least we knew who to ask for help. One day at a time, and all that.

"All of a sudden I really want a drink," I said.

"Me, too," Leda said. "And I want *you.*"

Back at my little house, instead of having a drink or even a shower, we fell upon each other like funky famine victims attacking a buffet. The course of true love never did run smooth. There was much taking of comfort and some receiving of sadness. These are the tears of things. For all that my house overlooked a colonial graveyard, at least here no psychic traces of old disaster seeped into our minds. Year after year people die, but life on Earth goes on. That's the way it's supposed to be.

Isn't it?

Finally, a little reluctantly, Leda and I reached out in our thoughts in response to the gentle presence of that third mind we'd felt since we returned to Earth.

Aimee?

Hello, Jerry. Pleased to meet you, Leda. Thank God you're both all right.

Pleased to meet you, too, Aimee. We should meet, shouldn't we?

Um, I just arrived in your living room. Don't worry, I didn't hear a thing! I checked for surveillance. Nobody else heard anything, either.

[Smiles all around]

Aimee waited patiently while we showered and made ourselves presentable. Once we sat down in the living room, Daniel entered the mind-space from afar. I was thinking that it was funny how quickly I'd gotten used to mind-to-mind communication.

Careful, Jerry, Daniel teased, *you might find yourself becoming more than just an Elf Friend.*

I felt Leda's panic and looked at her. *I won't go anywhere without you,* I thought. *I promise.* She knew I meant it; you can't lie mind-to-mind.

I kind of want to want to go meet you face to face, Daniel, Leda thought. *But I'm really scared to go.*

You can't be any more frightened of the journey than I was, Daniel thought. *Aimee once scared me so badly that I almost threw up.*

You're not talking about the time I propositioned you, I hope, Aimee teased.

After a bit more silliness, the four of us got down to the business of the evening. Leda and I told our stories. Actually, we *recalled* the memory of what we'd done in the Other World, all the memories of what had happened to us, everything we'd thought and felt, everything we'd perceived around us. We went over every detail, sometimes more than once. To have people like Daniel and Aimee examine your past with you is to discover how little of your experience you attend to. Humbling, is what it is. I guess it takes humility to learn anything new.

Daniel and Aimee learned something new from our memories of the Old Gods and the Other World, things about Earth's violent secret history that had been hidden even from the elves. Leda and I felt their shock as all of us relived the sadness of the many sand-covered ruins.

Self not different from world. What Daniel learned from us he shared in a flash with others in his own world whose minds were so deeply quiet and so filled with light that I would have been afraid of them if they weren't also full of compassion. Speaking of humbling.

Finally, Aimee and Daniel helped us figure out what we needed to do next.

At the end of our little meeting, Daniel thought, *Okay, you guys did great. We know things about the bad guys we didn't know before. Now Aimee's gonna come home to me. We've got people we need to talk to. Once we figure out what has to be done on our end, we'll be in touch.*

Aimee thought *Bye*, smiled happily at us, and faded out of my living room.

"Huh, just like any business meeting," I said.

Leda bounced over to my side of the couch, put her hand on my thigh, and commenced kissing me.

Being a gentleman, I kissed her back.

45

An Officer of the Court

The secretary ushered Leda and me into Steve's office without an appointment and unannounced. Another smart woman. She knew nothing good would bring a client in the door five minutes after the office opened.

When he caught sight of us, Steve's mouth dropped open for a moment, but he shut it quickly. "Holy crap!" he said.

"See," I said, "*that's* the kind of considered legal opinion I was counting on." I introduced Leda to Steve, who of course had already figured out who she was.

Steve came out from behind his desk and shook her hand with both of his. "I'm very glad to meet you, Ms. Clayton. May I ask where you've been all this time?"

I butted in. "Before we get into the details, can you agree to represent both of us, Steve? I'm quite sure we're going to need legal help."

"Um, can I assume you had nothing to do with her disappearance, Jerry?"

"You have my word on it," I said.

"Mine, too," Leda said. She gave me a level, affectionate look. "Some bad people kidnapped me and were holding me against my will. Jerry

221

got me away from them."

Did it just get hot in here? I thought. I didn't feel at all heroic today. "Here's the thing," I said, "thanks to some friends of ours, Leda and I have legal counsel available in Boston." I named the firm I mailed my rent check to every month. "But *you're* my lawyer, so I wanted to talk to you first. I mean, we knew each other as kids, for God's sake."

Dismay was all over Steve's face. He was a smart guy. He saw that Portsmouth's metaphysical undercurrents were about to sweep him up, as Leda and I had been swept up. And all of us against our will. Being a lawyer, he rarely asked a question he didn't know the answer to. "May I ask who these friends are?"

"You've probably heard about the Elf Friends. I've been with them for years," Leda said. She smiled at me. "Jerry's a new member."

Steve waved us to the guest chairs in front of his desk. Looking lost, he wandered around to his own chair like he wasn't sure where it was or even what chairs were for. He slowly figured it out and sat down heavily.

"Holy crap," he said again softly. He shook his head.

"So ... you're our lawyer?" I said.

Steve looked up at the two of us sitting there sympathetically watching the outer signs of his inner struggle. "I *am* your attorney," he finally said. "Both of you. I guess I can kiss my regular life goodbye."

Until that moment, I hadn't thought much about my own regular life. *Our* regular life, Leda's and mine. Chilled, I reached out to her and she took my hand. We reassured each other silently that everything would be okay. "Think of it as eating fruit from the tree of knowledge of good and evil," I said.

Steve tried to make a joke. "*Portsmouth* is the Garden of Eden? Who knew?"

46

A Refusal to Cooperate With the Authorities

Escorted by Steve, Leda and I walked into the police station where the deer-hunting detective had tried to interrogate me. The story we gave the cops was that while hiking the Odiorne Point State Park, disconsolate, I'd met Leda wandering around, cold, disoriented, and unable to remember where she'd been. It wasn't much of a lie, but the truth would have been even less well received.

We were not entirely surprised to learn the feds were "assisting" the local authorities with this investigation. The locals called them when we walked in the door. As our attorney, Steve closely examined every identification the Washington guys proffered. He took the time to write names, ID numbers, and purported agencies in a little leather pocket notebook. Lawyers can be so irritating, with their persnickety insistence on the dotting of *I*s and the crossing of *T*s as regards the rule of law and the rights of the accused—or in my case and Leda's, the rights of the not-accused-of-anything.

Steve told us he'd be calling the headquarters of any federal officers who showed up—to be sure they worked for who they said they worked for. Judging by subtle signs of discomfort, two of the five feds were off the books.

Steve would not allow Leda and me to be interviewed separately, the way the feds all wanted. The two sides were at impasse until a female FBI agent asked Leda, "Ms. Clayton, do you feel safe now?" Leda agreed that she did. "Do you feel safe at your house?" Interesting. The same questions emergency room nurses and doctors ask.

Leda looked at me, burst into tears, threw her arms around me, and buried her face in my neck. "I only feel safe with Jerry," she said. "I was lost, didn't know where I was. But he found me, he found me, *he found me!*" I saw in her mind that it wasn't all histrionics.

I threw my arms around her protectively, hugged her, and patted her back, *there there, honey.* I kissed the side of her head awkwardly, a guy whose girlfriend's tears are running down his neck and soaking his collar. I glared at the minions of law enforcement and the American surveillance state: *Now see what you've done! How dare you insult my lady's good character?*

"No crime has been committed, as far as anyone here is able to determine," Steve said. "Is either of my clients charged with anything?" None of the cops and federal agents was able to come up with anything we might allegedly be guilty of. "Although we haven't solved the mystery of Ms. Clayton's disappearance and return, Mr. August and Ms. Clayton are going to resume their lives. Do we have your assurance that they may do so unmolested, or must I raise the issue with your chains of command?" None of the federal agents wanted to answer that one. They reserve the right to mess with the citizenry arbitrarily.

"Just to satisfy our curiosity, Mr. August," said one of the questionable feds, "where have *you* been the last few weeks?"

"Was I missing?" I said. "I had no idea."

The agent gave me one of those you-haven't-seen-the-last-of-us looks. I was unimpressed. Seeing an Other-World deity absorb your uncle elevates your fear threshold. But I'd received the guy's message: *We're watching your ass, citizen.*

47

Unintended Consequences

Miracle Max's phone rang and rang without going to voicemail. I showed Leda my surprised face. It wasn't like my friend not to answer his phone.

Finally after about twenty rings, I heard a slurred voice, "'lo?"

"Max? It's Jerry. And I've got my girlfriend Leda on speakerphone."

"Hi, Max," Leda said.

"*Leda?* Don't know any Leda, Jerry. Loose lips sink ships, y'know."

I mouthed the words Leda heard me thinking: *He's drunk.* "You haven't met Leda yet, buddy," I said. "Um, are you okay?"

"Until you called and woke me up," said Max with exaggerated dignity, "I was blissfully sleeping off indulgence in excessive alcohol."

"That's not like you on a work night," I said.

"Got no job to get up for. They fuckin' *fired* my ass, Jerry. The best code monkey they had, too."

"Did they tell you why, Max?"

"The day after those federal agents showed up at my door, I got called into the big guy's office. Asshole said something about *the appearance of impropriety* and called security. Security stood around, watched me clean out my desk, confiscated my ID badge, walked my ass down to human resources, sign here, sign here, and walked me out of the building. See ya later, *bye.*" Max sounded pretty sober now. He was rocking the righteous anger.

"Any luck finding a new job?" I said, remembering my own difficulties.

"*No!*" Max shouted into the phone. Then he calmed down. "Sorry, man, I shouldn't blame you for this. I did what I did for you because I thought nobody would see me doing it. Live and fucking learn, huh?"

I got his point. Apparently Max's researches into the August Association on my behalf had drawn the attention of those whose attention is better left undrawn.

"Look," I said, "I don't want to promise you something I can't deliver, but how would you feel about moving up here if I can find an IT job for you?"

"Hmm, let me think about that," he said. A long pause while he thought about it. "Yeah, no. Thanks, my friend."

"Girlfriend?"

"Several," he said. "Begging your pardon, Leda."

Leda laughed at that and Max laughed along with her. My ex-wife would not have thought multiple girlfriends were a bit funny and would not have laughed. Ironic, no? I thanked a God I didn't quite believe in that the woman had divorced me.

"Let me ask you this, then," I said. "How would you feel about a bit of contract work?"

"You have my attention."

"If you agree, a guy who knows Leda and me will come pay you a visit and talk things over. Only if you agree, though."

"All I have to do is talk to him?"

"That's it," I said. "If you like what he has to say, he'll get me on the phone and the three of us will figure what to do next."

"Ugh. What *I'm* gonna do next involves drinking water and brushing my teeth."

48

There's Something About Mary

Quincy didn't need a personal assistant/bodyguard because he was supposedly out of the country on business. With her services not needed at August Associates, all Myra had to do was to boss Quincy's household staff around and teach the Squad Leader English. Myra was reluctant to let Mary leave Quincy and Pepsi's mansion with me. But Myra believed that I, who looked exactly like Quincy's nephew, was actually Quincy. She *had* to obey me. The Old Gods had set Quincy above her in the Other World chain of command.

"Go with Mr. August, Squad Leader," Myra ordered. I managed to keep myself from smiling at that.

Mary bowed her head in obedience, Myrmidon-style. Wearing one of Myra's coats over one of Myra's business pantsuits, she climbed into my old Honda.

As we turned onto the coast road, Mary looked out at the quiet Atlantic shining in the sun. "What a strange world this is," she said in perfect English. "So *cold*. So much *water!*" She had only a trace of an accent.

I did a double-take but managed not to drive off the road. Had Myra done a superhuman language-tutoring job, or was Mary some kind of prodigy of languages?

"You speak English better than I do," I said.

Mary smiled at me. "The Captain was *very* insistent that I listen and repeat everything she said back to her. For *hours*. Also, she ordered me to watch *television*." She made a face and shook her head.

"Did you understand what you saw on television?"

"I understand most of what people say, but I can't tell what's real and what's made up," she said.

Everybody's a TV critic. "I had the same problem everywhere I went in your world. My eyes kept telling me things I couldn't understand."

She smiled. "Myra is very intelligent, but she doesn't understand what's right in front of her eyes—*you*, Jerry."

"My life is in your hands, Squad Leader." I wasn't joking. "Leda's, too."

"And mine is in *yours*," she said. "You drive almost as fast as Myra!"

I was barely doing the speed limit on the winding road, but I slowed down anyway. There were no cars behind me to get impatient. I couldn't imagine what it was like to upgrade from horse and cart to automobile in one noisy instant. I hoped we wouldn't have to take Mary on an airplane just yet.

"Thank you for slowing down," she said. She tightened her seat belt. "You can call me *Mary*, though. I like that name; it's not too different from my own."

Still with the name taboo? "I'm glad you like it," I said. There was no need to get into Quincy's reasons for naming her colleague Myra. And I thought *Mary the Myrmidon* sounded nice. Silly, but nice, like a children's story. "Mary, we're going over to my house to meet some friends of mine and Leda's. I trust *them* with my life, too. They're warriors of great power. I think you'll like them."

Mary was no dummy. "What do they want of me, Jerry? What do *you* want of me?" Her tone wasn't hostile, just curious.

I thought about what I'd told Larry, Moe, and Curly back in the Other World. "My uncle Quincy was trying to use his wealth to make our land over according to his will. He wanted the rich to have power over everything and the poor either to be slaves or to die. He may be part of the god of your world now, but in this world my uncle's ... confederates will want to continue his work. They steal from the poor and give to the rich, Mary. That's the real job of everybody who works in that building where we first walked into this world. And that's *Myra's* job, whether she knows it or not—because she works for Quincy and Pepsi. What I want—what my friends want—is for *all* our people to have a fair chance in life. You know what I mean?"

Mary leveled a gaze at me that was full of speculation and sorrow. "The gods summoned you and Leda to bring one age to an end and to begin another. Am I right that there will be no ... *divine child?*" I agreed that she was right. I hoped we wouldn't have to discuss human birth control and goddess gynecology. Mary continued, "Then the ceremony has yet to be completed. Now that you have looked upon *them* face to face—and the gods have seen *you*—they will never stop seeking you. *Never.* I'll listen to what your friends have to say, but I don't know how anyone can prevent *gods* from coming here and taking whatever they want."

Interesting. Mary didn't mention that she was sworn to the service of those gods, and from the womb.

"You know, what *I* wanted most was to bring Leda home safe again. I'm in your debt for helping us, but I can't help wondering why you agreed to come to this world," I said. "And I wonder why you chose not to betray me to Myra."

Mary was quiet awhile, thinking. Was it hard translating thought in the language of dreams into English? And why did that translation happen so ... *automatically* in the Other World?

"Jerry, did you see the gods' faces when they looked at you?" I nodded. She said, "They *approve* of you. They *love* you both."

"And yet the gods were planning to *absorb* me and Leda. Whatever that means to you, to me it meant the death of us."

Mary was silent for another long moment, thinking hard. Then: "I wonder if it was not the gods themselves seeking your lives, but your aunt and uncle somehow still working their will—*through* our gods."

Jeez, if one of the gods' own Myrmidons didn't have the answer, how would I know? I glanced at Mary. Her face had gone rigid with distaste. I thought I might know why. "When Leda and I were lying there on the altars of the god and goddess, I learned that Quincy and Pepsi aren't just rich, arrogant, careless aristocrats. They're cruel and selfish, too. *Needlessly.*"

Mary turned her face away from me. She looked out the window as the tires rumbled across a low bridge over a little tidal creek. Ashamed? "Myra *wept* when she told me this," she said. I found that hard to imagine. She paused. "They made Myra *take comfort* with them—both of them at once. Myra didn't want to, but your aunt and uncle were— *are*—the gods' *legates* in this world. Your uncle took some sort of medicine for his manhood. Then he *took* Myra. When Myra's body ... *responded* to being taken, your uncle ordered her to *take* your aunt. There was no comfort in any of that for Myra—no love, little desire— but she was under orders and could refuse them nothing. As if a Myrmidon officer had no more dignity and worth than a *slave.*" Mary's voice was harsh and low with anger and shame. "Your aunt and uncle are not *worthy* of being called up into the gods. *You* are worthy of the gods, Jerry. You're *loyal* to those you love, as a warrior should be, as your Leda is. I choose to fight on your side and help you if I can—even if, as it seems, you reject the gods' will."

Overwhelmed by all that, I just nodded. Would the gods destroy Mary for disobeying them? I felt a heavy burden of responsibility. Yet another entangling alliance. The rest of the ride passed in silence.

"Aimee Amory of Earth, more recently of the next world over from Earth," I said, "allow me to introduce my friend from what we call the Other World. There I called her *Squad Leader,* her title; here she allows me to call her *Mary.*" *Other-World people don't share their names easily,* I thought to Aimee. She nodded in acknowledgment.

"I'm pleased to meet you, Mary," Aimee said. She observed Mary with real interest and affection, as elves do.

Mary bowed her head to Aimee as if Aimee were a superior officer. She looked closely at Aimee and shook her head, unable to understand what her eyes told her. Aimee was dressed in black jeans, soft boots, and a black shirt, so whatever Mary was staring at, it wasn't Aimee's outfit. "What *are* you, Aimee?" she said. Her voice was reverent. "Are you a *god* that such a light shines out of you?"

Aimee laughed. "I'm no god, believe me. No, what you're seeing is the light that shines through us all from the source of all being."

Mary looked skeptical. "Jerry said you were a warrior of great power. But I can see with my own eyes that you have power I do not."

Myrmidon eyes, I remembered, saw more clearly both in the dark and in the light.

Aimee's rueful thought to Leda and me: *Sorry about this, but some things can only be said in Elvish.*

"*Mary,*" Aimee said softly in the Unfallen Tongue, "*you see me with the eye of the spirit, not the body.*" That, at least, was the sense of the words that danced and shone and lit up my living room. The words hinted at more; they promised a deeper knowledge to anyone with the courage to follow where they led.

"*Oh!*" said Mary and she knelt on one knee before Aimee on my threadbare rug, like a samurai. "If you speak the secret tongue of gods, I am yours to command."

Aimee, who read the thoughts and hearts of men, women, and also Myrmidons, spoke in English again. "Stand *up*, Mary." Like a good soldier, Mary stood up. She was taller and heavier than Aimee, yet in that moment less substantial. "*Mary,*" Aimee both said and thought, as much for Leda's and my benefit as for Mary's, "*will you trust me with your life?*"

"I will," Mary whispered. She took Aimee's outstretched hand.

Mary and Aimee disappeared from my living room: *pop.*

Leda and I bent our shaky knees and sat ourselves down on the cabbage rose couch.

"I'll never get used to that," I said. I meant people appearing and disappearing in my house.

"Me neither."

"We may *have* to get used to it."

"Could we not talk about *that* right now? And would it kill you to hold me?"

"I'll be happy to hold you," I said. I was as good as my word.

Leda and I snuggled on the couch. At odd intervals one of us would shake with an involuntary shiver and be held tighter by the other, although the house was warm enough. Elves can't help how they affect the rest of us. Something about the impact of their presence, their thoughts, their luminous language, and their impossible mode of transportation.

I kind of want that power Aimee has, I thought to Leda, *but I'm scared of what I'll have to do to get it.*

Me, too, she thought back. She shivered again, and I held her.

Before we could take ourselves off to the warmth of bed, Aimee popped back into the living room from wherever she'd taken Mary.

She grinned at us sitting there with our arms around each other. "God, you two are just *adorable* together," she said.

"Are *not*," I said.

"Are *too*," Leda said, elbowing me gently in the ribs.

I saw that Aimee was alone. "No Mary?"

"As you saw, she chose to come with me to the next world over," Aimee said. "She'll learn everything she needs to know there. After that, we decided, she'll be going back to the Other World. The Old Gods won't be able to see her. They won't even know she's there."

I did the math, not that I understood the result. "In Earth time, she may have returned home already."

Aimee smiled. "Very probably."

"So she's going on a recruiting drive for you?" Leda said.

Aimee nodded. "For us in the next world over, for her own people. And for Earth."

Leda was pretty smart. "For us, too," she said. "For Jerry and me."

Leda didn't say what Aimee already knew about us. That we were drawn to the idea of going where Mary had gone. That we were afraid of what would happen to us if we left Earth with our friends to walk the Invisible Mountain into the unknown.

We were more afraid of what *wouldn't* happen to us. Our ordinary American lives were probably over. We clung to them anyway.

49

Bob, Bob, Bobbin' Along

I thought Bob was going to have a heart attack when I walked into his office. He jumped backwards, as much as that's possible for a sitting man. The back of his chair hit the wall hard. Fortunately the expensive chair was stable enough to keep him from hitting the floor on the rebound.

"Jesus Christ, Jerry, where you *been*, man? I been sweating bullets for weeks. I can't get in touch with Quincy August, and nobody will tell me how to reach him. I get no word from the August Association about exactly *how* they want to execute the contract they signed with me. *What about all these employees?* I ask them. The best the Association's lawyers can do is cut a month-to-month interim contract for *me* to manage this operation—in the puzzling absence of Jerry August." Bob put both hands palm-up on his desk: *I eagerly await your explanation.*

"Kind of a long story," I said. I went through a little game of charades. I pointed to Bob's phone, shook my head, and put one finger over my lips: *Shh.* I cupped one ear: *Is somebody listening?* I shrugged to indicate I didn't know. "Want to go get a cup of coffee?"

Bob looked at me like I was nuts, but he said, "Sure, why not?"

I took my cell phone out of my jacket pocket and set it on Bob's desk. Bob looked at my phone, then looked at me, confused. His eyebrows went up as he understood what I meant. He put his own cell phone on the desk.

"Mind if I drive?" Bob said.

"Not at all."

At my suggestion, we avoided Starbucks and instead grabbed a table in a bar that also served decent coffee. In china mugs, not in paper cups. I didn't see anything that looked like a security camera, but what do I know? I could only hope the August Association and its co-conspirators hadn't bugged the sugar dispenser or the napkin holder.

I decided to get right into it. "Portsmouth has gotten kind of a weird reputation the last thirty years or so. Ever hear anything about that?"

Bob made a face. "We moved here a few years ago. Good schools and a favorable tax climate for business. I've heard a few things, sure. But my property taxes are too damn high for me to *believe* those weird tales you're talking about—any more than I'd worry about the Mothman or the Jersey Devil." He stopped smiling when he noticed I wasn't smiling back.

"I'll give you the short version of my story," I said. "But first, what did you know about the August Association when they asked you to hire me? What did you know when you sold your company to them?"

Bob's hands rose up as he formulated a self-justification, then dropped as he abandoned it. His hands rose and fell a couple of times. Finally: "Eh, at first all I knew was they were arrogant assholes with too much money. By the time I sold out, I'd done enough due diligence to know they were *dangerous* assholes with too much political power."

"Figured you'd take the money and run?" I said. "I don't blame you."

Bob held his coffee mug in two hands and sat back in his chair. "So where *were* you?" He was ready to hear whatever I had to tell him.

"Does it seem possible to you that an August Association employee might also be an officer in a ... *foreign* paramilitary organization?"

"Let's say I think it's at least *possible*."

"You probably heard about Leda being kidnapped right in front of me on Thanksgiving?"

"You kidding? It was all over the news."

"This paramilitary organization I'm talking about kidnapped her. I went after Leda, and got captured myself. Long story short, I got us both out of ... where they were holding us."

Bob looked skeptical. "Heroics?" he said. I didn't blame him. I mean, look at me.

"Nah, I made friends. My friends helped us escape."

"*That* I can believe," Bob said. "You really do know how to talk to people."

We talked around the underlying issues until we had to ask for more coffee. Bob couldn't understand how the August Association could be evil enough to kidnap somebody but stupid enough to have no contingency plan for Uncle Q's absence. I was pretty sure Bob wasn't ready to hear about bird-god adventures and body-swapping. Not yet, anyway.

"Good, bad, or indifferent, Bob, they're just people," I said. Probably a partial untruth there. Whatever Quincy and Pepsi were now, they weren't *just* people anymore, were they? But as far as I knew, the Association was made up of human beings. Even including Myra the Myrmidon. Not that I wanted to get into a big discussion of who the Myrmidons were—and whose.

"You think those people might have bugged my office—or my phone?"

My turn to pause for thought. "That depends on what they want," I finally said. "Look, what's happened to the company is no financial hardship for the Association. They can afford to maintain your—our— business in a holding pattern forever. Or until Quincy shows up to make his wishes known. Ever wonder why they picked *your* company to force me on—and why they ended up buying it from you?"

"I assumed it was all about you."

I shook my head No. "I don't think it was entirely about me. You— we—have some expertise and some proprietary software that they also want. Eventually somebody in the Association is going to remember that."

"Okay, *why?*" said Bob.

"Ever hear of Miracle Max?" I said. "*He* knows why. We need to go talk to him face to face."

"You've talked about Max before. He's almost famous in our little world. Maybe 'notorious' is a better word. I suppose a conference call is out of the question?" Bob was trying to tease me, but I wasn't having it.

"Hey, if Max is afraid to discuss something on the phone, that means he thinks the feds are involved—and not on our side."

"Dammit, Jerry, what the hell have you gotten me into?" Bob didn't say No, though.

⚓5O2⚓

Are We Having Our First Fight?

"I don't *want* you to go to Washington," Leda said. "I *hate* when we're not together."

I knew what she meant; I didn't want to leave her, either. She was reluctant even to leave me long enough to go to work; she had to, though. We had to keep up two different sets of appearances. First, that we were Jerry and Leda; second, that we were Quincy and Pepsi *pretending* to be Jerry and Leda. Most of that masquerade fell on me, but she was still scared. We both were. We felt safer together.

Leda's office had welcomed her back to work like a heroine or a celebrity. Now she had to show up at her desk every day like nothing had changed. My job gave me more freedom of movement. While I was gone, my projects had been offloaded onto other colleagues. I could shake loose and go to Washington for a day or two, but Leda had to stay in Portsmouth. Appearances. And the fact that the work she did was indispensable to her company.

Also there was the mundane but necessary matter of money. Leda needed a regular paycheck. Thanks to Bob, my salary continued to be deposited into my bank account. Uncle Quincy's Association paid Bob according to the interim contract they'd signed, but Bob's accounting service was still handling the payroll. I'd gotten a big raise as soon as I'd signed Quincy's employment contract. I was shocked at how fast my bank account had grown while I was traveling in the Other World. There was a lot left even after I paid all my overdue bills.

Money had stopped mattering to me.

Leda and I sat side by side at the kitchen table. "I hate leaving you, too," I said. I covered her hand with mine and left it there. It's comforting just to touch someone you love, and we both needed comfort. "But I've started getting phone calls from Quincy's lawyer. Dude sounds like he's on a fishing expedition. He keeps using obvious code words that I have to pretend to have forgotten the responses to. Then I get phone calls from Myra. The poor woman's bored and lonely rattling around in Quincy's mansion, feels useless. She keeps asking *When is Mary coming back?* I tell her Mary's on assignment for me, very hush-hush. What Myra wants to know is when we—I mean Quincy and Pepsi—are coming back to the big house. She wants to know when she and Quincy can get back to work at the August Association robbing the poor and giving to the rich—and maybe silencing dissenters and atheists."

"I don't suppose we can continue on the way we are," Leda said.

"Well, don't start singing 'The Way We Were' just yet," I said.

"Only if you promise not to sing 'Never Gonna Give You Up'."

"Dammit," I said, "Barbra Streisand and Rick Astley have ruined *everything.*"

Leda looked away from me for a moment. "I'd like to move back in with Beth and Janjan while you're gone. You said it was just a couple of days, right? I miss them and they miss me."

I miss my old life, is what she meant. I would have pointed that out to her mind-to-mind, but since we'd come back to Earth our mental connection had become hit-or-miss. I looked at her sadly. "If trouble comes looking for you, do you want it to find Beth and Janjan?"

She looked shocked. "I'm so selfish. I never even thought of that."

"Are they at least Elf Friends?"

She shook her head. "I've always kept that part of my life to myself. So I can be just one of the girls when I'm with them."

"Would you be hurt if I said it's only human to want to have it both ways—always?"

Leda knew what I meant. She stroked my face. "I'm not hurt," she said, "I'm just scared all the time. I'm so sick of being scared."

"Would it help if we put our minds together and asked Aimee to keep a close eye on you?" I said. "Daniel is going to sit in on the meeting at Quincy's Washington law firm. *I'll* know he's there, but nobody else will."

Leda took a deep breath. "I suppose I *deserve* this for getting you mixed up with the elves."

"Jesus, sweetie, look what I got *you* mixed up with—rapist bird gods from outer space. There's always plenty of blame to go around."

After a little canoodling, we reached out our minds to Aimee. She'd been waiting for us. The barriers were all on our side, not on hers. She thought, *Oh, boy, sleepover!*

That brief contact restored the mental connection between Leda and me. Huh.

This is what I want, I thought to her. *To be this close to you all the time.*

I want this, too, she thought back.

We spoke the truth right from the heart. Uncle Q was right. Once you know what you want, you know what to do.

🦢 51 🦢

Oliver Twists

Myra picked me up at my house in Quincy's Mercedes. She opened the door so I could sit in the back like a captain of industry, or maybe an admiral of financial jiggery-pokery. She stored my suitcase in the trunk next to hers.

WWQD: *What Would Quincy Do?* He'd put his employees on the defensive.

"Don't suppose you've managed to find Mary yet, have you?" I said.

"No, Mr. August," Myra said. She sounded alarmed. Had I ordered her to track Mary down? Had she forgotten that I had done so?

"Hmmph," I said. It's so hard to find reliable mind-reading minions these days.

We drove in silence to the August Association offices, where she badged us into the building and cowed the daytime guards into submission with her war face. Formidable woman, Myra, daunting even to those who had no idea what a Myrmidon was or that she was one.

Up the elevator we went, where Oliver met us when the doors opened. I noticed Quincy's secretary was missing from her desk in front of Q's office. I gave him a puzzled look: *Where is she?*

"Don't you remember, sir?" Oliver said. "She's on leave until, well, *arrangements* are finalized here in the office."

I sighed. The three of us walked into Quincy's office, but remained standing. Myra shut the door so we could talk privately. She and I kept our coats on; we wouldn't be staying.

"It's no use, Oliver," I told Quincy's attorney. "I know that you and I arranged *something* before Pepsi and I ... left the country, but damned if I can remember what we agreed to. A lot happened to me over there, as any fool can plainly see. Getting my ... health back was more traumatic than I expected. It's played hob with my memory. Can't remember the signs and the countersigns." My tone suggested this problem was entirely Oliver's fault for failing to foresee it, not my fault for causing it. Would Oliver have known that Quincy planned to use supernatural leverage to evict my soul so he could move into my body, like a hermit crab moving into another crab's shell?

Oliver got the message. Despite looking exactly like Jerry August, I'd just convinced the lawyer *Quincy* August was standing in front of him. "Then I'm afraid I don't quite know how to proceed, Mr. August," he said. For once, the guy looked neither supercilious nor peevish, but *frightened.* He was on his own in kind of a bad spot. I almost felt bad for him. Almost.

Quincy August never hesitated, so neither did I. "Here's what's going to happen," I announced. "This is above your paygrade, no offense." (Hah! As if Quincy ever worried about offending the lesser beings who served him.) "Now that Pepsi and I have established the return of *Jerry* and *Leda,* Myra's going to drive me down to Washington. I want to meet with your firm's senior partners and with the Association's, er, *stakeholders*—your superiors will know who they are—and we'll map out the way forward." I peered at Oliver skeptically. "You can at least make *that* happen, can't you, Counselor?"

"Certainly, sir," Oliver said. "Myra, I'll call you with the details." He was pathetically grateful to be assigned back to gopher status and relieved of legal sentry duty. I wondered if his life was in danger. I decided that was his problem for choosing to represent dangerous clients.

For all that she'd been born in the Other World, Myra drove superbly, fast, smooth, consistent and courteous. I imagined she'd had expensive anti-terrorism evasive driving training. I would have asked, but I wanted to limit the number of times I played the Quincy-can't-remember-this-detail card. Myra was a lot smarter than Oliver. What I did to discourage further conversation was nod off in the back seat.

Sleep came easily. Leda and I had had a busy night. The poor girl was going to have a tough day at work unless she drank a lot of coffee. I hoped she wouldn't spend the day cursing me. But in my defense, it was Leda who started ... something we then had to work hard together to finish. A robust exchange of views regarding matters physical and spiritual, let's say. I didn't know how we'd ever live long enough to learn everything there was to learn about each another. In the morning she sang "Getting to Know You" from *The King and I* in the shower just to make me laugh.

I love you so much, I thought to Leda as I focused my attention in the quiet center of myself and listened.

I love you, too, came her loving, but distant thought.

Our mental connection was limited by distance in a way that Aimee's and Daniel's was not. That was the least of all the mysteries we were up against.

While Myra drove me to D.C., Bob was driving himself, ostensibly to visit his parents in their senior citizen community in Virginia. And Steve was flying out of Manchester to meet us in Washington. I'd be sneaking out of my hotel to meet with them and with Max.

After I snuck back into the hotel, Myra and I would be attending a second meeting in the lions' den of Quincy's arguably-criminal associates—and I didn't mean just his law firm.

52

They Hate Our Freedom

Daniel had given me the address. Bob, Steve, and I met Max in the empty function room of a sprawling Chinese restaurant in Suitland, Maryland. A slight man I hadn't met greeted us and served as host, conveying our orders to the waitstaff in Mandarin. The stranger was possibly Eurasian, of indeterminate late middle age with short salt-and-pepper hair, even more unprepossessing than me. I knew what he was, though, by his inner glow, which is shorthand for how his presence affected me, or maybe how my mind experienced his: as *light*.

He saw me see him for who he was, grinned, and thought: *Isn't this fun?* I grinned back. I am not so made as to find chicanery entertaining, but his enjoyment was infectious.

He asked us to call him Trevor. None of us bothered with last names. He spoke the Queen's English with the Received Pronunciation. Sometimes his accent shaded into ironic self-parody. Once, he said, he'd worked for the U.S. Central Intelligence Agency. More recently he'd traveled to the next world over and become ... whatever those who go there become. Fully human, maybe?

If anyone knew the secret history of the world and of the Portsmouth Wars, it was Trevor. He'd fought on the right side, the side of the good angels. I knew some of Trevor's history, but it was all new to the rest of the Portsmouth contingent and to Max, the local boy. Wherever you live, you will have heard *something*. Like Max, you will have thought it unlikely.

The five of us sat at the far side of the function room, away from the interior door to the restaurant. We were still talking in low tones, getting to know each other, when a sixth man just *appeared* two tables over. I'd seen this phenomenon before, so I was less rattled than poor Max, Steve, and Bob.

"Gentlemen," I said, "allow me to introduce Daniel Ryun, formerly of Portsmouth, now a resident of the next world over from Earth."

Trevor of course knew Daniel from the last Portsmouth War, one of the three wars nobody in Portsmouth ever talks about. The two men hugged with real affection. Elves don't worry themselves about machismo or about proving anything to anyone. Gay, straight, and everywhere in between, they conduct their love lives with honor and treat everyone with respect, even people who think the elves are their enemies.

I'd already met Daniel in my mind, so I recognized him when he showed up in the restaurant. Personality and self-concept seem to be anchored somehow in the physical body. I knew Daniel Ryun was from my father's generation and had also fought in Vietnam, but I was surprised all over again to see that Daniel didn't look anything like his Earth age. Lean, strong, centered, golden skin, dark almost-Asian eyes, white-streaked black hair, inner stillness. I'd wondered if Daniel and Aimee were some kind of May-December romance, but those age categories don't seem to apply to people from the next world over.

Now that I thought about it, Trevor was even older than Daniel in Earth years. I simply *could not tell* how old he was. I guess it didn't matter. It would have gratified my mother no end to see how my new friends all had good posture and perfect teeth.

Max looked fascinated. Bob looked stunned. Steve looked sick. I sympathized with them all. But they said hello to Daniel and shook his hand as if he'd just walked in the door like the rest of us, instead of popping into the room from another world. He grinned at them, and they grinned back, even Steve. It was a very *Fellowship of the Ring* moment. Daniel was a natural leader, and we were all in this together.

I gave the man a hug. "Dan," I said, "I'm very happy to meet you face-to-face, but I'm surprised to see you here. I thought maybe you couldn't come back to Earth."

He grimaced. "Oh, I can come back okay—with a bit of extra effort. It's *remaining* here for any length of time that's the problem. *But!* When I talked to my elders and betters, they reminded me that nobody has more experience than I do of those beings we call the Old Gods. So here I am where I'm most needed. I'll stay as long as I can, but don't be surprised if I disappear without warning. When that happens, I'll have to go home to ... recharge for a while before I can come back."

Steve still looked shaky, like he was grateful to be sitting down and drinking strong tea. Bob looked fascinated by what he was hearing, like he was trying to fit this new human data into what he knew about math and physics.

But Max gazed at Daniel like he was suffering from the onset of a serious bro-crush. "Man," he said, "you hear about this kind of thing on the internet, but it's hard to separate the signal from all the noise."

Daniel cocked his head to one side and observed Max with great interest. "Would you like to see where *the signal* comes from?" he said.

Max nodded Yes.

"Do you trust me with your life?" Daniel said.

"I think I *do*," Max said, surprised to hear himself say it.

"Give us a couple of minutes," Daniel said to the rest of us. "Max and I will be right back." He reached out his hand to Max. Max grasped the hand, and the two men disappeared from the room.

"Best part of the job, that," Trevor said. "As long as we're waiting, anyone else want to make a quick visit to the next world over?"

"Maybe later," Bob said, sounding like he just needed to think it over first and have a family meeting or something.

I thought about Leda. *Mmm, Leda...* Then I reluctantly dragged my thoughts back to what had to be done *today,* smiled at Trevor, and shook my head.

Steve didn't say anything. He'd started to look seasick again. I threw an arm around his shoulders. "It's okay," I said. "Daniel and Trevor are the good guys."

"Psh, like *that* helps," Steve said. His color started to come back, though.

Trevor lightened the mood by telling us how the owner of the Chinese restaurant we were sitting in was a known agent of the People's Republic of China. Paradoxically, this knowledge made the restaurant a safe place for American intelligence operatives and retirees to meet ... whoever they met. No cameras, no microphones. Beijing, Trevor said, had an American restaurant that worked under the same rules. Both restaurants provided deniable back-channel communication between the two governments and saved face all around. It was a good story, but thinking about all that spy-versus-spy stuff made my head spin. It was confusing enough having a secret identity of my own—depending on who I was talking to.

It was actually more like five minutes before Daniel and Max reappeared. Daniel looked just the same, no surprise there. Max had looked indoor-pale and slightly drink-bloated before, but now he looked tan and fit. He seemed to have dropped a few pounds. His face looked thinner. He didn't glow as strongly as Trevor and Daniel, but there it was, Max had the unmistakable inner mark of the next world over. Five minutes of Earth time to us could have been years of time to him.

"The Garden of Eden?" Steve asked.

"Dude, it's *way* better than that," said Max.

"*Old Gods?*" Steve asked Daniel. He couldn't possibly have put more skepticism into the words without sounding rude. I think people go to law school to learn how to walk that fine line with a judge and jury.

"Just a way of talking about something that baffles our human senses," Daniel said. "Something our minds can't accommodate."

"So they're *false* gods, surely," Steve said. His parents had made him study Torah. The Hebrew Bible has nothing good to say about substitute deities.

Mind-reading abilities aside, Daniel was smart enough to know what Steve was getting at. "They embody real power," Daniel said, "but they're still false gods. There's no salvation to be gained from them. *Worshiping* those we call the Old Gods is like praying to a nuclear reactor."

"Peter Brown told me the Old Gods were dangerous to human beings," I said.

Daniel looked around at all of us, to see if we were following him. Nobody dismissed his story out of hand. "They seem to relate differently to our physical reality," he said. "It's like they're partly with us but also mostly elsewhere." He paused, thinking about how to continue. "I was actually *inside* one of the Old Gods. He was deep inside the World Mountain. He'd been there ever since human beings first appeared on Earth. You have only my word for this, but inside the creature was *a completely different universe*. The laws were so different there that he was able to transform my human body, to kill me and resurrect me in a *steelbody*. Think nuclear-powered cyborg."

Bob looked baffled by a story that sounded so much like an internet conspiracy theory. Trevor and Max who had been in the next world over long enough to confront wonders with equanimity, listened calmly. Steve was shaking his head, not because he didn't believe Daniel, but because he did—he just didn't want to.

"But here's the thing," Daniel said. "The Old God *responded* when I showed him kindness. All sentient beings respond to that, unless their wills are given over to evil. Despite all his power over physical reality, the Old God was a simple creature—and lonely. Jerry, tell everyone what happened when those Other-World gods looked at you and Leda."

I really did not want to tell the whole story of what had happened in the temple tower. It was too intimately entwined with all that Leda and I meant to each other. More prosaically, gentlemen don't kiss and tell, especially when the kissing is spirit-to-spirit. But Daniel's question was safely specific, so I said, "This is hard to explain, but when the god and goddess *looked* at us and looked *into* us, they seemed to *approve* of what they saw."

Daniel came to my rescue, "The gods approved of you and Leda even though they were about to absorb your lives so that your aunt and uncle could return to Earth in your bodies?"

I nodded agreement. "Is it possible that Quincy and Pepsi managed to pervert or distort the god and goddess?"

Daniel, Trevor, and Max all grinned at me. Elves can laugh at all the sickest jokes of human existence, because they've found a way out of the sickness. "That's what *I* think," Daniel said. "The Old Gods are bad for human beings, but some people seem to be bad for the gods. And that, my friend, is why the ceremony didn't work. Even after Quincy and Pepsi spent so much time and energy sucking you and Leda into the Other World so they could steal your lives and youth."

That made a weird kind of sense. "The gods were set to act according to whatever physical laws govern them," I said, "but Quincy and Pepsi are so twisted that they deformed the god and goddess. So the age *didn't* end in catastrophe for Earth and for the Other World."

"Well, not yet, anyway," Trevor said. "Where are your aunt and uncle now, I wonder?"

Everybody got a chance to talk. Bob and Max talked about the software Bob had created and I and the other employees had perfected. Specifically, they talked about why the August Association would need our talents as an in-house operation.

"Holy crap," Bob said, "you really think the bad guys want to take over the internet?"

"Probably not the whole thing," Max said, "just the parts that handle money."

"I'm afraid it's worse than that," said Trevor. "You may have heard a lot of muttering lately about the *surveillance state*, the National Security Agency, and all its private contractors. Traitors, whistleblowers, telecom and internet service providers, all pawing through your phone calls and emails—looking for what, exactly?"

"Terrorists?" Steve said.

"Locating jihadists is just a side benefit, believe me," Trevor said. "No, what your uncle's associates want, Jerry, is to leverage *your* company's expertise, Bob, to dial the world economy up or down. Mostly down, actually. Think of the nozzle on a garden hose or the dimmer switch on a lamp. If they have to drive the United States to default on its debts and pauperize the population to gain the whole world, they won't hesitate."

Daniel spoke up. "There's a coalition of *very* bad people supporting the August Association and its corporate allies in their endeavors." Daniel just let that hang in the ensuing silence. Those we call elves are not much given to exaggeration. Everybody stared at him, afraid to ask the obvious question.

Now it was my turn to feel sick, but I had to know. "Are we talking about the *black-magic* sort of badness?"

Trevor nodded agreement. "We want you to know who you'll be going up against when you meet with your uncle's law firm and his fellow conspirators," he said. "One of the people you'll meet is almost certainly a Materialist Magician. I wish it were otherwise."

"He's not going to be much of a threat in the great scheme of things," Daniel said. "The Order has fallen on hard times in recent years." A classic elvish understatement. "But you can expect that he'll know how to fight and won't hesitate to deploy magic against you."

Some things actually are *problems*, not "issues." What we faced were real problems that had to be solved.

In addition to me, who should attend the meeting at Quincy's law firm? I hated to walk into the place alone, but I would if I had to. Aimee had taught me enough that I might be able to escape a physical attack as I had in the Other World. But I knew nothing about magic, black or white. At a minimum, we decided Steve should attend the meeting as "Jerry August's" attorney. Why? There would have to be some sort of legal conveyance to transfer ownership of Quincy's estate to the "nephew" who was actually Quincy himself.

How could I convince the bad guys that I was actually Quincy, returned from the Other World in Jerry's body but with an imperfect memory? Daniel laughed and assured me that was the easy part. If Steve and I agreed, Daniel would attend the meeting with us—in our minds—and read the thoughts of our opponents. Knowing from experience there was nothing to fear in that, I agreed right away. Steve asked for a moment to think about it and wandered off to stand in a corner by himself. When I saw him gently rocking back and forth with his lips moving in prayer, I looked away out of respect for his privacy. He wasn't gone for long.

"I'll do it," he said to Daniel. "The idea scares the hell out of me, but I'm pretty sure if anybody's on the right side, it's you guys." He meant the elves.

Okay, fine. Now should Myra attend the meeting? She was Quincy's personal assistant and bodyguard. She did believe I was Quincy, although she clearly had some lingering doubts, as who would not. We argued for way too long, finally deciding that it would look suspicious if Myra *didn't* attend the meeting with Quincy.

"I'd keep an eye on her, lad," Trevor said. No kidding. Myra was a trained killer devoted to the gods of her world—and to Quincy's vision of turning Earth into a place like the Other World, with a few nobles like himself—and their Myrmidon enforcers—in charge of a lot of sorry-ass peasants.

What about Bob and Max? We decided they would go with Trevor to a location where the cybernetic problems might productively be addressed. And never mind *who* they planned to visit. Neither Steve nor I would be told where they were going and what they might be up to there—on the sound principle that we couldn't divulge what we didn't know.

There was a political problem here, too, and none of us were in a position to solve it. The August Association had fellow travelers and agents of influence in government law enforcement and intelligence agencies, and who knew how many card-carrying Association lobbyists twisting arms, making off-the-books campaign contributions, and even drafting legislation for Congress to enact. Trevor made no promises, but said he *knew people who knew people*. That would have to be good enough. I mean, we could spill the beans to the news media, but at this point there were damn few beans to spill. All we had were suspicions of a vast faux-libertarian crypto-fascist conspiracy, but no evidence of any wrongdoing.

Was I an *agent provocateur*, then? Not really. I was going to walk into the presence of my enemies to convince them I was one of them. Whether the bad guys did anything illegal was up to them.

Best case? I'd wind up in charge of the August Association.

Worst case? My friends would have to say prayers over the corner of the Fort Totten landfill where the bad guys had buried my body. My friends would have to find a way to make sure I hadn't died in vain.

53

Wretched Excess

Myra was dressed in black and wearing the short jacket that covered her holster. She was not happy when Steve met us in the hotel lobby. Myra was prepared for anything except surprises. When I introduced Steve, and Myra learned she'd be driving both of us to the meeting with Quincy's attorneys and associates, she showed us her war face. It was pretty scary, but I was in charge here, wasn't I?

I apologized to Steve for the apparent rudeness and took Myra aside for a word. "What part of this is confusing to you?" I said. "He's *Jerry August's* lawyer. For all I know, he's executor of Jerry's estate. You can see how it might be useful to have him on *our* side, can't you?"

Myra looked quickly over at Steve to be sure he wasn't about to launch a surprise attack against us or possibly file a lawsuit. He stood there looking patient but perplexed next to one of the shiny granite pillars that held up the lobby ceiling. The rich are very different from the lawyers and other members of the vanishing middle class who serve them: lawyers learn *that* right after law school.

"But what if he finds out who you *really* are?" Myra muttered. She had a point. At this meeting, that disclosure was inevitable.

"Dear girl," I said in my most condescending Quincy tones, "by the time he finds *that* out, he'll either be working for us, or not. What happens to him if he should decide *against* us will be his responsibility."

"You're right, of course, Mr. August," Myra said. "I apologize for doubting you." She didn't sound at all contrite.

"Fair enough," I said. "Shall we go?"

Energized by the fact that her employer had just outlined the conditions under which she had permission to kill his nephew's lawyer, Myra led the way. She tipped the valet who fetched our car and opened the door for Steve and me with a flourish.

For all that it takes itself with extreme seriousness, the District of Columbia is not a vast place. The worst of the morning commuter traffic was over by the time Myra drove us across town and into the parking area beneath a fairly new midsize office building.

On the way over, Steve, Daniel, and I had done a mind-space communication check. Steve's initial seasickness at direct mental contact quickly gave way to excitement: *This changes everything!*

No kidding, right?

Myra called from the garage to let our hosts know we'd arrived. She knew which button to press in the elevator. She'd taken Quincy here before—all the way to the top, baby.

The man who met us when the elevator doors opened had Managing Partner written all over him: tall, white-haired, fleshy, expensively besuited, sixtyish, with a face as smooth as a baby's. Unlike my Aunt Pepsi, he'd *had some work done.*

Daniel fed me the guy's full name and I greeted him with his nickname, as I assumed Quincy would have. The lawyer's reaction was very telling: a look of restrained surprise that a shorter, younger man he didn't recognize called him by name—in Quincy August's overbearing manner. The lawyer had a pretty good poker face. "Good to see you again, Mr. August," he said. He nodded to Myra, "Ms. Breck." Myra nodded back impassively. She was in bodyguard mode, eyes scanning the deep-carpeted entryway for trouble.

The lawyer's eyes fell upon Steve. He looked puzzled, so I quickly drew him aside out of Steve and Myra's hearing. "That's *Jerry August's* attorney," I said. "At the moment he thinks *I'm* Jerry August. Can you see how it would be to our advantage to let him *go on* believing that? Once you, the other partners, and I come to an understanding this morning, I'll want to meet with the Association's other stakeholders. Perhaps you lawyers can hammer out the details and just bring me the documents to sign—after *Jerry's* lawyer reviews them, of course." The secret of impersonating Quincy was to treat everyone as a lesser being. So far it was working.

"That does make sense," the partner said. "And if I may say so, *well-played*, Mr. August."

I led the lawyer back and introduced him to Steve. For a moment the lawyer had that fastidious Oh-dear-a-Jew look on his face. Steve saw it and managed not to laugh at the guy. *You might as well laugh*, the elves say; I think they have a point.

The partner led the three of us to the door of a large conference room where four other men were sitting close together and talking quietly. Large windows with motorized shades currently lowered against the sun. Polished antique oak conference table. Comfy chairs. Sideboard with coffee urn, china coffee cups, water carafe and glasses. Large-screen TV/video conference monitor, currently switched off. You know the drill. The four looked up, saw me, and all looked shocked, to varying degrees. The plain fact was that Jerry August looked nothing like Quincy August. I really did not want to take another step into that richly-appointed lions' den.

"If you'll all wait here," the managing partner said, "I'd like to caucus with the other partners for just a minute before we start our meeting. I'm sure you understand."

None of us did understand, but I made a gracious gesture of agreement all the same.

The five men in the room put their heads together and manfully resisted looking at me again—or at Steve.

Daniel's mental voice spoke in my mind and Steve's: *They knew*

Quincy would look different when they saw him again, but most of them don't see how you can possibly be Quincy. You'll have to persuade them, Jerry.

I thought back to Daniel and Steve: *Let's do this, then. Steve—Jerry's lawyer—will wait out here while I go set my hired functionaries straight. Once they understand that I'm Quincy and I'm in charge, we'll invite Steve in to handle the paperwork on behalf of the man he believes is Jerry.*

I don't like it, but okay, Steve thought. *What about Myra?*

She goes where Quincy goes, I thought, *and I'm Quincy, dammit!*

We felt Daniel's smile. *I'll have most of my attention on the people in that room, Steve. Give a holler if you feel threatened. Otherwise, may I suggest prayer?*

There's nothing like the psalms in Hebrew, Steve thought.

54

A Granting Clause

The managing partner politely returned to the door to escort us in.

"If it's all the same to you, Counselor," I said, "I've asked my, er, *Portsmouth* attorney to wait out here for the first part of this meeting. I'm sure you understand." I spoke loudly enough for the other lawyers in the room to hear. "Steve, have a seat over there, if you would, please." I meant the luxurious waiting area outside the elevator. "I'll come get you once we come to some agreement in here."

"Sure thing, Mr. August." Steve said it with a straight face. Like any competent attorney, he was a pretty good actor. The Elf Friends were paying for his time today, but it wasn't just about the money anymore. All our lives were on the line here.

Myra and I sat on one side of the conference table. Actually, I sat at the table while she sat up against the wall behind me and to my right where she could see everyone and watch both the door to the hallway and the door leading to the inner offices. The five law partners sat on the other side of the table. I took charge of the meeting, like Quincy would have.

"Gentlemen, I'm sure Oliver, your Portsmouth man, has informed you that I came back from my, er, travels much improved in health as you can plainly see. What you *can't* see are the gaps in my memory. I'm

261

sure Oliver also told you about that. I *know* that we arranged passwords or countersigns or something of that sort, but I cannot for the life of me remember what they are. I'm hoping you smart people can figure a way around this problem. Otherwise the August Association and its important work will have to cease operations. Bad as that would be for the United States and the Western world, imagine how it would be for me to have to go on pretending to be Jerry August for the rest of my life. I'd have to work for a living again, if you can imagine it."

Polite laughter from the legal contingent. They watched me sympathetically but carefully. I had their attention.

One lawyer surprised me by addressing Myra directly. "Ms. Breck, were you present during the, um, *procedure* Mr. August underwent in your, um, country?"

"I was," Myra said.

"To what extent, if at all, did that procedure succeed?"

Myra leaned forward and put on her war face. "I will not subject the sacred rites of my faith to your profane inquiries," she said. *Growled*, actually. She didn't have to reach for a weapon. Everybody on the other side of the table slow-rolled their chairs as far away from her as they could.

"Forgive me," the lawyer said hastily, "I didn't mean to question your beliefs, Ms. Breck. It's just that your employer looks *nothing* like he used to look. My duty—*our* duty—is to determine that he's still Quincy August."

Did I feel Myra's gaze on the back of my neck? "Of course he is," she said simply. "How could my god and goddess ever fail in anything?"

The discussion ranged back and forth. I felt Daniel's presence in my mind. He gave me information he'd gleaned from our opponents— details which I then relayed to the lawyers as if I'd just remembered them.

My performance as Quincy seemed to be probative but not

dispositive. If lawyers and IT people have anything in common, it's a willingness to get into the details and stay immersed until a problem is resolved. Quincy's lawyers also had a strong motivation to restore the status quo at the August Association—and to ensure an uninterrupted flow of legal fees from New Hampshire to Washington.

They were greedy, not stupid. To establish that Quincy was really Quincy, they'd established a sign-and-countersign process that would have involved a conference call with these men as they sat here in Washington while Oliver sat with me in Portsmouth. That would have required too much long-distance reading of too many minds even for Daniel Ryun.

With Daniel's help, though, and with all the heavy hitters here in one room, I gradually won the lawyers over to my side. I might have *looked* nothing like Quincy, but who else would have been able to "remember" a twenty-digit international bank account (possibly Swiss)? Two of the partners put their heads together over a sheet of paper inside a file folder that only Superman's x-ray vision could have seen through. They confirmed that the code I rather hesitatingly gave them (and then repeated) was correct down to the last letter and number.

Also this: I sat as they remembered Quincy sitting and spoke as they remembered Quincy speaking. Daniel fed me each man's specific memories of my uncle, turns of phrase, posture, and manner of gesture. I used what Daniel and Aimee had taught me to replicate Quincy's outsize personality whether I was moving and speaking or sitting and listening impatiently to these lawyers who were, after all, only Quincy's hired help. The body moves as its energy prompts.

I watched the body language of the men across the table as, one by one, they relaxed and sat back looking in my direction with little nods of approval. *You've convinced them you're Quincy,* came Daniel's thought—*all but one.*

That one skeptic, the youngest of the partners, sat forward leaning on the table. The conference room had gotten warm. During the proceedings he'd removed his suit jacket and rolled up his shirt cuffs to reveal meaty forearms.

"Mr. August," he said, "we very much appreciate your patience with all our questions."

"I *expect* you to be thoroughgoing," I said. "What else do I pay you for?"

The other lawyers smiled at that; this guy didn't.

"Then you'll understand our reluctance to rush to judgment," he said.

I made one of Quincy's magnanimous gestures: *Do go on.*

"What's happened to you is *far* outside the bounds of any area in which my partners and I have experience," the lawyer said.

"Believe me, Counselor, it was like nothing *I'd* ever experienced, either."

Again, smiles from those I'd won over to my side, but none from the skeptic.

"There is one more of our associates, I'd like to call in to this meeting," he said. "If you agree, of course. We rely on him for his ... knowledge of the, ah, *metaphysical* matters at issue here—expertise the rest of us lack."

"How can I say No?" I said. "I placed the fate of my—of *our*— enterprise in your hands before I left the country to see to my health. By all means, call in your associate. Let's get this over with so I can get back to New Hampshire and get back to work in my own damn offices."

The lawyer smirked and left the room by the interior door. I heard the sound of voices, but not what was said.

This'll be the magician Trevor warned us about, came Daniel's thought. *Center yourself, brother. The first meeting with evil is always a shock.*

55

I Perform With the MMs—You've Probably Never Heard of Them

My skeptical thought was, *Evil? Really?* But I took Daniel's suggestion and centered myself. It was more like remembering I was centered already and had always been so. I sat in relative calm watching the inner lights, curious about what was unfolding in the world inside and around me.

There was a lot to observe. Distant sparks of the elvish network exchanged thoughts. Daniel touched base with Aimee. Aimee agreed with him about something and went into action back in New Hampshire with Leda. I got a sense of Leda's love and she got a reassuring sense of mine before that signal faded, or my attention turned...

...turned to Daniel who gave Steve, waiting out in the hallway, very specific instructions: *Head off like you're going to the men's room, then duck into the stairwell down to the lobby. Leave your rental car where it is. Walk out of this building, take the Metro to the airport, and catch the first plane home. We'll be in touch.*

Daniel's attention flashed to Trevor. Two calm, amused, compassionate minds shared information in their own language. The sense of it was: *Time to take action, my brother. Shit's about to get real all up in here. Go with God.*

That all happened in the few seconds it took for the skeptical lawyer to usher in his associate. As the lawyer sat back down at the table, he introduced the new guy. I didn't catch the young man's name because a roaring started up in my ears. A roaring as of mighty rivers, coupled with an all-too-familiar sense of *immanence* and the imminent arrival of ... *something.*

The new guy remained standing, the better to stare at me rudely, the way idiots challenge other idiots to bar fights. I held the center and returned his gaze calmly. The young man wore his hair short on the sides and long and oily on top. He was going for the West Coast Cad look, judging by his designer beard stubble. He wore some sort of new-made vintage-looking suit with a long, tight jacket and tight pants. Oh, and a bow tie. I couldn't see his shoes, but vintage patent leather 1920s dancing pumps were clearly not out of the question.

I wasn't at all tempted to laugh at him. His appearance was a *costume*, a way of deflecting attention from the true, dangerous self that reached out from him invisibly to manipulate the world around us. This hipster douchebag magician had brought—or was bringing—the Other World into the conference room with him. The sound of flooding rivers thundered through my sensorium, but no longer made me dizzy. Travel, it seems, is broadening. I swayed a bit, but stayed centered inside.

The hipster addressed himself to the lawyer who'd brought him into the room. "I don't know what this guy's been telling you," he said, "but he has *elf-stink* all over him."

Daniel thought: *He's bluffing. Dude hasn't mastered the reading of thoughts. He's playing another game here.*

Taking offense the way Quincy would, I addressed myself to the skeptical lawyer. "You brought this fella in to *insult* me? I have no time for fantasists."

"Oh, Mr. August," the lawyer purred, "*this* is no fantasist, I assure you."

Still staring at me as if he could see my inmost thoughts, the hipster magician began to speak, and I learned that I was wrong about the language of dreams. It *did* work on Earth when it was used to invoke the Old Gods—and when those gods came riding upon the invocation from the Other World. The room became a Nexus connecting that world to Earth.

Like the rush of air that precedes a subway train into a station, the sense of the god's and goddess' arrival filled the conference room. The *spiritual space*, call it, became so overwhelming that it fairly intoxicated all of Quincy's lawyers. A room full of drunken lawyers would have been kind of funny, but I was too preoccupied to laugh.

In the language of dreams, the young magician in the silly clothes addressed himself to Myra. "You have been derelict in your duty, Captain," he said. "You *helped* this man escape the god and goddess. Bring *Jerome* August back to the Shining City and redeem yourself."

So as not to alarm anyone, I stood up from the table very slowly, like a man taking a stretch after sitting still too long. I kept most of my attention on the magician, but I took a quick look at Myra. What would she do? She'd been trained to follow orders from her chain of command without hesitation. I saw her wondering why she should follow this guy's orders and act against me, the man she believed to be her employer.

More to the point, what should *I* do? I wondered. Once the language of dreams rushed into the conference room, it severed the mental connection to Daniel with a snap or a click. One minute I'd felt his presence, the next second it was gone, as if one of us had hung up the phone or the network had dropped the call. Can you hear me now? Nope, no bars, no signal.

I had no sense of any mind but my own. My only ally in this room was the guidance I'd had in the Other World, intuition. Elf-enhanced, but still.

The magician stayed where he was on the other side of the table. He kept talking and talking, rippling words, flowing sentences, entire coherent paragraphs, bringing the laws of the Other World to bear in this time and place. I sensed *a being* behind and above him. And behind and above that being were other, fainter beings, like a series of Russian nesting dolls. So many faces. There were Quincy and Pepsi, (both furious with me and thirsting for revenge), along with many others I did not know, all talking and talking the language of dreams in unison, working the magic that came from erasing the ordinary wall between subject and object. The magic that came from union with the god and goddess and with the Other World they had fashioned around themselves.

And I wondered: Had the Old Gods made that world from the uncounted thousands of worshipers they'd absorbed?

Word not different from thing. Perceiver not different from perceived. Self not different from world. *Numinous* equations that worked differently in the world of the god and goddess than they did on Earth. That mystical participation in the *wholly other* was coming to Earth.

As if in slow motion (was that slowness an artifact of my accelerated mental state?), Myra turned toward me to do the magician's bidding as the language of dreams opened her eyes. She saw that the man occupying Jerry August's body was Jerry himself, not Quincy.

Gulp.

56

Brenda Lee Sings "All Alone Am I"

A physical fight is a lot like crossing a busy street, or maybe like running across a six-lane interstate highway. Abandon the idea that you'll ever be safe again and deal with each immediate threat. Set your intention to get to the other side. You have to keep moving toward the goal while you avoid getting injured or killed. You have to get there before you're so exhausted from dodging traffic that a random car takes you out.

The bad news was that Myra was a stronger, more experienced fighter than I was. The good news was that she'd been ordered to take me back to her world, not to kill me. The bad news was that she'd injure or cripple me to follow that order. The good news was that her style of combat was very direct and relied on linear physical strength. She knew far less about the inner energy than I did.

Myra tried to grapple and bring her strength to bear on me. I used what Aimee had taught me to deflect and redirect each of Myra's attempts. She knew enough to block anything that looked like a physical blow, though, so there we were in the midst of traffic, smacking and grasping at each other while punch-drunk lawyers goggled at us from their cushy chairs with no idea what they were looking at.

I moved toward the hall door.

Myra moved to intercept me.

She kicked at my knee.

I moved aside and struck her kneecap with both palm heels.

Her leg buckled and she fell against the table.

I wrenched the door open.

Ignoring the pain, Myra got both feet under her and threw herself at the door, slamming it shut.

The magician walked around to my side of the conference table at an unhurried pace. Not even for a moment did he stop speaking the language of dreams, but his attention was on me, not on his words. The atmosphere congealing in this Washington office building felt as turbulent as when Leda was stolen away (so long ago) on Thanksgiving Day at Odiorne Point. A confluence as of mighty rivers roiled the air around me.

With the conference room becoming a Nexus, I had to get out that door before I got pulled into the Other World. Myra was more than capable of keeping me in the room single-handed; all she had to do was wear me down. And here came the hipster Materialist Magician slouching toward the fray, speaking the magic words that cut my mind off from communication with every source of help...

...except whatever it was that had awakened inside me. Whatever was so far beyond words that I had to translate its guidance into words out of the images it sent me.

What should I do? I asked. Images came.

[At my urging, the Red Sea parts, that I might escape the oppressor.]

[In the desert a burning bush speaks to me for the source of all life.]

What could I do? I put my attention in the center of myself and surrendered to whatever it was, beyond thought and judgment, that guided me as to when and how to move. Words came to me, not in the language of dreams, but in English. I moved toward Myra and the magician as the inner impulse prompted: (move, strike, move, elide, redirect, feint, strike, push, pull, deflect, step, slide). What came out of my mouth while I did what was before me to do were the words Abraham Lincoln spoke in 1865:

With malice toward none, with charity for all, with firmness in the right as God gives us to see the right, let us strive on to finish the work we are in, to bind up the nation's wounds, to care for him who shall have borne the battle and for his widow and his orphan, to do all which may achieve and cherish a just and lasting peace among ourselves and with all nations.

It startled the magician to hear me speaking English without inhibition. He'd counted on my following him into the language of dreams where he had all the leverage. Perhaps he'd never encountered resistance to his magic or to his will before. It made him petulant and hesitant. Or was it simply the word "God" that made him flinch?

Myra had never heard Lincoln's words before. She may have thought they were some sort of priestcraft or magic. She also hesitated.

Lincoln's words created a sandbar of calm where I could stand amidst that confluence of mighty Other-World rivers. Paradoxical ripples reached out from me, flowing from the ocean that births all worlds and all beings. From my own unsuspected depths I cried out.

In answer, Mary materialized at my side.

57

Lynyrd Skynyrd Sings "Gimme Three Steps"

Sometimes good guys wear black; elves often do. I'd met enough elves to recognize what my Myrmidon friend had become.

Mary grinned at me. "You did great, Jerry. I'll take it from here." Murmuring words of power in the language of the next world over, she waded into the fight. Without apparent exertion, she moved Myra and the magician away from us. Myra drew her pistol; Mary stripped it away from her. The weapon went spinning under the table. Myra fell back. The magician pulled some sort of wavy-bladed fantasy knife from inside his suit. What a tool. Mary slapped the knife out of his hand. Wincing as much from the words Mary spoke as from his stinging wrist, he skittered back away from her flashing hands.

The final outcome of the fight was far from certain. I still had no sense of mental contact with Mary. The magician continued speaking the language of dreams. Other-Worldly power bore down on the room.

As the process he'd initiated unfurled, the hipster magician's face began to change. (The sense of nesting dolls, one inside another.) There was Uncle Q's head atop a body that was not his own. And behind Q was the winged god from the Other World. The god who had been the power behind so much destruction watched me from far behind the scenes, from one of the circling orbs in that astonishing purple Other-

World sky. Watched me with *approval* at whatever I was embarked upon (it remained mysterious to me), watched with great interest to see what I might do about the mighty rivers of power that flowed at the very heart of himself and his goddess.

As if Quincy and Pepsi were merely incidental to the relationship Leda and I had innocently forged with those ancient beings during our time in the Other World.

But in the forefront of all those aligned faces and beings there was Q glowering at me out of the magician's face. I wondered why he hated me so much. I mean, apart from the fact that I'd somehow denied *him* life in a new human body by trying to save my life and Leda's.

Quincy's hatred, operating in and through the hipster magician, triggered a stupid tactical error. He stopped speaking the language of dreams through the magician's mouth and reverted to English, the better to taunt me.

"Think you're safe from me *on Earth*, Jewboy?" Quincy said. "You'll never be safe *anywhere*. Give it up and come back to the Other World so your aunt and I can finish what we started. We've already got your little slut. There's no hope for you."

Without the language of dreams to power it, the magician's spell wavered. I felt the touch of Mary's mind on mine, amused, focused, compassionate:

He's lying, Jerry. Now get your ass out of here. Go home—I'll see you there.

Mary hip-checked Myra away from the door—the same way Myra had hip-checked me into the Other World. Payback's a bitch. Not that I'd ever use that word to describe a Myrmidon.

I was out the door, into the hall, down the stairs, and out of the building in short order. Everybody in the District is always in a hurry. My focused core of energy deflected curiosity. Nobody noticed another driven, badly-rumpled, ordinary-looking man on a mission.

58

Tikkun Olam

I'd hoped I could persuade Quincy's lawyers I was Quincy.

What? With Daniel's help, it totally could've worked.

Okay, fine, it *was* a long shot.

If it *had* worked, I was hoping to persuade Quincy's criminal associates that I, Quincy, despite *appearing* to be my own much younger, leaner, shorter grandnephew, was now ready to climb back in the saddle and lead the bad guys. They'd think we were about to ride the American republic into the ground in the sacred name of Ayn Rand and the Austrian School of Cowboy Economics. *Yahoo, kleptocracy! Kew! Kew! Kew!* In reality, the good guys and I would be collecting evidence we could take to the media and to the Justice Department.

But no battle plan survives first contact with the enemy; my vague hopes certainly hadn't. The Materialist Magician was kind of a wild card. Now I had a better idea what kind of evil-doers I—we—were up against. But I didn't want to go home before I—and the people I'd dragged into this mess—figured out how to respond. If the good guys didn't work together, the bad guys would just pick us off one by one. Given the level of resources and political access arrayed against us, arrest, prison, and even Guantánamo were not out of the question.

Don't get me wrong. All my heart wanted was to get back to Leda in

Portsmouth and hold her close. But both my head and my heart knew it would be dishonorable to abandon my friends here in Washington.

A few blocks away from the law firm's office building, I waved down a gypsy cab, the kind that keeps no records and reports to no dispatcher. After a bit of haggling, I agreed on a price with the driver. He'd have been suspicious if I didn't haggle.

He dropped me off in Suitland at the Chinese restaurant where we'd done our battle planning. I guess it really was one more battle in a long war.

A well-dressed woman I didn't recognize stood at the host station just inside the restaurant's front door. She recognized *me*, though. She held up a finger: *Wait a minute*, and disappeared through an interior door. She returned with an Asian guy who was obviously her boss. I'd barely noticed him the first time I was here, but he remembered me. A good memory for faces is probably an occupational requirement for spies—and a matter of survival.

The host beckoned me to follow him and led me back toward the empty function room. After the fight with Myra and the magician, I looked rather the worse for wear. My shirt was ripped under my necktie and my suit coat had lost buttons and loosened a shoulder seam. My dress shoes were all scuffed up. My face felt bruised, my knuckles were abraded, and my hands and ribs ached. I'd feel even worse tonight after all the adrenaline wore off.

The guy looked me over and shook his head sympathetically. "Bad business," he said.

He knew, then, or at least he knew something about what was happening here in Washington. He and Trevor would have traded information and favors. The Chinese, I now remembered, had been involved with the elves since the 1980s. With political factions that worked for or against the elves, the same as in the American government.

"*He who is in battle slain can never rise to fight again*," I said.

He grinned at me. "That's the spirit."

He left me at the door of the function room. Inside, I found Trevor,

Bob, and Max, but not Daniel.

Daniel had tried to send him home, but Steve was there, too. "Idiot," he said, but he had a big smile on his face. He got up and hugged me.

I hugged my fellow idiot back. "Is that your considered legal opinion?" I said. "I'm glad to see you, too, brother."

We all sat down at one table and, as best we could, hashed out who would do what. Steve taught me the Hebrew words *tikkun olam*: healing or repairing the world. Less grandly, I guess you do what you can to figure out what would make a bad situation better. Steve trusted his rabbi. I trusted the elves.

After this second meeting, Steve and I rode back to Portsmouth with an Elf Friend who took no toll roads, hoping to avoid surveillance cameras. The Elf Friend dropped Steve off near one mall, then left me near another. I imagine Steve called his wife to come pick him up.

Naturally, I called Leda.

59

Freddy Fender Sings "Wasted Days and Wasted Nights"

Nobody expects reality to be soft and fuzzy like a kid's stuffed animal collection. We don't expect life to be barbed and prickly like a cactus garden, either. Neither Leda nor I had unrealistic expectations about our little lives in the world. Now even those modest hopes and dreams seemed as unattainable as interstellar flight.

And this was the origin of our second fight, not really much of a fight at all, and actually a continuation of our first non-fight. Whether we would grasp the nettle and do the difficult thing. How much we would mourn the life that started with our first kiss and our first embrace, the life the Other World had taken away from us. How much we would rage against the dying of the light of everything familiar.

We sat on the edge of my neatly-made bed. The world might be crumbling around us, but I felt no need to live like a rat in a bowling alley. As long as I lived here, the bed would get made and the dishes would get washed. Our tears had dried. We felt the ache in each other's hearts. Leda and I were more alike inside than appearances would suggest.

"Dammit, Jerry," she said, "I just want to make a life with you. Have a lot of sex. Go to work. Have a career. Take vacations together. Have kids someday." She looked around my bedroom. "More than any of that, I want to live with you, buy you a new couch and paint these pastel puke-green walls any other color at all."

She made me smile. *That's my brave girl*, I thought. "I know, babe. I want all that, too." I didn't insult her by pointing out that we could still have many of those good things. We just couldn't have them in Portsmouth. If Quincy had told the truth through the hipster magician's mouth, we probably couldn't even have those things on Earth.

I heard her thoughts: *It's so unfair. Why me? Why us?*

I thought back: *Sometimes war just finds people. We're not exactly innocent civilians anymore.*

"Well," she said aloud, "we can't stay here, can we?"

"Would you like me to sing 'There's a Place for Us' from *West Side Story*?"

Leda started laughing and crying again at the same time. She hugged me hard. "You are such a *shit*," she said. "I love you so much."

I hugged her back. "There's *nothing* like a good shit," I said. "Maybe even more essential than the musical theater. I love you, too, by the way."

We were both mostly laughing. If you don't think poop jokes and musicals are funny, I don't know what to tell you.

"I'll miss my family," Leda said. "Even the relatives I don't like. I'll miss my friends. I'll miss most of the people I work with."

"I'd hate to do anything that would send the bad guys after anybody else," I said. "We'll probably have to touch base with friends and family, um, *later*."

She looked at me in feigned bewilderment. "And not even update *Facebook?!*"

I stopped talking abruptly. Dread struck my mind like a gong and reverberated in Leda's: the imminent arrival of something unwanted. No time to lose. We were no longer alone in the house that was going to be *our* house.

"Oh, crap," I said, "it's the Eye of Sauron again. We're not even safe in our own bedroom."

"I thought it was *me* at first," Leda said. "It's very handy being able to check my perceptions against yours. Also you'll never be able to cheat on me."

"Wouldn't think of it, sweetie," I said, grabbing her hand and leading her out the door. "Can we get out of here before the bad guys come calling in person?"

At least I won't have to repaint my bedroom, I thought. *I hate painting.*

I love how you always look on the bright side, thought Leda.

Neither of us took the time to call our employers. We're not stupid.

I did take the time to lock the door on the way out. You never know.

60

Eddie Money Sings "Walk on Water"

Sails on the sea-swell,
Ghosts on the grey wave,
Drift past the eye's pledge,
Dip at the sky's edge;
Gone, while the gulls grieve.
Gone. Hear the sea-knell.

- (Robert G. Tucker, "Sea Poem")

It was early on a weekday morning. Cold and damp, thanks to the Atlantic Ocean and the Labrador Current. The sun was up, but we couldn't see or feel it. We saw a few adults walking out of the state park as we were walking in, then nobody else. Our nerves were on edge. We would have noticed anyone who looked like a threat.

Exhausted and chilled, Leda and I stood alone on a huge chunk of granite at the end of the Odiorne Point breakwater. The same place where one cold, dark November night I stood shivering, holding winter coats and watching Aimee Amory lead an old couple across the water and into the next world over. What I'd seen still seemed impossible.

But on the other hand: the Other World.

I wondered how Leda's friends were doing now that they weren't just Elf Friends, but the real deal. I hoped they were doing better than me. I was scared sick.

Before I'd even driven past the cemetery, we were talking to Daniel and Aimee mind-to-mind. We swallowed our pride and asked for help. Our friends were happy we'd finally asked. They told us to meet them here.

Gulp.

The obstacle to *accepting* that help was in Leda and me. It was the wall we all build around our ordinary selves to protect us from the miraculous.

Some who want to visit those we call elves simply *go with them*. They enter the next world over in a flashing instant, like Max did when he took Daniel's hand—and trusted Daniel with his life. The thought of giving up control like that made me sweat. I've never been a leap-of-faith kind of guy.

Peter Brown had offered to take us to safety, and we'd turned him down. Months later, we were smart enough to know we *had* to make the trip, but we were still less trusting than Max. We were reluctant travelers, refugees. It felt like we were throwing away ... *everything*. The only way we could bring ourselves to approach that other, better world was to walk there on the surface of the sea. Even to save our lives, we'd have to go under our own power, at our own pace. With magical assistance, sure. The elves would meet us where we were and help us get past our fear. Free will and all that. They were the good guys.

So where were the bad guys this raw, stinging morning? It seemed they couldn't fix their perception on us after we drove away from my house. Now that we were standing still and waiting, we felt a sense of impending heavy weather once again. Was it just the barometer dropping? The weatherman on my car radio breathlessly predicted thundersnow today. Clouds massed above us, very melodramatic, gothic, and corny. But the bad guys really wanted to take our bodies and our lives away from us, didn't they? They'd failed once, but felt entitled to keep trying. They knew where we were; they'd be coming for us, were probably already on their way. They didn't worry much about free will.

And here came the good guys, walking toward us out of the morning sea mist. We spotted their tiny figures in the distance and saw the towering mass of the Invisible Mountain behind them, as if the Mountain had also just appeared.

I won't lie, my heart leaped up when I saw them. Then my heart sank. I felt both my own uncertainty and Leda's.

"Are you as scared as I am?" I said.

"Yeah, and it's making me *horny*," she said. "I want to do things on this breakwater that would make you lose all respect for me. For example, I'm thinking I should show you my breasts right now, right here in front of God and everybody. You know, maybe just to see if you still *like* them?" She pointed her chest at me to be sure I understood what she meant.

Frightened as I was, she made me smile. "I've never respected you more," I said. "I've never *wanted* you more, either." I wasn't lying; something was *happening* to us. I directed my thought at her: *Remember what we did in the Other World, how we joined our minds together? I think maybe we should do that again and keep our clothes on. Just for now.*

The thought became the deed. Our energy centers lit each other up. At least today we could hold hands. She felt so warm. Whatever may be wrong in the world, it's wonderful to love and be loved. A very good thing, indeed.

Daniel and Aimee got closer, footsteps barely dimpling the water. In their minds, they saw us following our own best instincts, our intuition. Their smiles said we were doing the right thing.

Some things you only learn in the moment. Having free will meant Leda and I couldn't wait passively for our friends to save us. We had to *act* to reach the only safe place in all the human worlds. We had to work from the most essential part of our being. We had to follow our intuition to its source.

To put it another way, it's easy to think love is just sex, easy to stop with sex when love is what you also need. Body and mind are good things, maybe, but not the best things; they point to something beyond themselves.

Leda and I shone upon each other. We entered the bridal chamber of the heart where the Song of Songs is sung, where lovers find each other always new, desiring and desired.

Oh, my God, Jerry.

Oh, my God, Leda.

Daniel and Aimee climbed up onto the breakwater. Aimee took my hand, I held Leda's, and Daniel took Leda's other hand. The light from the next world over linked up with the light inside Leda and me. Why would it not? It was the same light. We were welcome to it, welcomed into it.

A hush enveloped us; there was no need to speak. We all stepped off the stone ... and onto the river. Sharp smells of seaweed and salt struck me. A cold wind. Still a bit of fear there; we were only human. I wondered distantly if we'd sink, but no. The words Aimee and Daniel murmured focused their energy—and ours—on the seawater under our feet, turning it yielding but solid enough to walk on, step by step.

You're doing fine, thought Daniel to Leda and me.

I'm so happy for you, Aimee thought.

With each step, we walked further out of our ordinary minds. It was hard to turn thought into English words, but I needed to express my gratitude for this unexpected happiness. *This is how it's supposed to be, isn't it?* I thought to Leda and to our friends. I meant life itself, and they knew what I meant. *This is what it's all about,* I thought. I suppose that's what every stoner thinks when the first blast of marijuana passes the blood-brain barrier. You have only my word that this was different.

Remember this connection, Daniel thought. *Whatever happens, hold tight to each other, hand to hand, mind to mind.*

That sounds like a warning, I thought. Or *did you just pronounce us husband and wife?*

Daniel smiled, but Aimee pointed south out into the open water. *Uh-oh,* she thought.

A distant dot sped in our direction. A small boat. It would intercept us before we reached the lower slopes of the Invisible Mountain. With elvish help, Leda and I could walk on water, but we couldn't run on or above it the way Aimee and Daniel certainly could—if they didn't have us to shepherd.

Uh-oh, indeed.

High above us, the clouds congealed as if they were made of something thicker than water vapor. Light grew brighter inside the cloud, quite unlike a lightning flash. I heard the sound of mighty rivers in the air as they rushed toward the sea. Unseen rivers converged. The Nexus between Earth and the Other World was coming for us.

The speedboat held its course, spraying a tall rooster tail of wake. It was no coincidence, not here outside the shipping lanes on a cold day before the proper start of New Hampshire's brief boating season. Nobody goes pleasure boating when it's still painful to be out on the water and even tough old lobster fishermen keep their survival suits handy.

No, Leda and I were the target. The question was, what could we do about it out here on the water? We loved Daniel and Aimee, but we weren't able to trust them with our lives. We couldn't enter the next world over directly, like Mary and Max both had.

We wanted to go to the Invisible Mountain, but we had to walk there. We could only approach its strangeness gradually in our own familiar bodies.

We knew the Mountain was there. We saw it whenever the mist parted.

I recognized what was happening because it had happened to me before. Through a sudden break in the cloud cover I saw again the rich, dark, predawn purple ... *firmament* of the Other World.

Hold on to me, I thought to Leda. *You're going to feel stoned, but you're not. You and me, babe, mind to mind, heart to heart.* Wordlessly she agreed.

Our thoughts wanted to float like the stars or planets we saw high overhead, swirling in their stately courses high in the heavens.

Everywhere we looked above us was beautiful as a Van Gogh painting. Beautiful but dangerous. We didn't stop walking to gawk. Aimee and Daniel exchanged an unbroken stream of Elvish, the language in which only truth is possible, a sure defense against illusion and evil. But what we saw was no illusion; it was the actual sky of the Other World. Beautiful, morally neutral, but not evil.

As the boat drew closer, I caught a first glimpse of the winged god and the goddess high in the clouds. In the Other World they'd descended toward their altars as if on invisible stairs. Here on Earth they plummeted toward us like raptors determined not to let their prey escape a second time.

You're right, Leda thought, *I do feel stoned.*

It's their ... anesthesia, Daniel thought. Along with the words came a complex and bitter sense of what the man had suffered inside another Old God deep beneath another human world. He was the right man in the right place today. I wondered what this mission to Earth would cost him.

Aimee looked at Daniel sharply, wondering the same thing. At this point, none of us had any secrets.

How do they live like this? I thought to Aimee.

She knew what I meant. *They're ... transparent all the time,* she thought back. She meant not only Daniel and Aimee, but all the people of the next world over. The world we weren't ready for. The world we could enter only by walking the gently-sloping foothills of the Invisible Mountain.

The Mountain we'd never reach before our enemies intercepted us.

Accepting the reality before them, Daniel and Aimee conferred in Elvish and in images. We changed course slightly to the north. We couldn't get to the Invisible Mountain ahead of the bad guys, not at our walking pace on top of the water. But there was an islet of tumbled rocks poking up out of the ocean. It was covered with algae and seaweed. Waves slapped gently against it.

It wasn't much, but it was the only place to make a stand. Daniel and Aimee hurried us along toward the rocks as fast as we could go.

61

The Island of Doctor Moreau

An altar is erected in between two separate people, on which each seeks to kill his self, and on his body raise another self to take its power from his death. Over and over and over this ritual is enacted. And it is never completed, nor ever will be completed. The ritual of completion cannot complete, for life arises not from death, nor Heaven from hell.

- (*A Course in Miracles*)

On top of the little rockpile, the Coast Guard had set a marker to warn ships away from the underwater hazard. It was a red-and-black-banded pole, maybe thirty feet tall, with two black balls at the top. Bright lights flashed from it at regular intervals, too painful to look at. The four of us scrambled up onto relatively solid ground. Even slick rocks felt good under my feet. I wondered if I'd ever get used to the slippery, uncertain feeling of walking on water.

I wondered if I'd have to get used to being pursued by magicians and by my aunt and uncle doing business as bird gods from another world. I figured there probably wouldn't be time. We were between the devil and the deep blue sea this morning. I mean, the sea was all around the islet, and the magician's boat was close enough for us to see his contemptuous, unhappy face. And the god and goddess had dropped low enough for me to see traces of Quincy and Pepsi in their faces. Plenty of devils, then, and the vast gray-green Atlantic.

One way or another, things would sort themselves out in the next half hour. *Dans la vie tout s'arrange*, my father used to say, just one of the helpful phrases he'd acquired in Vietnam.

But being who I am, I had a stupid question. "I don't remember this island from the last time I was out here in a boat. Granted, that was years ago, but is this new?"

Daniel and Aimee shared a look with Leda: *Tsk, who wants to tell the idiot?*

Leda stepped up to the plate. "Jerry, most of the continental shelf is *gone*. It *fell away.* At the end of the last Portsmouth War, Daniel and Aimee saved the East Coast from the tsunami." She barely managed to keep pity for me out of her tone, but I felt it in her mind. She was thinking this was a bad time and place for me to go into denial.

I shook my head. How dense could I be? I'd read about this, too, how the two vaguely Asian-looking human beings who were trying to save us had shaped white magic using what they called the Unfallen Tongue to save the whole city and most of the Eastern Seaboard from a parade of massive rogue waves. I still had trouble believing that.

But on the other hand: water walking.

"Oh, so this island is what's left of the continental shelf?" I said. "How stable is it?"

Daniel's eyes went distant. I felt how his perception reached down and down into the ocean, right through the rocks we stood on next to the flashing danger marker. Then his mind returned from the deep places where my mind couldn't follow.

He grinned. "Not *entirely* stable. "We probably shouldn't tap dance up here."

Then, because our time was running short, what with the gods and the magician, I thought, *What should we do?*

Best possible question, Aimee thought.

Our thoughts flew back and forth in what I guess was the elf style. A consensus quickly emerged. *The best you can do is the best you can do*, we say in the IT world. Of course, we only say it behind the clients' backs.

So the god and goddess came down out of the sky on the god's lovely white wings to the islet. And the magician leaped nimbly off the bow of his boat while two large, unpleasant-looking men with machine pistols held the craft steady and glared at us. When all you have is a gun, everything starts to look like a target.

The bad guys had a battle plan. Killing Leda and me was not their objective. Not right away, at least, and not with bullets.

The god and goddess, we now noticed, were speaking, had been speaking for some time. We had not heard them because the four of us were linked in thought.

This speech was no mere conversation. The two Other-World deities exchanged calls and responses with the magician in the language of dreams. I felt the minds of Aimee and Daniel fall away from mine and from Leda's.

Leda and I, more intimately linked deep in our minds, watched as Daniel and Aimee began an ordinary conversation in Elvish. They spoke of their longing for warm weather and friendship with everyone in the simple beauty of the next world over. They spoke of grasslands and highlands, love's home country. The air around the four of us *lit up* with the Unfallen Tongue, and our four-way mind connection came back on line.

The good guys seek to bring people together. The bad guys seek to drive people apart. It was exactly that simple.

Two streams of language met. The god and goddess began looking less like their old selves, as I'd first seen them, and more like Quincy and Pepsi. My aunt and uncle looked *very* displeased with me. The language of dreams shaped the power of the Old Gods to express that displeasure. Hearing the Unfallen Tongue rocked the magician back a step, but he retreated no further. Streams of Other-World power supported him and he directed that power by *talking over* Daniel and Aimee.

There was a maelstrom of energy in play. It became too much for Daniel. Abruptly, he stopped speaking Elvish. He bent at the knees and took shallow, painful breaths as if he'd been punched in the solar plexus. The outline of his body began to waver as he stood back up. No, that's not quite right. Something half-seen began flickering around him like flames. *Is that his spirit?* I thought to Leda. *I think maybe it is*, she thought back.

Aimee continued to speak her wonderful language, but now directed her words to her husband: *Are you hurt? How can I help?*

Centered, grounded, but still outlined in clear light, Daniel looked at us and spoke in English. "Guys, I'm about to *fall out* of this body. I'm sorry I have to leave you now when you need me most." He vanished.

"You know what to do," Aimee told us. "Go deep. Look directly. Tell the truth. Love each other." Then she vanished, too.

62

Lorde Sings "Royals"

Often I would find myself entering those crypts, deep dug in the earth, with their walls on either side lined with the bodies of the dead, where everything was so dark that almost it seemed as though the Psalmist's words were fulfilled, Let them go down quick into Hell. Here and there the light, not entering in through windows, but filtering down from above through shafts, relieved the horror of the darkness. But again, as soon as you found yourself cautiously moving forward, the black night closed around and there came to my mind the line of Virgil, "On all sides round horror spread wide; the very silence breathed a terror on my soul."

- (Saint Jerome, *Commentarius in Ezzechielem*)

The elves left: *pop.* The light, cold East wind died. Little waves splashed at the rock of the islet. One of the armed thugs tied the boat's stern line around an upthrust black rock. The fiberglass hull bumped with a hollow sound against a chunk of bedrock that had once been down on the seafloor. Gulls flew inland below the gray clouds: storm coming? Leda and I held hands tightly and watched the world together in shared wordless mental rapport.

The Materialist Magician watched us closely, ready to attack with magic if the need arose. We could guess his thoughts from his sneer: *Beating you was too easy. Elves are nothing. Without elves to help, you are less than nothing.*

The false gods whom the magician served now stood on the rockpile before us. The god's wings folded back gracefully behind his broad shoulders. He was clad in white feathers, though he looked more man than bird. The goddess wore shining white raiment. They were in charge of this show.

Below the surface of their more-than-human faces, I saw the merely-human faces of Quincy and Pepsi, as if they swam on the underside of a sheet of ice. How did they breathe? I wondered. Were they running out of air? Did they even *have* to breathe?

I bowed my head courteously to those strange creatures and spoke to them in the language of dreams, the only words that wanted to come out of my mouth. "Welcome to Earth, O gods of the Other Land."

The god and goddess smiled regally at me and at Leda. They were perhaps a foot taller than us. It was hard to see them clearly, as if what our eyes reported and our minds understood wasn't exactly what was here on Earth before us.

The god looked at the goddess. They both looked at the world around them, the ocean behind us, the river and the land behind them, the gray sky above.

"It has been many and many a year since our feet have touched this world," said the god.

"Not that it matters what world we dwell in," said the goddess. She put her arm around the god's muscular waist. His arm and its wing encircled her shoulders. The two shared a smile.

They love each other, I thought to Leda in English, as the intuition struck me.

She thought back, *Then why do they kill people?*

Good question, I thought. *Ask them!*

"I see how deeply you love each other, O god and goddess," Leda said. She was compelled to speak the language of dreams, as I was. "Does your love require that you *kill* people in order to live? Does my love for Jerome matter so little that you would take our bodies from us?"

"Your people die and are forever extinguished, daughter, but *we* do not die," said the goddess. Her tone was chillingly kind. "Only those few we summon to share our power and our lives continue on—*in us.*"

"Yet you have absorbed the bodies of my aunt and uncle," I said.

"They *serve* us," said the god, as if that explained anything. "For a time we preserve their old bodies within ours. They will *continue* to serve us after we give your bodies to them."

"Your *[life force]* will then become part of ours," said the goddess. "The flesh of your aunt and uncle, first given to you, will then become part of our flesh. This is a great honor we bestow upon you, that you help us continue to live and manifest ourselves to those who worship us."

"And what of the child you tried to get on me against my will?" Leda said. "Do you not know that your children bring death by the thousands of thousands to both our worlds?"

"The lower exists only to serve the higher," said the god, as if patiently explaining the obvious to an idiot. To him and the goddess we had no permanent existence and therefore we had no lasting importance.

Oh, fuck you, is what Leda and I tried to say, but we never got the words out. The gods expanded into our physical space and *took it away from us.*

"Come now," said the god to me as he surrounded me.

"Come now," said the goddess to Leda as she engulfed her.

With those words which were the same as deeds, my hand was once again wrenched out of Leda's and her hand wrenched from mine. Unlike the Thanksgiving kidnapping, at least this time we were taken together.

As the magician and his henchmen kneeled on the wet rocks and reverently bowed their heads, Leda and I felt ourselves *summoned* into the universe of the god and goddess, like scarecrows sucked into twin tornadoes.

Subsumed mind and spirit, and for all I knew, body as well.

63

Jethro Tull Sings "Inside"

Leda...?

Swirling egoless silence and yearning half-thoughts struggled toward mine (wherever I was). Finally I heard: *Here. Oh, Jerry, I'm so scared. Where are we? I can't see you! I can't see anything.*

Use this. (My mind pictured the center of my body's mass, or where it would be if I could only feel it. You have to hold your tongue just right.) *Use your inner knowing. It's in the mind-space where we talk to each other and where we meet the elves.*

Ah...!

And there we were. We beheld ourselves as two ovoid shapes of light. We swayed together in the center of that fluid knowledge. We stood as still as light can stand on a sandbar miraculously intact amidst the confluence of mighty rivers. At least here the roaring waters went silent, although we felt their force.

Where then was the ocean? A question for later. Unless we were *in* the ocean, yet somehow absolved of all need to breathe. Together we touched the envelope of our new condition. Learning together, our two minds shared idea, perception, and memory as one mind.

As in Washington, the images returned to me; I shared them with Leda. Or: the vision came to both of us from a place within us both.

[We saw the Red Sea part so we might escape the oppressor.]

[In the midst of desert a burning bush spoke to us for the source of all life.]

The source that had created us, the fire that had sparked us into being. The source whose image shone in the settlements of light within us where the highest did not stand without the lowest and where every light shone upon and cherished the light in all the rest.

We were as much created in the divine image, Leda and I, as the first man and woman. We were two, we were one. The simple fact that was beyond our understanding was the basis of all understanding.

Aimee had told us: *Go deep. Look directly. Tell the truth. Love each other.*

We could not hold physical hands because the gods had separated us from the familiar feeling of our own bodies. But from deep in the center of our love where we were wed in our own free will we looked out upon the rest of creation. We looked directly and saw...

How Quincy and Pepsi sought to finish the ritual of completion they had begun in the Other World.

How the power of the gods upheld and supported my aunt and uncle somewhere between flesh and spirit.

Quincy's and Pepsi's complete ignorance of what Leda and I were— and of all we had come to know.

The utter arrogance of their belief that nothing we knew, were, or possessed meant anything except as it served their purposes.

False gods. Great power. No sane person prays to a nuclear reactor. If false gods did not exist, it would be necessary to invent them.

Holding to each other's minds, Leda and I dove deeper still. Faced with death, our lives reviewed themselves. *But wait, there's more!* Before this current birth, we had both lived other lives. Those lives also flashed by in review, and all the times in between one life and the next. *Now how much would you pay?*

Nothing in the past mattered as much as the here and now. When *here* was uncertain, all we had was *now.*

I love you, Leda.

I love you, Jerry.

As we had at our first physical encounter, we gave the gift of ourselves, unfelt body, mind, and spirit, too. *Whatever I am I give you. I'll see your you and give you me.*

Human love is a very good thing, but it's not the best thing.

It's a gateway to the best thing.

As Leda and I looked into ourselves, we saw also into the power of the god and goddess. How over uncounted millennia human greed for endless unchanged life had colored and misshapen that nonhuman power. To retain their forms, the Old Gods now *required* worship and propitiation. Under their mythic surface appearance, the flying gods were imprisoned with their devotees in the Other-World religion that had sprung up around them.

Would an impersonal power *need* to reproduce? No. That human need was projected on the god and goddess by those who sought their power.

Body-stealing required that the gods conceive a divine child out of human raw material. But the child was really neither fully divine nor fully human. The child grew like a thundercloud, unleashing the lightning of catastrophe, striking the innocent on Earth and on the Other World.

> *You purchase pain with all that joy can give,*
> *And die of nothing but a rage to live.*

When lightning struck, the cloud-child dispersed like a dream, but not before the demigod clawed immortal symbols out of the collective unconscious. The underworld symbols etched themselves into the flesh of dying human beings as they sculpted the stone of dying human cities. And all was soon covered by the lone and level sands. Again and again. How many times had this futile cycle pointlessly repeated itself?

In the Other World, civilization moved on, consolidating itself closer to the Shining City of the gods. On Earth, the population grew and grew, and new cities were built atop the ashes of the fallen. People forgot or denied what had happened, believing that they would go mad and destroy themselves if they faced the truth.

Go deep. Below where our ordinary minds danced and craved things was a place of no fear. The place all true guidance comes from, to lead us from our ordinary ephemeral lives to our true lives.

Look directly. We looked together. There are no words for what we saw.

Love each other. We saw where our human love came from. Where all love comes from. We saw that we loved each other more than words could express. We saw also *that we were loved.*

Tell the truth. The truth was too good not to share. How many lives would we have to live to finish sharing it with everyone? The truth was inexhaustible. It was embodied in paradox, things we knew, but which we did not understand.

Everyone dies, but everyone lives forever.

Everyone in a human body feels pain, but suffering is unnecessary.

Why not end the suffering? Why not have life and have it more abundantly?

We saw that the fight for survival was as nonsensical as sacrifice. Jean-Paul Herold had seen the same truth. At the root of all human experience there *was* only the one truth.

Leda and I chose to do the task before us as well as we could. Free will and all that.

Together we two embraced the best thing. And together we vowed to give this best thing to all the world. To give the gift of truth that brings peace.

Starting, if we could, with every being on the little rockpile where our bodies lay, insensate.

Like divers pushing off the sea bottom and returning to the surface, we came back up to a first tentative feeling of our human bodies. Those bodies—we—lay on slick black rocks surrounded by swirling clouds of the god and goddess. Our eyes, which is to say, the eyes of the body were closed, and yet we saw everything from outside those bodies. Saw it together.

How long have we been gone?

Doesn't matter, does it? We're back. Sort of.

I figured we hadn't been gone all that long. At a distance, the magician and his gunmen still knelt like the Three Magi, heads bowed respectfully.

Quincy, naked, slick, wrinkled, wet, and hairless as a newborn, distilled out of the bird god's side. Eww.

Blinking even under the overcast sky, Pepsi, equally bald, equally old, emerged naked from the side of the shining goddess. Ick.

You don't want to hear about the sound of their rebirth, if that's what it was.

My aunt and uncle crouched next to Leda and me where we lay side by side. Quincy beckoned to the magician.

"Bring your medical kit, Nurse Nancy," Quincy said to the magician.

Medical kit? I thought.

Ugh, Leda thought, *they want to take my IUD out. I'm not ready to have a kid with you. I'm not about to have a divine child for your aunt and uncle.*

The magician scowled, but did as he was told, rising to his feet. He pulled a folding leather surgical pack out of an inside coat pocket.

"Hey, Abbot and Costello," Quincy said to the two thugs, "get your asses over here and cut these kids' pants off." He meant Leda and me.

The thugs scowled menacingly, but also did as they were told. He who has the gold makes the rules. They holstered their machine pistols and drew ugly little boot knives.

♫ 6 4 ♫

Beyoncé Sings "Listen" from *Dreamgirls*

So the ritual of completion would be enacted upon Leda's body and mine here on this last, precarious piece of the vanished continental shelf. The transfer of soul-self would proceed from rape. It made me furious. We weren't fellow human beings to Quincy and Pepsi. To them our bodies were just *raw material* to be appropriated by the kleptocracy. We were *meat*.

Did they believe in our souls? If they did, they didn't act as if that mattered. They used magic, but all they cared about was matter. No wonder they'd teamed up with the Materialist Magicians.

Jerry, Leda thought, *I'd rather die than get fucked by a duck masquerading as a god—or by your uncle masquerading as a duck god.*

I'm with you, babe, I thought. I'm not letting Aunt Pepsi or the goddess, um, have their way with me.

Always the gentleman, she thought with an inner smile. *What do we do, then?*

The Invisible Mountain is somewhere out there to seaward. Let's swim for it.

That's your plan—swim for it? So sarcastic, my Leda.

Would you rather get raped again or drown trying to escape? Bad as the rape would be, it's just foreplay for something worse.

You have a point.

On the level of energy, Leda and I were aligned so closely that our physical eyes opened at the same time. For a moment I saw the world through her eyes and she saw through mine. It would have been dizzying, but we were already lying down. Did I mention that every breath brought us another wave of inner orgasm?

Yow! I thought.

No kidding, she thought back.

And away we go, we thought together.

We both rolled over onto one elbow (I felt her roll in unison with me), and scrambled to our feet. Quincy, Pepsi, the hipster magician, and the two gunmen were all momentarily startled to see supposedly comatose patients sprint down the sea side of the rocks, and dive into the cold, cold Atlantic.

Gimme Three Steps, I thought. We took deep breaths and swam below the surface of the water to give our enemies less of a target. They would be tempted to shoot us out of spite. Quincy and Pepsi needed us alive because they needed our bodies, but when spite and stupidity are well-armed, it's best to watch your ass.

I heard Quincy screaming on the islet. "No, you idiots, do *not* shoot them! You—Haircut—get the boat ready! Do I have to do everything myself? Did you at least bring clothes for me and Mrs. August? We're *freezing* on this rock!"

"Aaaaaaaah!" Pepsi's voice rose in a wordless scream of rage, as if she'd lost all human mentation and abandoned any pretense of being human. It was chilling.

Speaking of chilling, Leda and I felt our core body temperatures dropping. Not a good sign, given how much effort it took to keep breathing and to swim toward a mountain we hoped might be out there, but couldn't see. The mind and spirit have much to say about the body, though. Our travels to the Other World and the things we'd had to do to escape it had awakened us to what might be called the inner alchemy.

Banal as it sounds, we had our love to keep us warm. We encouraged that heat to suffuse us.

Our awareness focused in on ourselves, sure, but at the same time our spirits now saw further outside us. We heard the sound of the freezing ocean around us as we swam through it. Sharp sea salt burned our eyes and stung our nostrils like tears. We heard the sound of our breath as it entered and departed, the human body's constant converse with the air. Voices carried sharply over the water behind us. And we heard-and-felt the shining wordless presence of the god and goddess. They watched our efforts with great curiosity, but did not intervene. As if they didn't *know* where their interests lay.

All mystical knowledge aside, we hadn't swum far cocooned in the inner heat before we heard the speedboat start up behind us on the landward side of the islet.

Aimee's words came back to us: *Look directly.* We looked directly at our memory of walking on the water with Aimee and Daniel. We saw the deep place that ability came from. Aimee had spoken Elvish words which were unknown to us, but surely even words in the Unfallen Tongue were only a finger pointing into the sky and not the moon the finger pointed to.

Floating in the water, resting in the gentle waves (hearing the speedboat getting louder), between one breath and the next.

Stand up! Leda thought.

I held her hand and stood up, not worrying for the moment about how such a thing might be possible. The seawater seemed to push us up out of itself.

Now walk! I thought.

Holding my hand, Leda walked with me. It wasn't terribly different from walking on ice, careful step after careful step, upon a cushion of the energy that flowed through us into the world and through the world into us.

Wait, ice? I thought. *Let's skate!*

We began gliding across the surface of the ocean in great swoops. Faster and faster we skated. It was exhilarating. Our bodies warmed to the work, and there was a lovely sexual quality to the rhythmic movement.

Oh my God, Jerry, I am so wet right now.

Of course we were both soaked from the swim. Despite our speed, it was still water we were sliding on and naturally some splashed on us. *I am* begging *you not to make me laugh*, I thought. But I did laugh. I laughed for joy, and she laughed with me. We were so deep in this new wisdom that, even laughing, we stayed on top of the water.

Behind us or perhaps on the border of the mind state we occupied, we felt the god and goddess smile. They *approved* of us because our love mirrored theirs. Yet still there was neither help from them nor opposition.

652

Janet Jackson Sings "Go Deep"

The language of dreams created a kind of power-bubble around the rockpile. Once Leda and I got clear of it, we reached our minds out to seaward.

Like heat shimmer on a summer highway, there was the Invisible Mountain before us, still miles away in the distance. The speedboat was coming up fast behind us. Not exactly *The Great Escape*.

I kinda feel like despairing right now, Leda thought.

Can we at least make love first?

When did we stop making love?

She was right. The inner alchemy took our sexual energy and painted the world with it. *The heavens declare the glory of God*, I thought.

Yes, she thought. *Yes, they do.*

In finding each other this way, we'd discovered something about the human worlds and about their creation and our place in all that. Such a waste to learn something so wonderful, only to have our enemies snuff our lives out. Such a shame not to share this wonder with others. Life is so short; ours were ending too soon.

Two distant lights came toward us across the gray-green water from the Invisible Mountain under the low gray clouds: Daniel and Aimee?

The lights moved faster than we were able to skate on the swell. The lights moved almost as fast as the boat.

The speedboat throttled down so as not to hit us. The Materialist Magician's voice rose in the language of dreams to work the sad magic of separation once again. Perceiver not different from perceived. Self not different from other.

Inside the spheres of elflight, we saw Mary and Myra smiling happily at us.

The Myrmidons have come to our rescue, I thought.

They look different, Leda thought. *They're elves now, not just Myrmidons.*

I saw what she meant. First off, Myrmidons don't walk on water, duh. Also Myrmidons unquestioningly follow orders. Elves simply determine the right thing to do and then do it. I figured Mary had won Myra over to the good guys by bringing her to the next world over. They'd help us, even if it meant disobeying the Old Gods of the Other World.

There came a clash of languages on the ocean. The Unfallen Tongue, the language of the next world over, once again met the Other World's language of dreams. The god and goddess' language perfectly mirrored their thought-and-action. But the magician's knowledge of the language of dreams went no further than his desire to bend reality to his will. Mary and Myra had deep knowledge of the gods who had shaped them in utero; they had spoken the gods' dream-language all their lives. Now they also spoke the language of the elves, a deeper language still. They spoke the original human speech which conveys only truth.

Bit by bit, spell by spell, Elvish undid the illusion of separation as Myra and Mary spoke easily together. The magician barked out sentences, then phrases, then mere words and fragments of words, as his grip of the dream vocabulary faltered. Finally, he fell silent. He bent over, rocking and holding his ears: *la la la la la, can't hear you.*

Irresolute, the two gunmen stood in the speedboat. They had their weapons out, but didn't aim at anyone. They were waiting for orders. No orders came.

Quincy had forgotten about his troops. Like the magician, he struggled to remember the language of dreams to give him a weapon against his enemies. Myra and Mary's shining Elvish words lit up the air over the cold Atlantic. The very idea of power over others was revealed as a foolish mistake. Uncle Q opened his mouth a couple of times, but nothing came out of it. He left his mouth open, like one of those sad old wandering men you see gaping at a world they no longer understand.

Pepsi couldn't summon any language at all, even English. Her vacant expression said her mind had deserted her, poor woman. She was my sort-of aunt, after all, or had been. Did I mention she was as hairless as a Chihuahua? At least she had some clothes on now, men's oversize pants and shirt under a big pea coat with her bald head poking up out of the collar. Not her best look, I thought. Again she screeched like a bird. It wasn't chilling this time, just sad.

Quincy backhanded his wife across the face. She sat down hard in the bucket seat with a *woof* sound. Possibly the ugliest thing I'd seen today.

"You're no gentleman, Quincy," I said.

"Neither are you, Jewboy," Quincy said, "despite all your pretensions."

"What is this 'Jew' business?" Mary said. "How could a religion be an insult?"

"Kind of a long story, honey," Leda said. "By the way, are those your gods coming up behind the boat?"

6 6

Someone was here to see you. With a bill? No, just a regular nose.

Leda saw the Old Gods before I did. Sure enough, here they came walking toward us just above the surface of the water. The god had no need to deploy his wings. Nor did he and his mate comport themselves according to the laws of Earth physics. They cast no reflections on the water beneath their feet.

The god and goddess approached the speedboat where the magician cowered and the two gunmen kneeled. Leda and I felt their unvarying presence in our minds. We felt the gods as a loud soundless sound or as a light that dazzled without illuminating. They meant us no harm, approved of us, even, but there was something *withering* about their mere proximity. Their presence was intoxicating because it was literally toxic.

Mary stood by Leda and me atop the water and effortlessly bolstered our fledgling waterwalking with an occasional shining whispered word of Elvish. She looked directly at the god and goddess. Her expression as she observed the divine couple was not angry, not sad, not frightened or overawed, but *resolute*.

She never took her eyes off the nameless god and goddess, and she finally answered Leda's question. "Not my gods, no. And not Myra's, either, I think."

"Not anymore," Myra said. "*Our service to you is at an end, O gods,*" she called to the shining bird god and his mate. "*We are your Myrmidons no more.*" That was the sense I retained from the Elvish.

WE THANK YOU FOR YOUR SERVICE [Myra] AND [Mary], came the twinned thought from the gods. The thought came in whole concepts and in images which simply *arrived* in our human minds. I experienced the thought as if it swam up from the depths of my own inner knowing.

WE FIND WE HAVE NO FURTHER NEED OF SERVANTS, thought the god.

WE FIND WE HAVE NO FURTHER SERVANTS, thought the goddess wryly—EITHER IN [the Other World] OR ON [Earth]. She and her husband shared a smile. Odd how human they acted. Odd how nonhuman they seemed.

Thought pictures also flashed to me and Leda from the two new elves. How Mary had persuaded Myra to travel with her to the next world over. How the two of them had returned to the Other World and persuaded others that there might be a better way to live—and a better world. How those new elves soon returned on a recruiting drive. At the end of this elvish chain reaction, only a stubborn few aristocrats and no Myrmidons were left to the god and goddess.

The Old Gods talked on—or thought—for quite some time. Myra and Mary got answers to their questions, as did Leda and I. Well, the gods *thought* they were giving us answers, but I didn't always understand what they meant. The touch of their minds showed us how very different they were from us. Still sentient beings, sure, but differently embodied. They were both more than human and less. They were more immortal than we, but somehow also less.

Look, I know what I know about the Other World god and goddess. I don't claim to *understand* this knowledge. Once they saw how things were going in their world, the gods said, they'd commissioned a parting gift there for Leda and me. I didn't understand that, either. Not till later.

Leda, the elves, and I and talked with the god and goddess. Quincy and Pepsi slumped in their seats in the boat in a kind of torpor. The two gunmen simply passed out. The Materialist Magician rocked back and forth muttering spells, trying to work some sort of magic to turn back the overwhelming tide of reality rolling into him. Dark streaks ran down his face and dripped off his chin with his tears. Dude should have used waterproof mascara. Finally he too slumped over in a coma of denial. It was too much unwanted information for all of them. It was almost too much for me.

There being no further business, old or new, on the agenda, the god and goddess bade farewell to Earth and to us. They walked, or flew, back up into the sky and were lost to view. Who knew where such creatures would go and what they would do? Really, they needed nothing. What, in addition to each other's company, did they want?

As the gods walked or flew upwards, they grew larger. Thousands and thousands of shimmering lights departed from their huge, cloudy forms. The lights flew away like birds, but silent.

Those lights are the spirits of those who sacrificed themselves to the god and goddess over all the ages, thought Mary.

Men, women, and Myrmidons, thought Myra. *They're free now to go on to whatever is next for them.*

If such a god and goddess did exist, it would be necessary to uninvent them, I thought. Nobody argued with me.

Myra piloted the boat back to shore. Her job as Quincy's assistant was to get her nominal employer and his wife safely back home. I didn't worry about her ability to handle the magician and his men.

Mary escorted Leda and me, not to my rented house across from the cemetery, but to her new home and ours, where there were no cemeteries. Together the three of us walked across miles of yielding water and at last stepped onto solid ground, the gradual foothills of the Invisible Mountain.

We were finally ready now. We were more than ready.

67

Good Grief, *Another* Child's Birthday in Portsmouth

A few months later as time flows on Earth, Leda and I went to Chicago to meet her family. Leda's brother saw the world in terms of challenges to his ego, status, and manliness. *Do you even lift, bro?* I didn't—and don't—look like much of a threat, so he managed to be civil.

Leda's mother thought a pretty girl like her daughter could do better than a mutt like me. Mrs. Clayton also speculated about my race and ethnicity: was Jerry August just *tan* or was he *a person of color?* What color would the *grandchildren* be? What prejudices would they face? She was too polite to verbalize any of this pearl-clutching, but I saw it in her thoughts. Reading people's minds happened more and more often on Earth since we'd hiked into the next world over with Mary.

I guess that meeting went as well as it could go. Mrs. Clayton made a point of *not* asking about our engagement or wedding plans. She hoped Leda would find somebody taller and ... more *suitable*. Leda didn't have the heart to tell her that we were already thoroughly married. That in the green pastures of the world of the elves Daniel and Aimee had blessed the marriage that we'd first entered in our hearts and minds on the altars of the Old Gods of the Other World.

At Phyllis' house back in Portsmouth, my family embraced Leda immediately. They loved the way she dived in and helped serve food, shepherd children, clean up spills, and so on.

"She's lovely, Jerry," Phyllis said in the midst of the chaos. "So exotic! She almost looks Chinese till you look a little closer. And you both look so *tan!* Have you been on vacation?"

Before I could formulate either a truthful answer or an evasion, a minor incident of child-on-child aggression pulled Phyllis away.

That's life on Earth, I thought to Leda. *Everybody has questions, but they're too distracted to hear the answers.*

Leda was rinsing dishes in the sink and stacking them in the dishwasher, but of course she caught my thought. She thought back, *Did you tell them about the money?*

As it happened, I didn't get around to that conversation with Phyllis or any of the other cousins. Instead, I floated around the house and told all the adults to expect a good-news phone call from Steve, my lawyer. I told them they'd be invited to a meeting regarding the estate of the late Quincy and Pepsi August. I didn't tell them I wouldn't be there; that didn't really matter.

After our odd little conference around the magician's boat, Myra had piloted the craft back to a marina south of Portsmouth. She'd left the magician and his gunmen still unconscious in the boat, asked the harbormaster to call the police, and driven Quincy and Pepsi back to their mansion.

When the police arrived at the August mansion, they found Quincy and Pepsi tottering around in reasonable health, but not altogether lucid. They didn't refuse to answer questions, exactly, but they didn't comprehend what they were being asked.

My aunt and uncle had abandoned all hope. They had no faith and no love left, not for each other and not for themselves. Myra offered them passage to the next world over, but they would accept no help from the hired help, neither transport nor teaching nor healing. If they couldn't have their own way, they would have nothing. They'd embraced the self-destructive, fascist nihilism of the very rich. Myra watched over them and nursed them for the few days it took their stout old hearts to stop beating.

"They died in their sleep," she told the police when they showed up at the mansion the second time. The medical examiner confirmed it. Cause of death: *failure to thrive.*

Shortly thereafter, two federal officers rang the bell at Quincy's mansion. Imagine their surprise when the door was answered not just by Myra, but by Miracle Max and Steve, their attorney. These were the same guys who'd visited Max in Washington; Steve had met them in Portsmouth when I brought Leda home. They still weren't exactly who their credentials said they were. The sketchy feds had hoped to interrogate Myra about what, exactly, had happened out there on the ocean. They left unsatisfied. They'd already gotten Max fired, and they had no leverage on anybody else. Things were falling apart in their world. If one of their dangerous Materialist Magician assets had gone missing, it was damage control time.

Quincy's will named me as his heir. He'd expected to *be* me, remember? Or at least to look exactly like me because the Old Gods had managed to incarnate his soul in my body.

Of course there was a huge legal foofaraw about all this. Quincy's Washington law firm and the August Association's silent partners represented the bad guys. Steve and the Elf Friends' Boston law firm represented the good guys. Long story short, the good guys won. The bad guys wisely chose to cut their losses and settle out of court.

Leda and I had this huge fortune, but being who we were, we didn't need money anymore, or not much. So how could we do good with those billions, undo the bad that Quincy had done, and prevent the bad he'd tried to do?

Long story short again, Trevor, Max, and Bob were on it. Nobody was going to be deliberately crashing the global economy on their watch. Quincy had bought Bob's company to execute a massive economic hijacking. Let's just say that the word went out through channels official and unofficial that certain *safeguards* were now in place to make that kind of theft impossible.

Word also went out that the names of those in government and in the private sector who had colluded in this coup attempt were now known and would be released along with all the supporting documentation—should the American surveillance state further exceed its Constitutional bounds. You've seen the news lately, so you know what I'm talking about.

Elves are all about fire control: minimum force for maximum effect. They could rule the world, but why would they want to? Free will, remember?

Leda and I said our goodbyes to my family. Thanks to trust funds Quincy had never intended, my relatives would be comfortable. If their kids had any brains, they'd be able to go to college or tech school.

My wife and I walked to the little patch of woods where Quincy and I had seen the flying god—and the god had seen me. I shared that experience with Leda mind-to-mind as we walked into the field. The Old Gods didn't scare us anymore.

The sky above us remained resolutely Earth's, blue with streaks of cloud.

"I feel so sorry for Quincy and Pepsi," Leda said.

"Me, too. Remember that dream Quincy told me about? He said that Pepsi was his lost love. But Pepsi as she was when she was young and they still loved each other."

"They lost each other even though they still had each other," Leda said. "What could be sadder than choosing that?"

"It's hard not to want what you can't have," I said. "You and I can probably have a long, wonderful life together. What we can't have is an ordinary American life on Earth."

Leda and I held each other tight there in the field where Quincy had begun trying to sacrifice me to the Old Gods. Our old lives had been mostly illusions, but our hearts still ached at the thought of what we'd lost. A good thing, but not the best thing.

Then, giving thanks for all we'd gained and for the gift of each other, we left Earth for our own true home. We traveled together as the elves do, in a flash of thought.

Coda: The Parting Gift of the Old Gods

Whole galaxies appear to drift away.
Even small illusions— Dippers, Bears—
At harbor here, will show us parting flares
Unless a way of looking makes them stay.

- (Robert G. Tucker, "A Way of Looking")

YOU HAVE IN SOME MEASURE FREED *US*, JEROME AND LEDA, thought the god.

FOR THIS SERVICE, WE THANK YOU, thought the goddess.

WE HAVE GIVEN THOSE FEW WHO REMAIN IN *[the Other World]* ONE LAST TASK, thought the god.

TO MARK OUR DEPARTURE, THAT THOSE WHO ONCE LOVED US MAY REMEMBER, thought the goddess.

Images arrived fully-formed in our minds.

At the base of the palace of the gods in the Shining City, we saw people painstakingly sculpting two statues out of the fallen stones of older, larger statues. The statues were of Leda and me, heroically larger than life. The style looked something like Cold War Socialist realism, ironically enough.

Side by side, the finished statues stood as lovers do, with my stone arm around Leda's stone waist and hers around mine. We wore stylized Earth garments of stone. Our statues held up their free hands, waving an eternal stone farewell to Old Gods who had returned to the sky. Never again would the god and goddess descend to walk the temple tower their worshipers built for them so long ago. Our stone faces wore sad smiles. Artistic license.

Our statutes commemorated the fate that had overtaken the god and goddess. They had summoned us together to end one human age and begin another. When they saw into us, they saw that we loved as deeply as they loved each other. They saw that our minds were freely joined, as theirs were. They approved of us. They had thought only they could confer immortality on human beings. But Leda and I had brought one of their Myrmidons to the elves. Thus, one by one, elves came to the Other World to offer its people a way to awaken from their recurring dreams of death and catastrophe. The elves showed the gods that they had only imprisoned their worshipers—and themselves. By refusing the gods' false immortality and by keeping faith with each other, Leda and I had brought the long age of the Old Gods to an end.

But the gods' lives would go on and so would ours. They were free of bodies now, free of war and sacrifice and death, free of all the human spirits they had imprisoned in themselves, free of the need for worship and physical immortality and offspring.

Our statues said that the god and goddess were gone and only the lovers remained. Human love is a good thing, but not the best thing. It's a gateway to something even better, something irrelevant to the Old Gods, but essential to humankind. Our statues said that the people of the Other World were now free to love and free to find the gateway.

In time the pennants of the winged god would flap themselves into rags and the sand would cover up our statues. *Look on our works, ye humble, and take hope.*

Dedication and Thanks

This book is dedicated to the memory of my uncle Robert G. Tucker (1921-1982), poet, professor of English, U.S. Marine. Grateful acknowledgment is made to his estate for permission to quote from his poetry.

Loving Leda is also dedicated to Judy, my wife of many years. Who better to dedicate a Portsmouth paranormal romance to? As Jerry August's Uncle Quincy says to Jerry's Aunt Pepsi, *These have been good years. I'm fortunate to have spent them with you.*

Author's Note

Loving Leda is a work of fiction. This means that it's *made up*, as are all the characters in it, except for some actual historical figures mentioned in passing. Abraham Lincoln, for example. Those who care about such things may notice that I have again taken some liberties with the geography of Portsmouth and even its borders and environs. Among other things.

The book is set in the same twenty-first century universe and shortly after the events described in *The Next World Out*, the third book of the Nextworld Trilogy.

The Trilogy contains all the backstory for those who want to learn more about the Portsmouth Wars and those who fought in them: the Materialist Magicians (who really are both those things) and the elves (who aren't really the elves of legend at all.)

The Next World Out takes place only a few years after *The Next World Under*, the second book of the series, and more than twenty years after the events described in *The Next World Over*, the first book of the trilogy in which the way to the elves is reopened once again.

If I've done my job properly, you don't have to read the first three books to enjoy *Loving Leda*. You might enjoy all four books, though. Seriously. I mean, you don't want to miss anything, do you? The Trilogy is available as e-books from Barnes & Noble and from Amazon.com.

I'm now writing a second Portsmouth Paranormal Romance.

Wish me luck.

Dave Barnette

About the Author

David Barnette is a lifelong resident of Portsmouth, New Hampshire, where he lives with his wife Judy.

He is a graduate of Syracuse University and served with the U.S. Navy in Vietnam. After working many years as a federal civilian employee, he now writes full time.

Loving Leda is his fourth fantasy novel set in Portsmouth.

www.ingramcontent.com/pod-product-compliance
Lightning Source LLC
Chambersburg PA
CBHW020218260626
47156CB00002B/438